Angela Sréter Spencer was born in Transylvania, raised in Hungary, but lived most of her adult life in the US. She showed early interest in art and literature, following in the footsteps of her ancestors.

Two Candles (2010, 2012) was her first published book of poems, beautifully illustrated by Dr. Laszlo Hopp's award-winning photographic art. (Available from the author.) She was acknowledged in the Who Is Who in International Poetry and her poems were included in the Anthology of Best Poems in 2011 and 2012.

Dating Games (2012) is her second book, a collection of short stories, originating from the many interviews she conducted both in private and professional settings. (Available from Amazon and directly from the author.)

Land of Cotton (2015) is her latest work, a suspense-murder novel, guaranteed to keep the reader guessing who the ultimate criminal could be.

Angela Spencer is also an accomplished and respected Florida landscape artist, using both acrylic and oil as media. Her paintings found homes in California, Florida, New Jersey, North Carolina, Oregon, Tennessee, Texas, British Columbia, Finland, and Hungary. She had several art exhibitions throughout Florida.

When she does not write or paint, Angela Spencer, MD works as the owner and CEO of Spencer Neurology Clinic in Melbourne, Florida. She is a cerebrovascular neurologist, certified by the American Board of Psychiatry and Neurology.

She resides in Bayside Lakes, Palm Bay, Florida. She can be contacted via email aspencermd@gmail.com or by her web site www.SundaysWithAngela.com

Dedication

Dedicated to all who touched my life:
Some giving joy by entering and some by leaving it

Angela Spencer

LAND OF COTTON

AUSTIN MACAULEY PUBLISHERS™
London • Cambridge • New York • Sharjah

Copyright © Angela Spencer (2018)

All rights reserved. No part of this publication may be reproduced, distributed, or transmitted in any form or by any means, including photocopying, recording, or other electronic or mechanical methods, without the prior written permission of the publisher, except in the case of brief quotations embodied in critical reviews and certain other noncommercial uses permitted by copyright law. For permission requests, write to the publisher

Any person who commits any unauthorized act in relation to this publication may be liable to criminal prosecution and civil claims for damages.

Ordering Information:
Quantity sales: special discounts are available on quantity purchases by corporations, associations, and others. For details, contact the publisher at the address below.

Publisher's Cataloging-in-Publication data
Spencer Angela.
Land of Cotton

ISBN 9781641820301 (Paperback)
ISBN 9781641820295 (Hardback)
ISBN 9781641820318 (E-Book)

The main category of the book — Fiction/Crime.

www.austinmacauley.com

First Published (2018)
Austin Macauley Publishers Ltd™
40 Wall Street, 28th Floor
New York, NY 10005
USA

mail-usa@austinmacauley.com
+1 (646) 5125767

Acknowledgments

Each one of us travels through life and experiences many memorable moments, both happy and sad. In retrospect, these revisited mosaics of the past could be seen as our creative, irreplaceable forces. Not only major, but even the once seemingly unimportant incidents, could lead to changes that integrate into the character which we ultimately develop. Without each and every event, contact, and impression we would not be who we became. I say thanks for them.

If life events were this important, then how many times more weighty was the contribution made by the people who entered or left our lives? Without these consequences and contacts this book would not have been written, but would have remained buried somewhere in the foggy past.

A heartfelt appreciation is due to each character and persona portrayed, because they blossomed from the seeds previously planted in my mind. What seemed to be unjust, painful, or abominable before, with time, lost the evil connotation. Now I consider myself fortunate to have experienced them. All who stepped into my circles and brought along love, kindness, and help deserve nothing but my deepest gratitude. I was privileged to have met and known them.

Special thanks are due to all my friends and relatives who encouraged and supported me throughout this process and who proofread and corrected my writings: Professor Robert M. Metzger, PhD, Chairman at the University of Alabama in Tuscaloosa, AL; Dr. Tom Fabian and Dr. Cat Fabian of San Diego, CA; Susan Stockwell Gauthier of Oakland, FL; Susan Zell Sander of Palm Bay, FL; Gabor Fabian of Downey, CA; Maggie Ostergard of Cape Canaveral, FL; Suzanne J. Smith of Pasadena, CA; Fred and Sonna Whiteley of Lawndale, CA; and Navy Commander Jeanette F.C.

Shimkus, D.O. of Virginia Beach, VA. They spotted what I missed. Their encouragement, recommendations, and help were invaluable.

Needless to say, this book could not have been done without the ever-felt support and love of my children, Thomas Z. L. Fabian, Ph.D., and Gabor E. A. Fabian, as well as their cherished families.

PS: If anyone recognizes a character in the story, he could consider it purely coincidental or possibly the result of the author's artistic liberty.

However, if the shoes fit, wear them.

Angela Spencer

Outline

During the turn of the century, our country and her people underwent a drastic transformation. The old measures deteriorated at an alarming rate, degrading morals escalated, and norms were neglected in pursuit of fast materialistic replacements. Gentle Southern life started to vanish along with previously treasured ethics, and gradually was replaced by broken down political ideas in a gravely damaged economy. The loss of the old values of individual respect for persons and properties, age and experience, increasingly resulted in generation clash, fragmented families, and innumerable crimes. These reactions were dictated by religious hypocrisy, selfishness, and uncontrolled emotions guided by need of self-serving, instant gratification.

These were the circumstances and times when Jeb Odum was found dead in his rural Western Tennessee home. It soon became evident that his death did not result from a natural cause but murder by an unknown assailant.

'Land of Cotton' was the name of the largest Tennessee cotton-grower's land. Jake Odum, the older brother of the murdered Jeb, had his own tragedy. His son fell prey to the changing times and morals of America, ultimately paying a heavy price for departing from his family values.

Through the process of a murder investigation, the rural Chief Investigator of Homicide at the Fayette County Sheriff, Ron McCarthy, confronted many colorful characters who seemed to have reason to commit the crime. He also learned the effects of changing times resulting in generation clash and personal tragedies. He discovered anger and betrayal triggered vendetta, covered by social niceties. He found the hypocritical religious practice, encountered anticipated or only believed assaults. Before the entangled relationships could be unwrapped, and the criminal found, the Odum family had to face their haunting past. During the course of discovery, Mr. McCarthy found an intertwined, secretive, and crime-ridden life in the Bible Belt.

Ron McCarthy, with the assistance of Captain Corky and Mr. Wilson, investigated several potential suspects, eliminating them one by one, until they found the killer. However, they soon realized the true tragedy was caused by criminals often hiding behind the scenes who had no morals or reverence, and overflowed with runaway emotions.

All circumstances considered, McCarthy and his team performed an almost miraculous discovery ending the crime investigation in this fascinating suspense-murder story.

Chapter 1

Jeb Odum's body was found sitting on an old sofa, slightly slumped to the left. His left hand was caught in between his checked flannel shirt buttons, his fingers firmly pressed against his lower ribs. In his right hand, he tightly clutched the remote control. The TV aired a religious program from the Bible Hour series. Jeb was a well-known supporter of the local Baptist church and it was widely known that he only watched golf and pious shows. There was nothing unusual in that.

The large kitchen with the breakfast nook had another area which Jeb used for a family room. He always called it a "gathering room". Although this sounded a bit pretentious, especially because it was sort of empty, it never seemed to bother him. He lived alone in the huge house, but casually kept referring to it as if he often had a large family gather there if not daily, then at least often. In reality, he never even had a visitor, and day after day he sat alone in the echoing house.

The room only had a lumpy sofa and a love seat in front of a large TV placed on an old console by the opposite wall. Below, the cabinets were neatly stacked with vintage LPs, new CDs, and all sorts of unused cables. One just never knew when they might come in handy, so Jeb carefully and precisely rolled each in perfect circles, tied them with rubber bands, and packed them neatly in old shoe boxes. The boxes were marked on each side by a thick, black, felt-tip pen. Nobody could say Jeb Odum was not running a well-organized, tidy home.

"Who knows how long this TV was blasting, among all the things, of resurrection?" muttered Ron McCarthy, Williston's Sheriff. Then, again, being almost Easter, one could expect this in the Bible Belt. Although he lived in Tennessee for ten years now, some customs reminded him that he was a stranger in the South. No matter how well he assimilated, at times he still had to consider himself Philadelphia Irish.

"The poor chap must have died alone watching this show," he continued louder.

"I beg to differ, sir," said his assistant, Detective Corky. "The glass in the kitchen sink has a faint color on the rim. It sure looks like he had company."

McCarthy quickly glanced at the glass and, bending forward, tilted his head first left, then to the right to see the mark better. Slanted rays from a setting sun filtered through the shade, and at one point, burst into hot pink on the glass. Indeed, Corky was right. The glass definitely was marked by lipstick. *But not by a lip*, he instantly noted. Someone intentionally wiped the glass and smeared the lipstick, leaving only a wisp of color.

"Better get the glass, it might be important," turned McCarthy to his assistant, "and save whatever was in it," he remarked as he noted dark red liquid dried to a crackled little spot in the bottom of the wine glass. He wondered how long it was left in the sink. "Also, you should bag that phone, charging by the stove. And get that laptop, too. We might get a break from the stored records. One never knows…"

By then Corky carefully lifted the iPhone, holding one corner between his gloved right thumb and index finger and dropped it into a plastic bag he held by his left. He repeated the same with the computer. "Done," he beamed at his boss.

A faint siren sound got steadily stronger as it approached the house, then suddenly stopped before it got close. The driver probably realized he was approaching the address and did not want the law enforcement questioning him about why he used the siren when it was not an emergency. Too bad, by then they had all heard the shrilling sound.

Why do EMTs, firemen, and rescuers love sirens? Wherever they go, whether picking up a pizza or taking a heart attack victim to the ER, they turn it on full blast. Must be their self-importance. Or it is the little boy who forever seems to live in them? Maybe they just want to avoid traffic and get ahead of everyone. Traffic? What traffic can there be on a rural road at this hour? McCarthy wondered as he pulled the corner of his mouth to the left and snorted in disgust. He disliked EMTs ever since they were late to arrive when his wife had her last asthma attack. *Yeah, they sure missed it, in spite of the sirens and all.*

After the body was removed, the whole Williston, TN Sheriff Department of five people burst into action. They measured, photographed, fingerprinted, and sampled everything, crawled into every nook and cranny, and left nothing unseen or non-explored. Loaded up with several plastic bags, finally they sealed the entrances and left. The curious crowd of neighbors stayed for a while and quietly talked about Jeb and his unfortunate end. A detective stepped outside and announced that their initial work was done and there was nothing else to see. "You fellows just git going, git quietly outta' here, and head home. We don't want no more trouble, do we?" The shook-up neighbors slowly turned and headed home.

The house stayed as impressive as it always did, attractively standing among the tall pines and cedars, wrapped in silence. The only difference was the bright yellow cordon announcing, "Crime Scene – Do Not Enter" and the heavy secret it harbored. Stirred-up dust started to settle once more to slowly cover the furniture.

Chapter 2

The dead man and his surroundings troubled Ron McCarthy. He had seen many homicides while in Philadelphia, especially before he was transferred from the Northern section to Center City. Not that the Center City people were all angels, but they were probably more sophisticated. At least near the Museum district the murders were limited to rare findings of a dead body, usually stacked away or covered by dry branches and bushes in the largest inner-city park in the entire nation. The famous Fairmount Park was renowned for more than just its natural beauty. Many early mornings, he walked the deserted paths and searched for the spot indicated by nameless informers where a body was to be found. Other times shocked couples strolled casually on the meandering walkways and stumbled upon a motionless human. Usually they backed away in horror then turned to notify the police of their gruesome discovery. He had his share of murder investigations in the City of Brotherly Love because it apparently had plenty of unbrotherly hatred, too.

More often, street accidents, reckless drivers, or even more reckless pedestrians were the victims. But those were not intentional deaths. Furthermore, it was obvious even to a rookie as to what caused the tragedy.

The Williston death of Jeb Odum was troublesome. Not only was the man far from being old enough to die of natural causes, but that glass with the lipstick was unexplained. When did he have company? He must have known her well if they shared some wine. Drinks go equally well with business discussions and lovers' quarrels. But where was the company now? And who was she? Why did she leave, and why did she not come forward when all these actions swirled around the house? Was she nearby, or did she not hear of Jeb Odum's fatality?

McCarthy only met the man briefly before but knew a lot about him. He remembered hearing the scandal that shook the farmland community when Charlotte Kay Odum shacked up with a younger man and left her husband of thirty-eight years. Jeb Odum was known to be tight-lipped. He did not talk much about anything, and he certainly had no plans to start venting about his feelings after his wife's departure. Whatever happened between them remained a subject of much guesswork.

Everyone paid attention to the Odums when their only daughter, Mary Beth, married Larry Bostwick. Larry had a heating and air-conditioning business and served the whole Fayette, as well as part of the bordering Shelby County. He 'personally' appeared at the most inopportune moments, interrupting TV programs with his commercials. By the time he proposed to Mary Beth, he was a household name in the area. Their wedding was a big affair, and rightfully so, as it was expected from two well-to-do families.

Quiet Jeb Odum had worked in St. Jude's Children Hospital for sixteen years in the finance department. Charlotte was a receptionist in the front lobby. They were in the midst of building a house in remote Williston, hoping to settle in a quiet countryside home, far from crime-ridden Memphis.

The house was planned to stand in the deep end of a 20 acres flag lot. A dirt road, at least a half a mile long, led to the construction site. The rainwater slowly seeped through the clay-laden dirt, accumulating in the deep tracks made by the heavy trucks, or washed sharply curving crevices at the step-offs.

Charlotte Kay Odum all but whipped the workers to finish her house by the wedding day. In the interim, she scavenged the antique malls and shops for furniture, old-fashioned fixtures, framed duck, and old English countryside hunting prints to decorate the rooms. After his work, Jeb's wife ordered him to level the driveway and fill it with stones. His truck was seen up and down the highway, making innumerable trips to the landfill and the quarry. Barely completed, the house was ready for the big day to host the wedding guests.

Too bad, the marriage did not last long. The Bostwicks lived in the outskirt of Memphis and had no desire to move in with Mary Beth's parents. Larry never missed an opportunity to ask what was the difference between 'in-laws' and 'outlaws'? To the questioning looks he laughingly added, "The outlaws were wanted." The more-than-embarrassed Mary Beth apologized for the tasteless joke once her husband was not within ear-shot. Almost as if to prove there was some truth in the saying, Larry never warmed up to his wife's parents. He absolutely rejected the idea of living anywhere within walking distance of his new in-laws.

Charlotte Kay and Jeb offered half of their property and unsolicited help to the young couple if they built a house and moved next to them. They reasoned this would be close enough to help each other, yet, not too close for comfort. They could do a lot for them once the grandchildren arrived. But youngsters can rarely see what the more experienced parents recommend. Mary Beth and Larry Bostwick were the same. They eventually settled in a small suburban home in a modest, middle-class neighborhood.

In the fall of 2006, the initial housing boom suddenly bottomed out. The banks tightened giving out loans, and the employers increased the job requirements. These measures initially helped a bit, but ultimately backfired in the community. There were nine to ten well-qualified applicants for every position. The market was good for picking and choosing among the best. Jobs got eliminated as the finances became tighter and tighter. Companies merged, and the large organizations swallowed the little guys. The new management always dragged their own people along, and the old ones soon found themselves demoted or let go.

The US had the highest company taxes, and in order to protect revenues, many corporations transferred their operations abroad or outsourced their work. Labor force participation plummeted. When Walmart advertised hiring three thousand people for their stores in various locations, they received over ten thousand applications within the first three days. Rural Western Tennessee was just as hard hit as anywhere in the mid-West. Probably Alabama fared the worst: in Hale County alone, the disability claims suddenly reached twenty-five percent of the entire population, and unemployment abruptly soared to a previously unknown level. As the economy worsened, people became dependent on government hand-outs. In seven years, one out of six citizens was on food stamps.

Meanwhile, houses devalued rapidly to half of their original cost, but the taxes and mortgage payments remained the same. People struggled, but inevitably they fell behind on their payments. When the heads of household lost their jobs, one by one the housewives entered the workforce. Not being trained or experienced, they got more menial positions and much less salary than their men were making. Most streets became peppered with neon-red foreclosure signs. Some families lost everything: jobs, homes, and the land they inherited and worked on for generations. Times were tough, for sure.

Eventually, Larry and Mary Beth lost their house and divorced over the on-going, daily bickering. Larry paid off his wife and continued his long hours of work. The difference was he did not have to come home to her accusations any more. Mary Beth took a job, and was thankful for not having children. At least that made the parting much easier. Eventually the gossip died. The news of the Bostwicks' divorce was dwarfed by the calamity brought on by the depressed economy.

Chapter 3

McCarthy finished his TV dinner, but did not feel like getting up yet. He sighed, recalling the time of his own misfortune. He almost always worked two jobs just to keep the house and pay the medical bills. When his wife died, he fell in a deep depression. Being a strong man in the blue force, he did not talk about his lonely, sleepless nights. He never mentioned anything of his private life, really. Only the ever-deepening dark circles around his eyes testified to his sadness. His valiant but desperate attempts to cover his pain did not go unnoticed. After the funeral, he got frequent dinner invitations, but these calls soon thinned out as the months passed, and finally they stopped altogether. He was left alone.

The McCarthy's did not have children. His wife was almost always sick, and the doctors did not allow her any further risk to jeopardize her life. His parents had passed long before. He had a few cousins but lost touch with most of them when he married a non-Irish girl. The clan all but disowned him. Not that it bothered him while his wife was alive, but after she was gone, he felt the isolation. He realized he needed to get away from everything and start anew. He could not face the constant reminders of happier times without the fear of breaking down one day. When the Tennessee job got posted, he applied, and soon moved to begin a completely new chapter of his life.

In Philadelphia, McCarthy was a respected and well-known detective. He attended Temple University in the evenings and learned all he could about criminal justice, psychology, and every phase of an investigation. He worked hard and was soon recognized and rewarded. His last promotion landed him the dubious honor of being the head of the Homicide Division. In the seventh year, he became a widow. It did not take him long to realize his much-loved wife's tragic death ended his career and life in Philadelphia.

According to his references, the department never operated smoother than under McCarthy's leadership. Surprisingly, it still remained within the budget. In reality, his new Tennessee position was a step-down from being the chief of a large number of detectives, but with the much lesser salary also came lesser responsibility. If he missed the detective work, he never mentioned it. His new superiors were thrilled to get him for the money of a sheriff. After all, they gladly rubbed their hands over getting a new addition with an extensive detective background who also had proven leadership, and knew all the administrative paperwork. What more could they get for the salary they offered?

Being new in a small community had its benefits, too: he was instantly known to everyone in Williston. Not only because he came as an outsider, but because he apparently liked the community enough to settle down there. To be the local Sheriff was a position respected by the town elders and law-fearing folks. It was dreaded by the speeding maniacs and would-be thieves.

Rural Williston seemed to be a safe haven for the sleepy residents. Most of them lived off the main roads, surrounded by large wooded lots. The few silver silos silently watched the parched corn fields and tufts of fluffy white cotton twirl in the wind. Here the white and black folks politely lived by each other, whether in newly built big, brick homes or in rickety, old trailers. Most of the houses were moderate in appearance and fairly well-kept, anyway. Quiet McCarthy blended in the community without as much as causing a ripple on the surface of still water.

His job was simple, and his colleagues respected him. A few speeding tickets, a few warnings, an occasional false alarm, and an even scarcer burglary was all that broke up the daily routine. He liked the peaceful neighborhood. He found his niche and home in the rolling countryside, among the polite Southern gentlemen and charming, well-mannered ladies. He lost his Philadelphia accent and eventually his naturally slow speech picked up the local slang and drawl.

McCarthy first met Jeb Odum when his newly installed home alarm kept going off. After the third or fourth such false alarm, McCarthy sternly recommended Secure Alarm to review the wiring, or he would issue a citation and penalty. Jeb was more than embarrassed by the mishaps, but quickly resolved the problem. He smartly avoided the necessary confrontation with the alarm company when he simply disconnected the Sheriff Department. From that time on, the accidentally tripped alarm did not bother anyone. The neighbors surely heard it but never complained. The shrill sound was quickly extinguished, anyway.

McCarthy was amazed to see the huge house among the pines and cedars, safely tucked away from the prying eyes. He wondered why an elderly couple would build a house that spread over four-thousand square feet when their child was grown, and they had no grandchildren. Not only was the building vast, it apparently also cost a lot of money because some of the rooms were barely furnished, and half of the upstairs was all but empty.

The sheriff was younger than the Odums, yet he would not have wanted to climb the stairs, clean the big home, and do all the work it must have represented. The lot sure was pretty with the green trees, but the romantic appearance hid the inherent labor it required for maintenance. He could not imagine a valid reason why anyone would commit himself to all this work at the brim of retirement. Then he met Charlotte Kay.

Chapter 4

Charlotte Kay Odum was a tall woman who must have been attractive with a lot of long, curly black hair before the color became unnaturally dark against her wrinkles. When she talked to anyone, she looked straight in their eyes without blinking and kept staring until she succeeded in making her opponent uncomfortable. She liked to be thought of as assertive but not aggressive. Little did she know that some people tried to avoid her company because her staring evoked in them the feeling she was casting a spell.

For a Pennsylvania Yankee, the aging Charlotte's frequent, coquettish eye blinking and long, false eyelashes instantly brought back the memories of Tammy Faye Bakker. After visualizing the mental image of that infamous preacher's wife, McCarthy relaxed and did not take Charlotte's smiles and frequent frowns seriously. Jeb usually stood silently in the background.

The next encounter was much less personal. Barely a year later, McCarthy learned that Charlotte Kay suddenly left Jeb and the barely finished house and moved in with one of her son-in-law's employees. The little community buzzed with the news. At the Sheriff Department everyone knew some intimate tidbits of the separation and discussed it in the lunchroom in gory detail. Gossip and tales were woven endlessly into an outrageously colorful tapestry of deceit and manipulation. They seemed to become wilder and more bizarre by the day.

Yes, Miss Charlotte Kay fell in love with a young man and abandoned her unobtrusive and simple husband in the huge house. She took everything she could move. At the end, even the curtain rods were unscrewed from the walls and removed from the bedroom. Charlotte Kay felt righteous and just in taking whatever the Odums purchased together during their long marriage. Yet, she never failed to point out to her husband that she remained friendly and gracious toward him, because she left her childhood white bedroom set and a few pieces of essential fixtures which she inherited from her parents.

Jeb was told these should tide him over, and he was free to use her furniture as long as he realized they were hers. When the house was eventually sold, she would take them all to her new place.

Essentially, she depleted the bank account, emptied the house, and left to Jeb the mortgage payment and all the work of the huge empty house. He would not need anything, anyway; he should keep himself busy with maintaining the twenty acres around the house. His departing wife insisted in splitting the expected profits equally once the house was sold. Jeb did not fight, but remained calm, and showed little emotion. He agreed to whatever Charlotte Kay wanted, without contesting a single word. He just wanted to get over this unpleasant parting as soon as he could.

Poor Jeb, said McCarthy to himself as he shifted his legs on the coffee table, *he seemed to end up with the short stick in everything. First the breakup of his marriage, then years of pointless slavery just to hang onto a vacant house, chopping wood, and always bushwhacking. And to do all these for what? At the end, he still would die alone.* He reached for his cell phone to answer a call.

"Yeah? McCarthy. Is that you Corky? What's up? Any news?" He knew Corky discovered something, otherwise he would not have disturbed him at home.

Corky's speech was faster than usual and, in his excitement, his voice became high-pitched. "I sure did; I mean I have good news. I mean good news for us, not for Jeb Odum. After all, he is dead, what news would be good for him?" he cackled. When he did not evoke a single chuckle at the other end of the line, he became serious and continued, "Well, I know for sure he was not alone. The glass in the kitchen sink must have been left by a woman. Lipsticks do not lie, do they? I figured I'd take it upon myself to investigate who used this glass. I am pretty convinced it was his girlfriend."

"Corky, you're either not making much sense or I am missing something big time," replied McCarthy. "Where did you get the idea of a girlfriend? Did you know for sure Jeb had a girlfriend? It could have been any woman, don't you think?"

"Nope," Corky was determined. "You see, Jeb had the same lipstick mark on the side of his neck, too. Sorry, boss, it was a girlfriend. No other women would have kissed him on the neck, no way. Jeb was divorced, so it had to be someone else, and not his ex-wife. I don't think she was a kissy-kissy type, anyway. I just don't know, yet, who this woman was, but don't you worry, it's only a matter of time and I will get her name, too. I already know what she was like because she had a closet full of shoes and clothes left in the bedroom. It was that woman who killed him."

"Oh, God, when will you finally stop watching CSI, Corky? The clothes could have been left by his ex-wife. He could have died of a heart attack or a stroke, or any number of natural causes, and not necessarily be killed. Have you thought of that?" McCarthy was getting annoyed with his overzealous assistant.

"You think so?" asked Corky. "Then where did the stab wound come from? The coroner found a small triangular hole under his left rib cage, you know," his voice confirmed a poorly masked victory: for the first time he scored over the new Chief. Finally, he surpassed the very man who stole his dream and aspiration by sitting in the position he thought was rightfully his. "The wound was right under his fingers, pressed hard in the position to cover it. I guess this is why we did not see it right away. Yep, it sure bled into his chest and belly, maybe a drop or two to the skin, but not out, not at all."

At last Corky proved to be a real detective, a shrewd gumshoe, almost like his idol Paul Drake in the Perry Mason series. Ron McCarthy had nothing but a rank over him. When Corky would single-handedly solve this murder, everyone would see the mistake made by passing him over. Who knows, maybe he would be named Chief after all. McCarthy could go back to Philadelphia or wherever he came from, Corky did not care.

McCarthy heard the soft click ending the call.

Chapter 5

The Shelby County Coroner's Office was busy this morning. Before Dr. James J. Johnson arrived, his assistants prepared the reports and printed out all the paperwork he needed for the three planned autopsies scheduled for the day.

After the pale bodies were laid on the shiny metal tables, they made several pictures from every side; then all waited for the Coroner to start. Their preliminary chores done, his assistants quietly chattered before starting work, and the dead patiently waited for their turn to be opened up to reveal their secrets. All Dr. Johnson was required to do was the usual observation and routine autopsy, then fill the lines of a form with his findings. His role ended with putting his signature on the death certificates. Nothing was too exciting after twenty-two years in the same job.

Accidents led to most deaths in Collierville and its vicinity, though an occasional unexplained passing also required his expertise. Ever since he attended medical school, pathology was Dr. Johnson's passion, but the mundane routine work quickly chiseled away any novelty in his job. All cases were brought to him to the Collierville's office from Fayette and Shelby Counties. He became a respected local expert by the time he turned fifty. Very few insiders knew how often he looked for help from the Memphis University scholars in determining a puzzling cause of death. Though he said a second opinion served only to confirm his findings, many times he secretly harbored a well-concealed insecurity in making a convincing statement of the cause, if not the estimated time, of death.

Jeb Odum's body was stripped of his clothes and laid on the polished aluminum table which had an inch-high lip all around. It slightly sloped toward a drain at the far end, right over a large bucket which would catch all waste and liquids. The initial survey did not show much more than a sixty-seven-year-old white male who appeared his chronological age. He seemed to be in good physical condition. Apparently, he either worked out or worked hard physically, because his muscles were bulging on his arms and his shoulders were rounded. He had no obvious trauma to his body and had no big bruises, fresh cuts, or wounds. His arms and hands had a few scratches and likely work-related injuries. All people who worked in the fields, among the wildly growing thorny bushes and low-hanging tree branches, suffered the same. He must have worn short pants and T-shirts to work outdoors, because his white thighs and shoulders sharply contrasted his suntanned arms and legs.

Dr. Johnson tied the blue paper gown around his belly and leaned over the lipped table. He reached for the measuring tape and quickly determined that the dead man was five feet, nine inches tall. Simultaneously, he noted this must have been a false height because the man's upper back had a noticeable curvature that must have shortened him by at least two inches. He was lean without a pot belly, probably weighed hundred-eighty pounds. When he checked the scale, he concluded with a lot of satisfaction that he had not lost his prediction skills and estimated only five pounds under the real weight. So far, all seemed to be on the smooth track of a routine day. He hoped to get done with his work by noon, so after lunch he could rest until it was time to show up at home for dinner. Not a moment before.

The dead man's arms and legs were all intact, though both hands had healed scars and fresh scratches. The right had a slightly soiled Band-Aid covering a small patch of torn skin between his thumb and index finger. He was bald, with curly gray hair on the sides and back of the head. He saw no injury to the scalp, only sunspots and signs of little, healed scars. The face was almost weather-beaten with deep wrinkles running diagonally down from his nostrils to the corners of his mouth. A well-trimmed mustache covered his thin lips. The mustache had a faint tell-tale strip of silver close to the skin, attesting to his vanity: he colored the mustache dark. Dr. Johnson lifted the eyelids to expose the dark greenish-blue eyes. They were covered with a bluish matte film and stared into space. That was what he expected; the eyes of the dead always stared as if they looked at eternity.

Looking into the lifeless eyes, he always had the recurrent questions: what they had seen last, and what if there was a picture frozen on them somewhere? Wouldn't it be fantastic to detect it?

Maybe one day someone would use a chemical or a unique process and develop the last images seen and preserved on the retina just the same way as they develop a film. Why not? Other, less fantastic innovations were done which no one dared to predict before. Or maybe someone could map the brain and project the last thoughts into a visible, tangible image. He knew a big emotion evoked some sort of neuro-hormonal production. He could not quite recall what they were called, but remembered distinctly he heard about them while being a resident. Would it not be possible to detect it and know for sure how a victim was affected in his last minutes of life? He should really think it through, and one day, work more on this idea. Maybe he could stumble upon a great discovery and change pathology altogether. Wouldn't it be fantastic? His name would be forever known, and he could retire in full glory to his Scottsdale, Arizona retreat sooner than he planned. There he could start a new life, leaving the past behind. He would divorce his nagging wife and once free, he would move with his girlfriend to Arizona. No more hiding and sneaking, just an open, honest relationship with her. Who knows, maybe he would even marry her one day…

His life as a caterpillar turned long ago into a cocoon, but with a life-changing discovery, he would emerge ultimately as a carefree, wonderful butterfly. Ah, Scottsdale and the butterfly life! They seemed not only a mirage but something attainable. Dr. Johnson was ready to spread his hidden wings to finally live life to its fullest.

He wanted to do, try, explore, and experience all he missed as a young man. First the innumerable, sleepless nights spent among his thick textbooks, then the tight corrals of an unhappy marriage prevented him. The relentless years passed, and he was over his middle-age when it suddenly dawned on him what he lost. He lamented his disappeared youth and silently grieved for what he longed for without ever experiencing. Just before the sunset, he had the gnawing urge to do something crazy, even if only once.

While his rambling thoughts freely roamed the possibilities of a limitless future, his face remained void of visible emotions. He swiftly moved his hands with well-rehearsed precision while he continued daydreaming of a completely new life in Scottsdale, a life with so far not known inner peace, love, and passion.

The pathology assistants, if they glanced at him, only saw him methodically continuing the sequential movements embedded in his brain and hands by hundreds of autopsies. They never suspected that under the docile, unaffected facial expression a turmoil was brewing with the ferocity of a volcanic eruption.

He opened the mouth of the dead man, and his penlight slowly swept across the man's teeth. He had much dental work done, caps covered most of his teeth. The right wisdom tooth was missing, and a clot of dark maroon blood covered the recent extraction site. Dr. Johnson probed the tooth in front of the wound and saw it needed much work, probably a filling and a cap, to complete the already started repair and restoration in progress. The rest of the oral cavity was intact.

He systematically proceeded down on the body and almost missed the tiny wound hidden in a skin fold under the left rib cage. He took pictures of the site before he decided to explore the wound. At first glance, it looked small and insignificant, hardly enough to hurt and certainly not enough to kill him. Besides a little red stain, there was no blood anywhere.

His probe did not proceed far, the track was somehow cut off. After opening the body cavities, he realized the man's torso must have been twisted when he was stabbed. As soon as he straightened out his body, the tissues returned to their usual positions and blocked the exit for any escaping blood. A classic z-track, just like he learned as an intern to administer iron shots. If he did not twist the skin and the underlying tissues before giving the injection, the seeping iron stained the surrounding skin permanently as soon as he withdrew his needle. He almost smiled at his discovery, it was so simple while totally explaining the lack of outward bleeding.

It was about noon when he finished the autopsy. He was amazed at his findings. The tiny skin opening continued in a narrow channel of a wound, pierced the diaphragm, crossed the left lower lung, and entered the covering sack of the heart slightly to the right from the tip. The wound finally ended in about the middle of the strong muscles which created the wall of the heart. He knew the seeping blood slowly filled the cavity between the heart muscle and the outside sinuous sack called pericardium, creating an awfully effective tamponade, which eventually prevented the heart from functioning.

"The poor bloke died of a cardiac arrest and probably did not even know it was coming," announced his conclusion in a barely audible way, "otherwise he was in remarkably good condition. A bit of hardening of the arteries, but everyone at his age would have that much, especially if he had high blood pressure."

Dr. Johnson estimated Jeb Odum lived most likely less than half an hour and certainly not more than one hour after the injury. By the state of the body, he concluded Jeb must have died between twenty-four to forty-eight hours before being discovered.

Dr. Johnson recalled from his first pathology course the fact of the so-called "cracking": the necrotic tissue separated from intact tissue, telling the length of time required for the changes. Suddenly he realized that was applicable as gross pathology only in someone who remained alive after a brain insult. Jeb Odum was dead and not affected by a stroke. Nevertheless, decomposition was evident, and rigor mortis already was reversed by flaccidity. Indeed, death had to occur more than twenty-four but probably less than forty-eight hours ago.

To be complete, he entered all measurements and weights of the inner organs onto a chart then replaced everything into the empty body cavity and closed the opening. The cause of death was clear, no mystery there. Just to be on the safe side, almost as an afterthought, he collected little dishes and tubes of a few tissue and liquid samples, so the laboratory next door also would have something to do. Given his findings, this was not necessary, but sort of a self-protective routine procedure. In a litigious society, every physician learned fast to protect himself by practicing overtly cautious, defensive medicine.

He tore off the paper gown and tossed his soiled rubber gloves in a can at his side. He took another glance to be sure he did not miss anything, then covered the body with a sheet. His assistants would do the rest. He entered the adjoining tiny office to start dictating his final report. Once the paperwork was completed, he dialed the Sheriff Department and asked to talk to Chief Investigator McCarthy.

Chapter 6

Charlotte Kay Odum nervously fumbled with her keys when she heard the shrill ring of her house phone. She was expecting a call and wanted to reach it before the caller hung up. By the time she managed to open the door, the phone had gone silent. Although she ran to pick it up, she only heard the familiar tone of a lifted receiver. In her rush, she dropped her purse and keys, and now all were scattered on the floor. The contents of her handbag spilled from the love seat to the floor, sending coins, lipsticks, mascara, mirror, and a bottle of Motrin all over the room. She started to collect her things and noted some rolled under the sofa. Reaching far under the furniture, she was on all fours when she heard a man's voice behind her.

"Ma'am, excuse me, Ma'am, I need to talk with you."

The startled Charlotte turned only to see a strange man in uniform standing in the doorway, one hand on the frame and the other holding the door open. She was frustrated, irritated, and her day was simply awful so far. Now she could expect it to get even worse: she might be getting some warning for her expired license tag, or could have been busted for clipping the old truck at Kroger's parking lot.

Well, she almost got away with it. It was getting dark, and the parking lot was practically empty. She did not think anyone saw her hitting the rear side of the truck parked next to her. As she quickly pulled away, her driver's front dented the truck's right rear panel. Not much, but enough to be noticeable. She quickly surveyed the parking lot and saw no one around, so she continued going. She nervously kept looking back, but since no headlight followed her, she assumed she got away safely. Who would have thought to stop and leave a note on that beat-up, old jalopy? On second thought, she decided she would say she left a note on the windshield, but the wind must have blown it off.

While these thoughts flashed through her mind, her stoic face remained stone-calm, and her piercing eyes did not leave the man's face. She heard of plenty of criminals preying on defenseless women while posing as a figure of authority. Charlotte Kay was enough of a Southern belle to project herself as a vulnerable, weak, little woman, even if she were protected by an impenetrable armor of sheer will and physical strength. Now she was ready to scream the moment the man moved an inch forward.

"Ma'am, I am Captain Corky from Williston. You know Williston, don't you?" The man pointed to his name tag and flashed an identification badge to her.

"Oh, yes, of course." As she said the words, Charlotte Kay felt the relief one gets when a proverbial ton of rocks roll off the shoulders. Evidently, the man knew nothing of the local mishap at Kroger's. He surely would have started the call differently. Obviously, he was not interested in her car tag, either, she was sure. He was not after her. She did not know yet what he wanted, but she was convinced it was not her. He said he came from Williston. Gosh, maybe someone broke into the house, or it caught on fire and burnt down. She never allowed a real fire in the fireplace, but she could not control Jeb once she moved out. He never listened, anyway. Never. He just went ahead without any argument and did what he wanted. Furthermore, he had two left hands, and two left feet, Charlotte was convinced. It seemed entirely possible he did something to send the local Sheriff to her door.

"Williston? Of course, I know Williston. I know it very well. I used to live there. Why? What's the matter, is there anything wrong?"

"May I come in? I need to talk to you in private. It's about your husband."

"My husband? You mean to say my ex-husband, don't you?" Charlotte drawled the sentence longer than needed. "You may come in, of course, just leave the door wide open. Let's hear it, I am ready for the blow, what did he do now?"

"Thank you, Ma'am. First, may I ask you when did you see or talk with your ex-husband last?" Corky emphasized the word 'ex-husband' to show he got the message.

Charlotte Kay did not need to think long, she knew the days well. "When? We met two weeks ago on Monday, and then I called him last Thursday. Why? What did he do? I know he must have done something really bad, or you would not just show up here.

Relax, you could not really surprise me with anything he did; I am well aware of his clumsy ways, trust me. He never was the sharpest knife in the drawer, if you know what I mean."

"Just a second, please slow down. Let me ask first, you are no longer married, but you are legally divorced, aren't you?"

"Of course we are. For over two years. First of all, you never could trust a man as long as he was lukewarm and breathing. Second, you further had to mistrust him if he was a Baptist hypocrite. I have learned the hard way that Jeb was both. You know, Baptists have no morals. That marriage was like playing cards. It started with two hearts and a diamond. At the end all I wanted was a club and a spade," snorted Charlotte with an unpleasant laugh. As soon as she noticed the man open his eyes in wild surprise, she instantly resumed her previously projected cool superiority. "Not that it matters, anymore."

"One moment, please. It might. Say it again, what was your relationship with him? Were you angry with him?"

"Whoa! Hold your horses, partner. Wait a minute," protested Charlotte indignantly. "What difference does it make what I felt toward him, or when we were last in contact? You asked me if I was angry with him. Not that it's your business, but let me tell you this much: eventually there is enough anger in every marriage. Yes, at first when you are in love, you are blind. Then when you get married, you think you are in a bliss. Later, when anger creeps in and replaces your other emotions, it's your choice to divorce or murder. OK, that's enough of that."

Charlotte Kay took a step forward and looked straight into Corky's eyes. "Now, you tell me what did he do? He must have done something really bad and was caught, or you would not bother to come to me. Am I correct? Either you tell me right now, or I will have to ask you to leave me alone. If you want me to answer, start talking. First you tell me what he did, and then we might talk about the rest; otherwise we are done."

"I apologize, Ma'am. I am in a very uncomfortable situation, I assure you. I am sorry to tell you the sad news, Ma'am. It might be a shocker, but Mr. Odum was found dead in his house. I am really sorry."

"Oh, my Lord. Oh, my God. I did not know that. Are you sure we are talking about Jeb Odum, the same man? He was perfectly well two weeks ago, quite the same as always. He was not sick, was he? What happened to him?"

"Sick? No Ma'am, not that I know of. He was found sitting on the sofa, in front of his TV. We were called by his neighbor for the ongoing alarm. That's all I know, Ma'am," Corky calmly maintained an expressionless face, in spite of Charlotte Kay's piercing stare.

"I don't even know what to say. I am stunned. Did you call anyone in the family yet? My daughter? No, don't call her, I will let her know. I think it would be better this way. She will be devastated. Poor Jeb. Poor Jeb, he did not deserve to be killed."

Corky looked sharply down at her shoes, to hide the sudden alertness and interest that flared up in his eyes. He was taken aback by the expression Charlotte Kay used because he was careful never to utter the word 'killed'. He spotted a lipstick and reached to pick it up from the rug, but it slipped from his hand and landed again on the floor. This time, it opened up, and the two pieces rolled in two different directions. They both automatically bent forward, but Corky was faster. He quickly grabbed it and looked at the content. It was hot pink. "Here you go, Ma'am," he pushed the pieces together to close the little tube as he dropped the lipstick into Charlotte Kay's open palm, "Sorry to drop it, but I am not used to these little things. What were you saying before? I didn't hear you."

Charlotte Kay calmly repeated: "Nothing. Now I don't even remember what I wanted to say. I was just stunned to hear what happened to Jeb. Is there anything else you want to tell me, Captain—what was your name? Corky? I should remember your name, because it's just like the restaurant we used to like to go to. Funny, that's where I met Jeb the last time, too. It would not be yours, or maybe your family's by any chance?"

"Oh, I wish, Ma'am. If it were mine, I would not be working in Williston, believe me." His faint smile seemed sincere.

"Don't be modest, it's entirely possible to have a steady job if for nothing else but the insurance and the benefits. You get them, don't you? In the meantime, you could let your wife run the business. You look like a smart man, I am sure you thought of that, too." Charlotte Kay clearly expected an answer.

Captain Corky pursed his lips and pulled it sharply to the side while shaking his head in disagreement. "No, Ma'am, I am a simple man who happens to love his job. This is the only thing I do. And I am not married."

"Ah, I am surprised," claimed Charlotte Kay, with barely noticeable satisfaction, "a good-looking man, in the best shape and age! It's hard to believe some woman did not already snatch you up!"

Corky smiled at the obvious flattery. Then he recalled the official business he was to conduct and became serious. But the odd remark of the new widow struck him as being weird. After all, she just learned her husband, that is her ex-husband, was found dead. Even in such an awkward moment she seemed ready to fish for an unattached man. Why else would she set him up to reveal his marital status? Or did she just like trim, single men in uniform? Some women fall for that, Corky knew. Maybe it was nothing else but the usual Southern flirting. Judging by Charlotte Kay's fluttering, long eyelashes, she was an expert in coquetry. Regardless, whatever was the reason, Corky decided he would later have to investigate that idea a bit more. It might be interesting personally, or possibly even relevant to Jeb Odum's death. Either way, he would not lose a thing, but possibly gain something by digging a bit deeper.

For a few more minutes, they talked about God's will and accepting it serenely, and then he said goodbye to Charlotte. He inhaled deeply and held his breath to make his chest appear larger than it really was. Shoulders pulled back and straight; he pulled in the noticeable beginning of a beer-belly. They shook hands briefly, and then he snappily turned and walked to the curb where his unmarked car was parked. He got in and immediately headed to Collierville, to Corky's BBQ and Restaurant.

As soon as the police car pulled out of sight, Charlotte Kay Odum dialed her ex-boyfriend's number. He was Doug Bullock, the same young man for whom she left her husband.

Chapter 7

A few months before Jeb's death, Jake Odum, the older brother of Jeb, worked in the barn the whole day, as usual. After putting in a full day's work for the needed repairs, he was tired and was glad to hear the bell calling him for dinner. His wife hung a large cattle bell by the corner of the porch, and she rang it when she needed him, instead of yelling for him. The clear tone traveled faster across the field than her voice could, and she did not have to repeat herself with the bell, either. She did not believe Jake would ever deliberately ignore her but, being a man, he got involved with his projects and tuned out distractions.

Kasia met Jake in Memphis. After WWII her parents settled in Tennessee. Their apartment was not far from the prestigious university buildings. They were DPs or 'displaced persons' during the war. Working for the old government as a high-profile attorney and the youngest mayor in the history of his city, Kasia's father could hardly be considered a proletarian. In the quickly forming new world, dictated by the emerging Soviet power and its Polish servants, he instantly became a *persona non grata.* His name was listed among the "Enemies of the People's Government" and posted all over town.

Posters pasted practically every corner of Krakow or, hanging on trees by the sidewalks, announced the names and crimes committed by those who worked for the prior government. If anyone had held a government job, that alone was enough to merit a 'crime' against the new ruling class of workers and peasants. Anyone who recognized one of the listed persons could have shot him dead without ever being questioned or held responsible for the murder. Their homeland was torn into pieces and bled from thousands of wounds. The intelligentsia either escaped to the West or was taken to German labor camps for either having assisted the Jews or resisted the German invasion.

The Germans decimated the Polish Army and the Soviets totally annihilated it. Twenty-two thousand Polish officers and civilian leaders were murdered in 1940 and secretly buried in unmarked mass graves in the Katyn forest. The West did not stand up for them. President Roosevelt did not want to anger Stalin, whom he referred to as 'good old Joe'. Since the Americans and Russians recently made a pact to fight together against the Germans and Japanese, Roosevelt could not attack his new ally. Poland, the little European country, located so far away from the American continent, was only a small problem in the uprooted world and its raging madness. The Katyn genocide was not mentioned, and the peace talks continued uninterrupted between the Soviet dictator and the President of the United States. Poland no longer existed the way her people knew it.

Krzysztof and Zofia Krupka hastily fled Poland with their small daughter on her mother's arm. Zofia held the chubby little Kasia close to her skinny chest, as if she were afraid to lose her the moment her grip lessened. Her husband carried a suitcase in each hand filled with essential clothes and food. Zofia's jewelry already purchased them the escape from Krakow. Whatever they worked for, accumulated, loved and treasured, they left in the house, as if they were to return at any moment. Fear and youth propelled them to a Promise Land that existed somewhere in the West, some place where they hoped to find peace and harmony once more. They were luckier than most refugees because they had each other. As long as their family held together, everything else was only material and of secondary importance.

They progressed slowly, barely keeping their distance of safety from the relentlessly advancing Red Army. They rode in cattle wagons, slept on bare floors of bombed-out cathedrals, and walked miles between crumbling buildings with the baby in their arms. Finally, they arrived at the International Camp in Mooseburg, Germany. The camp was strategically located near Munich, in the center of Bavaria. It was maintained by the super powers of the American and English military. Kasia's lawyer father was hired to be a cook, and her mother became a camp interpreter. Zofia was raised by her college professor father who spoke German fluently, and now the knowledge of the language came in handy. It meant a roof above their head and food on their table. It meant life.

With the war over, the camp was no longer needed to provide safety for the international refugees. The Displaced Persons became Dispersed Persons from a Dissolved Place. All the homeless and destitute men hastily applied indiscriminately to any place that offered a ray of hope of shelter and retreat. The Krupkas also looked forward to settling down in any country that would accept them. They knew well that the horrors of war destroyed their homeland, leaving only ominous insecurity which loomed above the heads of those who stayed. They could never return to their birthplace. They applied to every place that looked for newcomers, all the way from Australia to England. Finally, they were accepted in the US. A Memphis, Tennessee Baptist Church sponsored them. Ever since they arrived in the new country, they felt obligated to attend the Baptist service as well as the Catholic Mass every week. Although the ceremony of citizenship ultimately gave them a sense of pride, it also made them aware of slowly losing their previous identity.

Both Krzysztof and Zofia eventually learned English and got familiar with the Western customs, but all along they remained fiercely Catholic in their soul, and Polish in their heart. Kasia grew up as an American beauty with high Slavic cheekbones and translucent skin. She spoke both languages fluently and was considered more American than Polish. She felt perfectly at ease among the new American neighbors and old Polish friends alike. Her parents on the other hand, no matter how good the new nation was to them, remained Polish to the core. They only spoke their mother tongue at home and kept every holiday tradition just as if they lived in Krakow. Old Polish recipes were used to prepare the food on the table. Regardless of the years that passed since their arrival in Memphis, they always referred to Krakow as their "home" with a slight pang of pain in their hearts.

When Kasia announced she wanted to marry Jake Odum, her parents were dumbfounded. Their only daughter grew up in America, but the Krupkas instilled in her all of their old-fashioned European values. They felt she always was a bit of a rebel, but that marriage was too much dissent, even for her. Krzysztof and Zofia took her every year to Pennsylvania's re-enacted shrine of Czestochowa, expecting her to meet a nice, young, Polish man one day. They hoped she would settle down nearby, and they would gain a son in her new husband, instead of losing a daughter. They reluctantly agreed to accept Jake and learned to look forward to their visits with the growing family.

In rapid succession, Kasia gave birth to three boys and a daughter. She was happy and busy with her brood, especially after her in-laws died and Jake inherited the farm. At the funeral, the wife of the younger son Jeb openly attacked Jake for 'stealing his brother's share of rightful inheritance', ignoring the fact that for the last eight years only Kasia and Jake took care of the elderly Odums. In exchange for the care, the old Father left the land to Jake. Jeb agreed with the decision and, if it hurt him, he did not mention it. He continued to work long hours, often for six days, at St. Jude's Hospital.

Charlotte Kay never had time to visit her aging in-laws. After learning of their lopsided decision, she felt she was more than right to ignore them all along. Raised as an only child and being the wife of a quiet and tranquil man, Charlotte Kay felt the head-on collision was justified even though it tore the brothers apart. Their older sister kept out of the family feud, maintaining the same relationship with both of her brothers.

Although the two Odum brothers were two years apart, they always were similar both in appearance and nature. As they aged, they even started to look more and more alike. People sometimes joked that they looked like twins and, if Jake did not behave, one day Kasia might accidentally end up in bed with Jeb. Jake, just like his younger brother Jeb, was also a hardworking, quiet, God-fearing, and good man. Two generations of Odums grew cotton in endless fields that blended into the horizon. Jake continued the same.

One day he hung an over-sized sign above his fence, proudly announcing the name of his farm 'Land of Cotton.' He stuck two big US flags on the two sides of the sign, to announce that Jake Odum and his family were proud to be Americans. He also was grateful and pleased to own a property that grew nothing but cotton. Indeed, a land of cotton it was. Jake Odum was the biggest cotton grower in Western Tennessee.

"It takes a labor of love to grow cotton," Kasia always heard. Jake surely must have loved it, because he continued doing the same work that his father and grandfather did all their lives. He just got monstrous, modern equipment for every phase of the work, and did not use the hired help much. His sons were strong enough to pitch in and help. Eventually, they would inherit everything, anyway.

They might as well learn from their father how things were done while they were young, instead of learning later, on their own, from their mistakes.

The bell impatiently rang again, this time longer than before. Seemed that lately Kasia easily got annoyed with a little delay. Jake was not aware of all that laid heavy on his wife's mind and heart: between her age-induced aches and pains and growing responsibilities, she had more than a handful to tackle. There always seemed some unexpected problem cropping up. Lately, her son added to her daily worries. Her youngest boy suddenly acted like a madman; in a fit he threw a dinner plate down, and shattered it into pieces. Kasia knew there was no way to talk or reason with him when he was angry. Only Jake could keep him quiet. The boy was always afraid of his father. She urgently rang the bell for the third time to get Jake home. Hearing the insistent sound of his wife's call, Jake stretched his aching back once more, pulled the cap down on his forehead, and with heavy steps headed for the house.

Chapter 8

Jake bowed his head and, as the patriarch of the family, said grace before the evening meal. His eyes were closed, and he did not see Kasia's red eyes and strained face. He did not notice his first-born son's mouth tightly pressed into a thin line while his young wife's face seemed bored and ignorant. He did not look up at his middle son's humble expression, to note he was in agreement with whatever was to come from his idol and ruler of the family, his father. He certainly did not glance toward his younger son's quickly darting, fearful eyes.

Jake did what he learned as a child and continued daily as an adult: he was offering the day's labor to the Lord and asking for His blessings. His last "Amen" was usually echoed by each family member. This time, he barely heard those who repeated the last word, but among the mumbled sounds he clearly missed hearing Billy Bob. Jake raised his voice and with extra emphasis repeated the Amen, while his piercing eyes rested on the face of his youngest son. The young man finally raised his voice enough for his father to hear him.

Everyone was quietly eating and thinking what to say, should Jake ask what was going on before dinner. Christopher weighed the possibility of bringing his grandparents into the picture, hoping their remarks might defuse the ominous presence.

Being the first grandchild, he was his grandfather's favorite and he proudly wore the name he inherited from the old man. He knew each time they arrived for a short visit, everyone started behaving the best. His father was less morose and usually would take his father-in-law target shooting deep in the woods. They would spend a day alone, have a quiet man-to-man talk, and both would get back by dinner time in a more relaxed mood. In the interim, Grandma would bake up a storm in the kitchen, keeping their mother busy, and off of the kids' back.

Krzysztof's old voice broke the heavy silence. He asked Zofia whether she remembered the name of the small city where they broke off from the convoy of people marching to an unknown destiny. He said that no matter how hard he tried, he could not recall it. Krzysztof was usually quiet, and his mind turned the same thoughts over and over until he finally formed the sentence he wanted to say. Zofia was jolted by the question because she had no idea that the memory of such a long-ago incident was on her husband's mind. She turned to him, wondering what triggered the question. She looked at him for a long time, hoping he would cave in under her staring and say, "never mind, it's not that important", but he did not back down, and she felt obligated to answer.

"You know, it was in the countryside, I really don't know the name of the nearest town. It was somewhere in Bavaria, the most Southern part of Germany, that much I can tell you. Why do you want to know?"

"Really? I thought we were still closer to Austria. Maybe you are right..." his voice trailed off and he stared at the snowy pile of mashed potato on his plate. "We used to make mashed potato like this in the Mooseburg camp... We made it from dry potato flakes... but the soldiers never liked it. As soon as they spotted it, they got disgusted and started to complain 'not again, not this shit'."

Suddenly he smiled, "You know, for a long time I thought that word meant 'mashed potato'. All the kitchen workers called it the same, so I really thought it translated to mashed potato."

Christopher smiled, but Billy and Michael laughed out loud. "Oh, that's good!" claimed Billy and turned to Kasia, "Mom, from now on that's what you will make for us."

"Billy Bob, watch your mouth," came Jake's warning.

Billy stopped instantly, but he clearly was displeased. "Dad, how many times do I have to ask, no, not ask, but beg of you, not to call me Billy Bob? Can you respect me enough to call me Billy? I am not a Tennessee redneck, and Billy Bob implies only that. I hated it my whole life. Every time I hear 'Billy Bob', I curse Miss Dunphy for calling me that. Since age six, I have regretted every day telling you what she named me."

"What's wrong with Billy Bob?" Jake looked at his son. "You are named William Robert, aren't you?"

"Yes, I am. So, call me William Robert, but not Billy Bob. Miss Dunphy did not know what monster she released when she coined her so-called endearment. Endearment, my foot. It is more like a stigma or a curse."

Zofia soothingly interjected, "Not every stigma is bad, Billy. I am sure she meant well and thought you were the cutest little boy she ever laid her eyes on. It just expressed her love for you; I am sure."

"No, Grandma, you are wrong. Miss Dunphy never had any love for me. She always thought I was a country bumpkin. Dammit, I was just a kid, never had been in a big town, never had seen a big red brick building with a fancy stairway, of course I was impressed. I reckon I wanted to get on her good side when I blurted out 'You call this a simple school? I declare, this sure is the finest ol' house, if I ever saw one, Ma'am.' She turned and asked me my name. I said, 'William Robert Odum, Ma'am'. And she burst out laughing, 'So you are William Robert, huh? Why, you sure are a Billy Bob!'"

Michael quickly changed the topic by asking Zofia, "Not to switch the subject, but what happened at the place Grandpa questioned you about? Anything interesting? Maybe if you talk about it, the story would trigger more of his memory."

Zofia did not seem too eager to talk. "Oh, it would not help much, and it might even depress him. I have told him so many of the old stories, and he did not respond too well to them. I think he recalls some parts, but not everything, and the missing connection bothers him. It is natural, don't you think to be troubled by something that you don't quite get?" she looked around, clearly hoping to gather allies.

Christopher turned to the old man. "Grandpa, what happened there? How did you get there? By train or by car? I bet traveling was not as much fun during the war than it would be now. I wish we could go and see that part of the world. Don't you, Helen?" His wife silently kept watching him piling food on his plate in the meantime. To divert her stern expression, he asked his wife to pass the gravy.

"But Chris, you know what the doctor said: lay off the gravy and the fried food," protested his wife in a whining voice. "You don't need it. Do I have to remind you each time? Really, you act like a child, you don't need a wife; you need a mother." Not knowing when to stop, she turned to Kasia and continued, "Mom, I asked you before, please stop serving food he should not eat. You really should listen."

Kasia swallowed hard. Her voice belied her being offended at her own table for the food she made and served, by the daughter-in-law she poorly tolerated. "Christopher should just skip it if he cannot eat it. We all like gravy on our mashed potatoes."

Helen did not get the message, and felt challenged by her husband's mother. "If you truly loved him, you would help him." Getting a sharp kick on her ankle under the table, she turned angrily to Christopher "What? Now what did I say? Nothing more than what we have already discussed before innumerable times."

Jake slowly turned to Helen and in a parched voice barked, "That's enough. Repeat it and you can leave my table." The room got hushed instantly. The only noise was the outside chime as a sudden gust of wind made it dance on the long wire.

"So, Grandpa, tell us what happened," asked Michael quickly. Meek and mild in nature, ever a peace-maker, he was always able to cool any situation that was laden with gunpowder.

Kasia took the clue from her middle son and quickly added, "Grandpa Krzysztof may not want to talk about it, but I bet Grandma Zofia would if you asked her nicely. C'mon, Mom, since Dad started the subject but won't talk about it, could you tell us what it was about? See, we all want to hear you. We are all curious."

Zofia looked around, seeing excitement and anticipation around her. At last her eyes stopped on Jake's expressionless face. *Jake was always so stoic,* she thought, *it must have been hard on Kasia.* Yet, this time she was convinced even Jake would lose his passive expression. Zofia looked away as if looking back to the forties war-torn Europe, and started to spin the old tale.

Chapter 9

"I swore I never would tell it, but I guess the 'never' just ended today," Zofia begun. "Actually, we were transported by the Germans to a safe area, supposedly where there was no war. We had a lot of people in our convoy, mainly from Poland, but some came from Hungary, Transylvania, and Slovakia, too. All were trying to escape the advancing Soviet tanks. We all worked for our old regimes, working as doctors, lawyers, teachers, what they called the 'intelligentsia'. The Germans promised to protect us, but by then we became their liability. We got their help but, surely, that was not the kind of help we expected," she continued.

"First we could take our car to leave Krakow. We drove, heading west. Two days later, a German officer confiscated the car, claiming to act on 'higher orders'. Then the ordeal started. They gathered us in a large group and gave us orders to remain together for the sake of easier transportation. We ended in cattle wagons; some had straw on the floor, some only the bare, dirty, wood planks. Your grandpa was lucky to fight his way to the front of the line to get the more comfortable cart with the straw. The trains moved slowly as the locomotives puffed out angry, white smoke. The smoke carried coal particles to the eyes if we dared to poke our heads out. We all must have smelled like unwashed coal miners. Many times, we had to pull out to unused, dead-end tracks and wait until we let long, military trains pass. These had a few locomotives hooked up to the front to pull often fifty or more carts. You see, the trains carrying soldiers or supplies had priorities on the tracks."

She halted for a minute, then continued in the same tone, "Thank God, they let us out of the carts while we were at the rest stops. I found an old washbasin and always got the hot water off the engine, so at least we could wash ourselves. They let the excess steam and hot water out onto the tracks, so I just asked for it. The engineer was nice, and said if I have something to pour the water into, I could carry it off. What a treasure that beat-up, old wash basin became! Without it we could not get clean. The water was yellow and smelled like coal, but it was warm. Your mother was always the cleanest little girl in the convoy," she smiled at her grandsons, recalling the chubby little girl sitting and splashing in a basin of yellow water near the tracks. How wonderful that children cannot understand the gravity of situations, and keep enjoying life as if they lived the most natural day. Unquestionably, blessed were the little children.

"When we got to Germany, the situation got steadily worse. I understood German, but they did not know it. They spoke freely in front of me. I often overheard the uniformed escorts complaining of this 'human waste', indicating us, who became their liability. They had to feed us, would have to house us, get us jobs, and eventually settle us down, while they had barely anything to eat themselves, and their homes were all but in ruins. The mood had definitely worsened with each new group joining our convoy."

"How many people were in this convoy, Grandma?" asked Christopher.

"I don't know; a lot, probably over two-hundred. I never counted them," responded the old lady.

"Two-hundred ninety-eight, including the little ones," said Krzysztof. "I counted them."

Zofia raised her eyebrows in surprise, but, instead of responding to her husband's remark, she continued her thought, "So, the tracks got blown up at one point, and we could not go further by train. From that moment on we lost our last, little comfort. We slept wherever we found shelter. In Austria, we slept a night in the ruins of the cathedral in Graz."

Her voice trailed off a bit, then she looked at her grandsons to ask: "Did you ever try to fall asleep on a floor? Don't imagine a nice wood floor or carpet, but a cracked marble floor. No, I did not think so. We did. We slept on such a floor, while the stars stared at us, because there was barely any wall remaining around us, and certainly no remnant of the roof was left. And those were the better nights, because at least some parts of a building were protecting us. Though one night the cracked wall collapsed and killed a few people who slept beneath…"

Her old voice trailed off, then regained strength as she continued. "Anyway, your grandpa found half of a broken door, so at least Kasia and I could sleep on the warmer wood and not the cold, stone floor. I tell you, we were the envy of everyone. The next day we were told we had to march on foot, carrying the sick and young who had no energy or stamina. Also, we had to carry all of our belongings, just like a snail or a turtle carried its shell on its back. After a while, the roads behind us were littered by abandoned treasures we brought from home and cherished in the unknown world. With every mile the importance of these material items lessened until the only valuables left were the family pictures and food. Those were never discarded."

Jake turned to his mother-in-law for the first time since she started the recollection. It seemed he wanted to ask a question, but apparently changed his mind and remained silent.

"As I said, we marched on foot," Zofia continued. "Somewhere, approaching Bavaria, we had to stop and rest. We just could not continue without food, water, weighed down by luggage, desperate for the yesterdays, and uncertain about the tomorrows. We found a wooden bench in front of a little house and under the shade of a few, dusty linden trees we rested. Kasia played in the grass with her ragdoll I made from my nightgown. Nightgown! What was I thinking to pack a nightgown and not a pack of matches or a lantern? Amazing how stupid we can be when things spoil us."

"Ain't that the truth?" mumbled Jake, looking toward his youngest son without expecting an answer.

Zofia turned to her oldest grandson, who kept his eyes on her at all times. "You know, Christopher, in those days there were no automatic gates at railroad crossings. Usually, they had a gatekeeper who manually operated the gate when a train was to pass. They built a little house where he and his family lived, right off the tracks. Day and night, he was on duty, no matter if it rained or shined. Can you imagine that?" asked Zofia. The three young men and Helen just stared incredulously at the old woman, trying to accept what they heard. Jake and Kasia did not seem to be as surprised by the old technology.

"Anyway, we stopped at such a gatekeeper's house. His wife, I never forgot her, was a big boned, thick-waisted woman. She approached us and asked who we were and what was going on. People directed her to come to me because I was the only one who spoke German fluently. I told her we were displaced persons, and the German officers were leading us to a place to endure the war.

After the war, who knows what would happen. I asked her if she had any food to share. She said they had none, either, but she just picked the last of her spinach from the garden and cooked it, and could give us a little. At least, give enough for Kasia, I asked her. God bless her, she came back with a plate full of spinach, and Kasia ate it like she never had anything better. While we watched Kasia gobbling up the warm food, she asked me where we were headed. I did not know the place but showed her the slip we were given with our final destination on it. I never forget her face, how it changed. She read it, and her smile disappeared. Her ruddy face became pale, and the paper in her hands trembled. 'Don't go there,' she moaned."

"Why? What was this place?" I asked.

"I cannot tell you, but for God's sake, don't go there. I'll tell you what to do. Stay at the end of the group and when you get in the center of the town, there will be a 'y' intersection. You will recognize it, right after you pass the blown-up city hall, next to the ruins of the church. You cannot miss it; from a distance, the bell tower still stands visible. Instead of continuing with your group, turn to the left and run as fast as you can. There is a little alley on your left, maybe a block later. Turn there and hide. If no one is looking for you, continue West, always West, until you get to Mooseburg."

"But why? I didn't really dare to separate from the group. I repeatedly questioned if she seriously thought that's what we really should do. After all, we had no idea where we were, my husband did not speak German, and we knew not a soul there. We never hurt anyone. Why did we have to run and hide? Wouldn't it have been better if we just trusted our officers and marched where they promised us safety? At least the Germans could have protected us as they promised."

"'No, no, no, and a thousand times no.' She could not tell me more. She liked our little girl, because Kasia reminded her of her own child, who died around the same age of diphtheria. Did I want her to live? My God, of course, yes. I knew it fully then that I had to listen to her, and had to do what she suggested. The poor, simple woman was very convincing as she begged me. You have no idea how many times I gave her thanks in my mind since that day."

"So, what was this Mooseburg? I asked her. Was it a city?"

"It was a small town about thirty miles away. It had a large International Military Camp. They would have never bombed it; the Americans, English, and I thought even some of the French guarded it. We were to go there and ask for shelter. We offered to do any job they needed. Don't forget, it was the only chance of survival we got. But before we reached Mooseburg, let me finish what happened with the German gatekeeper's wife. While we talked, her expression and tone suddenly changed, and she flatly announced in a loud voice that they had no food and could not offer any help. I looked back to see an officer approaching, and I understood her. She immediately disappeared into her house, and I could not even hug her to thank her for the spinach or the help. Until today, I don't even know her name. But I tell you, God should bless her, and rest her in peace for she must be dead by now. She saved us."

"And thank God, for my father! Bless his soul and may he rest in peace!" added Zofia, as she made the sign of the cross on herself. "My father, your great-grandfather insisted on the importance of education and taught me to speak another language. Without that, we would have not ended up in the Mooseburg camp."

"Don't forget to thank God for your believing in the woman and insisting on doing what she recommended," interjected Krzysztof. "We did exactly what she said, and the roads were as she described them. It took us almost two days to reach the camp. They hired me to be a kitchen help, and your mother became the translator. Remember how many big cans of food they gave us from the kitchen? We would have been dead if not for that woman."

The old woman and the even older man looked back in time and saw the military barracks that served as their shelter and home for the next two years. They saw the long wood benches and tables, covered with oilcloth, surrounded by loud, boisterous, young men. Where were those young men now? Some laid to rest in quiet cemeteries scattered all over Europe. Some were buried in Germany. Some were never found in the torn-up battlefields or lost in the seas. The fields looked crimson forever from their shed blood, and not from the red poppies that grew wildly all over. Many were more fortunate to return to age and die at home. The room was quiet. They were all thinking the same.

Finally, Kasia asked her mother: "So, what was written on your order to be the final destination?"

One could barely hear her voice whispering in horror, "Dachau Concentration Camp."

Chapter 10

The room was still, even the air became thick and heavy all of a sudden. They all knew about the infamous concentration camps. This was not shocking news. What stunned Jake Odum's family was how close the destruction came to their home. Grandma, Grandpa, Mom, all sent to a death camp? It was incredible. They knew what happened there, what was waiting for everyone who entered the barbed wire fenced genocide. Americans learned about what was going on in those death camps first from the military which freed the remaining live prisoners, then from the news when the Nurnberg trials started. The radios and newspapers were full of stories that were hard even to comprehend. They had to be true, though, because eventually many of the captured Nazi officers were hung or imprisoned.

"A concentration camp? But you said the Germans protected you, being an old ally," Jake's voice was indignant.

"To a certain point they did. But they were also starving, and then they had to feed us. We were their responsibility when they could not even be responsible for their own. It was easier to wipe out the whole problem with one stroke", replied Zofia.

"I don't get it, Grandma. You were not Jewish, and the Germans only wanted to kill the Jews, didn't they?" asked Christopher.

"Oh, no, my dear. They targeted all non-Aryans. You know, anyone who did not have German roots. Anyone who was different than they were. They got the Slavs, Gypsies, Poles, Catholics, homosexuals, cripples, political opponents, you name it. They got them all. Why, their most famous prisoner was Father Maximilian Kolbe. A Polish Catholic priest of the Franciscan order, who volunteered to take the place of a condemned, young soldier. When three inmates escaped from the death-camp, no one revealed the names of their helpers. To punish the silent prisoners, the commander chose every tenth man from the line and condemned them to death by starvation. Poor Father Kolbe suffered for two long, agonizing weeks of horrible starvation and dehydration at the hands of his Nazi guards before he was injected with lethal carbolic acid. He was the last to die of the ten convicted men. He first helped all to leave this life with a bit of caring before ultimately, he lost his life, too. You see, these death camps showed the worst cruelty but also the best of humanity, too."

Kasia interjected, "Mom, I just read the Pope has elevated him to sainthood."

"I tell you, he sure deserved it as much as any saint did, if not more. At least someone recognized his sacrifice and honored him. No, Christopher, no, not only Jews died in concentration camps, but about five million others died, too. Almost two million were Poles. Most were punished for hiding and rescuing Jews or just being plain Polish. My own father, your great-grandfather, hid three Jewish boys from the school where he was teaching. I remember he took his students to the press-house and hid them in a large barrel. Every day my dad pretended to go to his vineyard to trim and spray his grapes. On his bicycle, he secretly carried a basket of food to them. On his way home, he brought a can of waste to be discarded at home. It was a pure miracle that he was not discovered. Otherwise, he would have made five million and one non-Jewish victims."

"And you still like the Germans, Grandma?" questioned Michael in an incredulous voice.

"Of course. Without that kind and noble woman, we would not be here. Neither us, nor your mother, and certainly not you," replied the old woman.

"Dachau's name most commonly was associated with the concentration camp. Actually, it was the first such camp built thus it became the prototype for all other sub-camps and death factories. In the first four months of 1945, over thirteen thousand prisoners died in Dachau. Further North, in Bergen-Belsen, in another death camp, by the end of the war almost twenty-thousand Soviet war prisoners and another fifty-thousand inmates died. The first months of 1945 brought typhus into the crowded camps, and more than thirty-five-thousand weakened prisoners died of the epidemic. In Dachau, malnutrition and typhus were the most virulent and deadly diseases.

"When the British 11th Armoured Division liberated the Bergen-Belsen camp in the middle of April 1945, they discovered over sixty-thousand half-starved inmates, some mortally ill, and another thirteen-thousand corpses lying unburied around the camp. The main Dachau camp was liberated at the end of April 1945, by the U.S. Seventh Army's 45th Infantry Division and a major Dachau sub-camp was liberated on the same day by the 42nd Rainbow Division. Don't believe me? You can see the documentary films and pictures the English and US soldiers made."

After a little pause she added, "And this is where they were sending us. Do you think we could have survived these horrors in our debilitated condition?"

"Mom," started Kasia, visibly shaken by the never-before-heard story, "why didn't you ever tell me, or tell us what happened there? I never heard you even utter a single word about this until today!"

"The past is past. We did not want to start the new life in America by harboring hatred in our hearts. Besides, what was the use in talking about it? When we needed help, God sent this German woman to our rescue. I was sure He would send help again when it was needed. You know Kasia, not all angels come in long flowing gowns and fly on sparkling white wings while playing a golden harp. Most angels are disguised as everyday people."

"But, Mom," insisted Kasia, "if it were not for you, we all would be dust by now."

"Now, Kasia, don't attribute too much credit to me alone. Don't you forget your father was there to do everything to protect us. Without him, we surely would not have survived."

Jake looked up sharply and stared at the old woman who was determined to delegate more than half of the tribute to her husband. To her mate, who did not understand a word of German, and who argued with her not to desert the security of the group by believing the words of a half-illiterate wife of an uneducated, county gate-keeper.

Christopher sat stunned. His wife Helen just looked from face to face, and gave a silly smile to the older folks. Michael had tears in his eyes, and he stepped up to Kasia to hug her. Kasia reached out and squeezed Billy's hand as if encouraging him to say something. But Billy was solemn and remained silent.

"Dear Lord, I have never heard this before," claimed Kasia. "Sunday, we'll invite the folks from church, along with all our friends, and we'll have a celebration to honor my Mom and Dad.

And to honor the nameless German woman who saved us. Is that OK with you, Jake?"

"Of course, it is. We should. All of you should be planning to stay for the weekend. You, too, Helen."

Chapter 11

Now everyone became animated. Zofia and Krzysztof were a bit embarrassed about being the center of attention, but seeing how easily Jake agreed, they became enthusiastic about the planned get-together, too. Only Billy seemed to be less than excited.

"Well, we are all not going to be here. First of all, Grace is away in Arizona and second, I promised to meet some friends in Memphis," Billy said. "More like business partners," he corrected himself, hoping that mentioning business would be a more acceptable excuse.

"You heard your mother," came the quiet warning from his father. "Your family comes first. Family comes before your friends or business dealings. You mentioned Grace being away. It is not an excuse for your not being here. Your sister is married, and she cannot just drop everything to travel home for a weekend. Grace's life is in Phoenix, and she is not a skip or hop away. You have no such excuse, though. You live at home and have no responsibilities. Besides, what business do you have suddenly? You had none for the last year. None."

"Father, you know I tried, but after I got laid off, I had no luck," Billy's voice took on the same high-pitched whine as when he was a child and complained about his older brothers. It always irritated Jake, but he let Kasia handle it. Billy was his mother's baby and remained the same, in spite of his age.

"Billy Bob, you are almost forty years old and have no job. Furthermore, you don't work. There is quite a big difference between a job and work. You have neither."

"What more can I say? You never, ever see my side. Nobody understands me here. I am trying to do my best. No matter what I do, I will never be as good in your eyes as Christopher or Michael," complained Billy with a dark face.

Jake slowly measured his words, but Kasia noted his rising anger. "Perhaps if you worked as hard as your brothers, you would appear to be as good."

"Oh, Billy, we all love you and try to help you. How can you say nobody understands you? Did your father or I ever harm you? Did Christopher or Michael ever do anything to hurt you?" Kasia's heart ached and her voice pleaded with her troubled child.

"Good God almighty, Mom, you don't understand me. You have no idea what I am talking about, do you? You know nothing of the world. You are scooped up in your kitchen and see nothing further than the cypress in front of your window. Sometimes I wonder if you ever got over not getting crowned at that ancient Cotton Ball. You were a first runner-up, and not the queen, right? And when was that? Fifty years ago? Get over it! Life did not stop there!"

Kasia's eyes filled with tears. She was deeply hurt, as her treasured, old secret got spread out in front of everyone. She never imagined Billy could ever wound her more, regardless of what he would say or do in the future. She pressed her trembling lips tightly and remained silent.

Billy was on a roll, and continued his tirade, ignoring his mother. "Dad works the farm with Christopher and Michael, from dawn to sunset, all year around. Do you think they know anything about the world? Nope, they do not. Christopher has not been further than Nashville, and Michael only went as far as Memphis."

At this point, he turned back to his stunned mother with his attacks. "You two did not stick your noses out of Tennessee. You only know this land and how to grow cotton, and even that you do in an old-fashioned way. You live with your blinders on! You are content in the kitchen and Father thinks the best life one could get is growing cotton and working the land. I had been in the Army and traveled quite a bit. I even went to Boise, Idaho. I saw the world. There is more to life than to claw the clay with your ten fingers, this dirt around here." Billy's heated words ignited a long-standing and ongoing disagreement, which rapidly escalated toward a final showdown.

"What did you call this land? Dirt? Watch it, boy, don't you insult the land of your father and grandfather!" Jake snapped. "This land gave you shelter, food, and education when you were a child. This land now supports your idle butt. Instead of you working it, what do you do? Nothing! Not a damn thing! This land is all we got, all you got. When all falls apart, when you have nothing left, you still have the land. This land is eternal. Don't you ever forget it."

Although normally Billy would clam up at his father's rare outbursts, now he felt angry and humiliated in front of the entire family. He particularly felt ashamed in front of his grandparents after his Grandma Zofia defended him for being called Billy Bob. His cup was filled to the brim with bitterness, pain, and frustration, and it overflowed. Billy was determined to pour out his embittered feelings that gnawed at his heart and guts, infesting his inside. The ghost that lurked in his dark soul was finally free, and it spread its ominous shadow on everyone around the dining table.

"Then I guess the experiments I do are nothing for you? I am telling you; there are ways to make more money. For Heaven's sake, I am talking about money, much more money than you ever saw in your whole life in one pile. More than you make in three years of work with cotton alone. But do you ever listen to me? No, because you think I am dumb and know nothing," Billy finally snapped. The family sat in terror, seeing Jake's face darken and knowing whatever came next, could not be good.

"Yeah, your 'experiment' and your preoccupation with money. Have you not heard the preacher ever say 'money is the Devil's Bible'? And that's what you want. You have no shame. Supposedly, you grow a new kind of crop, 'an experiment', you claim. Huh, an experiment. Don't let me go there."

"Yes, I heard the preacher say that," replied Billy hotly and could not resist adding, "yet, every Sunday he takes a good portion of it, doesn't he?"

"Billy, it is only right to give to the church. Don't forget, they sponsored your grandparents, and made it possible for them to come here. Without the church, your grandparents or I would never be here," Kasia barely could conceal her indignation. Zofia and Krzysztof nodded in agreement.

"Sure, Mom, I know it all. You would never let us forget it for a second. Let me remind you that was long ago, almost before Christ! You already paid enough through the years. Don't you ever think you have compensated them for more than your share? Why do you have to feel you are obligated even now? Does repayment never end?"

Kasia's voice came firmly, "No. Obligations and thankfulness never end. Never."

"Since you are so smart, thanks to the Army," started Jake sarcastically, "tell me just why you think I needed your new plant? My cotton is well known and respected here. I use the new hybrid seeds and produce the best cotton in Tennessee. I don't need your new crop. I don't care how much money it would bring or how much better off we would be if we changed to planting your stuff instead of cotton. I always said I don't care what everyone else does nowadays. I am not 'everyone'. Don't you respect anything? Don't you fear the law? Don't you fear God?" Jake's voice steadily got louder and louder, and by this time he was red all the way to his collarless shirt.

"Besides, what makes you a big agricultural scientist, all of a sudden? Don't you know I am aware of your actions? You say 'you have to risk it to get the biscuit'. Let me tell you, you are not getting any here. I saw your hothouse. I saw your pots and plants. I don't know what you and your buddy grow there, but that is not cotton. You are plumb shameless." Jake was more disgusted with his own outburst than with the unfaithful son who provoked him.

"It is the new crop, and 'my buddy' has a name: Roy. You could use his name instead of calling him 'my buddy'. I would appreciate a little respect, as I believe it is due. You can't stand Helen, yet you treat her with kid's gloves because she is Christopher's wife. So what? Roy is my choice and at any time he is worth as much as Helen."

Blinded by his anger, Billy did not realize he revealed his well-guarded secret. Everyone long suspected him of being interested in men, except his father, who was as far as the moon from the earth from the very idea of homosexuality, and his grandparents, because they were old and never thought such things could happen in their family.

Billy hotly continued, "Furthermore, the crop I propose you plant is not 'my stuff' and it is not my 'pots and plants'. It is marijuana. You should start it, too. I told you, there is big money in it. Everybody grows it, but you with all this land, you could make it a big operation, and rake in the money. Or plant poppy. Yeah, instead of 'Land of Cotton' we could rename the property 'Field of Poppy'. Even better. Poppy would make more money and much faster."

"Billy Bob, you are plumb crazy. That's it. I am done with you. You are not my son, you are the spawn of a devil. That's it." Jake was angrier than anyone had seen him before. They all sat frozen in fear.

Billy also raised his voice and his words cracked like a whip. "You never listen, do you? Well, enjoy your half-rusted, old truck and the leaking roof over your head." His face flashed dark red with anger and the veins protruded on the two sides of his neck and temples. He was way too upset to realize what he blurted out, or to listen to what the old man was telling him. All he heard was the usual way his father ordered everyone around him and worshiped his cotton-growing, God-forsaken farm that was handed down from generation to generation.

Billy suddenly hated the old man, and really wanted to hurt him. Maybe then he would abandon his preoccupation with his only love, his land, and start paying some attention to him. It was always this condescending, belittling, superior behavior that he hated as a child, and could not stand as a young man. The fire burning in him blindly propelled him to confront his father, to pay him back for all the injustice he imagined he suffered from him, to break his righteousness once. He sprang to action and turned to the old man. In his anger, he slammed his fist on the table so hard that the plates and glasses rattled. He really wanted to hurt his father but, in his frustration when he hit the table, he only hurt his own hand.

Before he could control his voice to even utter a sound, Kasia jumped up to get between her husband and son. She did not notice her dress got hooked on the crocheted edge of the tablecloth, and she pulled everything off the table. The next moment her dinner was spread all over the floor. The broken dishes and spilled food made a horrible mess. They all stared incredulously at the destroyed meal, unable to say a word.

Jake looked at the floor with a dark face before he got up with the heavy limbs of an old man. In a cold voice he turned to his family, "You can thank Billy Bob for your dinner". Then he faced his youngest son, "You should continue eating; all dogs eat from the floor." The door slammed behind him as loud as a gunshot.

Billy was ready to tackle him, but his frail mother put her arms around him and started to talk to him in the same soothing voice she used when her children got hurt, but Billy was inconsolable. In his uncontrolled and blind rage, he wildly pushed his mother away. She staggered backward, slipping on the spilled mashed potato. Her arm reached out to grab the table, and as she fell, her outstretched forearm hit the edge of the heavy oak top. All happened in a split second but seemed to unfold as of in slow-motion. They all heard the snapping sound of breaking bones in the eerie silence.

Kasia lay helplessly on the floor before Christopher and Michael managed to get the sobbing woman up and carried her into the family room. Helen silently began to pick up the broken china and glass pieces. Old man Krzysztof looked at his daughter with tears in his eyes while Zofia rushed to her aid.

Only Billy stood frozen. His guilt over his mother's fall and her obvious injury shocked him, but the fear of his father's foreseeable reaction petrified him. Billy finally shot a pitiful glance at the tear-soaked, pale, and suddenly aged face of his mother. He could not stand the heartbreaking sight. He turned away and ran out of the room, without uttering a word of apology. In the commotion, no one paid attention to his disappearance. Once out of sight, he quickly grabbed a few of his belongings and tossed them on the back seat of his car. His faithful Ford stirred up a gust of yellow dirt as he left the farm in a hurry.

When he turned from the gravel road to the two-lane highway, he suddenly jerked the stirring wheel to avoid a ditch. The skidding rear of his truck hit the weather-beaten pole that held the sign "Land of Cotton". That sign was the only outward expression of Jake Odum's pride, as if openly announcing to the world 'here started and ended Tennessee's Land of Cotton'. The old pole cracked in half, and the sign fell and broke in two when hit the ground. The two huge Stars and Stripes that so proudly waved in the wind on both sides of the sign now made a few death-twists in the dirt. Then, as if realizing their futile efforts, they gave up and laid wrinkled and motionless among the ruins.

"Good", Billy thought with bitter satisfaction, "he deserved, at least, that much. I don't care anymore. I will never come back, never set foot on this God-forsaken, cotton-growing dirt again. Never."

Chapter 12

When Mr. McCarthy called the Coroner's Office, instead of getting Dr. Johnson on the line, a young lady answered the phone. She took the message and promised to give it to her boss as soon as he returned from lunch. She hesitated a bit, then added, "Sometimes he does not come back, though. Would it be all right if he called you back in the morning?"

McCarthy's response showed his mounting frustration with all the delays and roadblocks he encountered ever since Jeb Odum's body was discovered. "No, Ma'am. Kindly contact Dr. Johnson, wherever he is, so he can return my call." He needed clarifications for his understanding and could not wait for another day. He was irritated with the girl's singing, happy voice, which meant nothing more to him but another annoying delay. As a county employee, he had to keep long working hours. It was not right that the coroner, another government employee, did not work, at least, until the end of the day.

He knew very little of Dr. Johnson. They met on official business once, but never socialized. McCarthy realized they did not move in the same social circles. Dr. Johnson and his artist wife belonged to the fancy, rich society, studded by country-club membership, art gallery exhibitions, and a mansion in the most luxurious section in Germantown. Their teenage son attended a private academy. Aside from the gross financial disparity, McCarthy never could warm up to the doctor. The divide was not only the different lifestyle they lived, but their difference in personalities. Dr. Johnson was not a person who invited small talk or friendship from anyone. He was unusually quiet; only his unhappy eyes indicated he participated in the ongoing discussion. Usually he appeared outright sad by his expression and forbidding in his mannerism.

McCarthy read the coroner's report a few times, but found no suggestion as to what caused Jeb Odum's death. He understood the heart was effectively stopped from functioning by the accumulating blood in its surrounding sack. So much was clear. What caused the bleeding? The entry wound was triangular and small. What instrument was used? It had to be made out of metal, because it skirted the ribs, but the bones did not stop it from proceeding deeper. It also had to be long, for it had to travel a bit to reach Jeb's heart. A knitting needle would do, except, that was round. What could make a triangular-shape hole? McCarthy needed Dr. Johnson's input, hoping he could shed some light on the possible assault weapon. Maybe the coroner had seen something similar before.

He raised his voice and called Corky in his office. "Did you go through the bags yet? You know what? On second thought, forget that stuff for the time being, just get to his phone and his computer first."

"That was already done," reported Corky.

"And?" McCarthy raised his eyes to look at Corky above his glasses. "And you found what?"

"Nothing much, but what I did find was sort of revealing. He had a complete phone list of mainly women. Among the most frequented phone calls were Vittoria DelRosario's and Lana Hadock's numbers. He made a call twice a day to Vittoria, morning and evening, like clockwork, or received a call from her. On the other hand, Lana called him a few times more within the last month, but not regularly. It seemed like first Jeb stopped calling Lana about a month ago, then made only sporadic contact with her. In return, there were no new incoming calls from her, either. I assumed, as he apparently did not make much effort to talk to Lana, in return she also stopped calling him. Except she made a few calls to Jeb this week, I think the last was three days ago. By then, Jeb was not in a position to answer any phone calls. I wonder what happened. Did she call him because he didn't return her calls or was she fed up with him for some reason? Anyway, this is something worth pursuing."

"How about other incoming calls? Were there any suspicious numbers?" McCarthy inquired.

"The last two weeks, only one number showed up, almost on a daily basis. It was Doug Bullock's cell phone. I have contacted the cell towers and guess what? He called Jeb from various places, but each a bit closer to Jeb's house. Obviously, he was closing in on Jeb. I wonder if he showed up at Jeb's house on the last day."

"Are you sure of that? This might be crucial."

"I am positive. Oh, yeah, and his ex-wife called him five nights before his murder. They talked for a few minutes, maybe five or six, that's all."

"Really? Didn't you say when you saw her at her house, she didn't keep much in touch with Jeb?"

"You're right, she forgot to mention this. As a matter of fact, she said she did not have any contact, except a brief call, with Jeb for at least two weeks after that infamous restaurant meeting."

"Very interesting. Anything else?"

"No, just the usual calls for an air conditioner repair, to the road paver, and to his brother and daughter. Nothing to get excited over, for sure." Corky was unenthusiastic, to say the least.

"How about the computer? Anything on that?" McCarthy hoped for some clues.

"No. It sure was not a treasure-trove, if that's what you expected. He had some web searches for Match.com and SeniorsDate.com, otherwise just the routine online banking, management of his retirement plan, getting directions to the dentist, that sort of stuff. Nothing. Nada. Jeb Odum was a bit of a bore, if I may say so. A very predictable man, for sure."

"Well, for me, that use of a dating service is not as boring as you think. Did you discover what he was doing there? I mean, I know, he was looking for dates. But did you find his profile?"

"I sure did. He posted three pictures of himself and signed-in under the pseudonym 'NeedAnAngel'. He wanted to meet professional, accomplished, financially stable, single women for long-term relationship, possibly leading to marriage."

McCarthy laughed, "Corky, you tell me, which woman in his age group would not want to be married once she had everything but a man? Or which women did not think of herself as an angel? Destined to save a lost and lonely man? You're wrong; old Jeb Odum was not as simple-minded as he liked to come across, for sure."

"Well, it certainly looks like it," agreed Corky.

"How about that glass in the sink? What did the lab find out? You know, that dried up stain in it. Was it wine in the bottom? Also, was it truly lipstick on the edge? What did you discover?" inquired McCarthy.

"Oh, that. The lab found it to be dried up wine, indeed. As a matter of fact, it was the same wine we found in the refrigerator. Twisted Merlot. The second glass was found half-filled with wine and stored in the refrigerator. It had Jeb's fingerprint on it," Corky became more animated as he talked.

"So, two people were drinking the wine. It was not a set-up. One of them was a woman, by the lipstick alone. Remember, we saw lipstick on the edge. You know, the funniest is that both his ex-wife and his fiancée used the same hot-pink color lipstick. I saw the same color at Charlotte Odum's place, myself, when I picked up her lipstick from the floor. Vittoria DelRosario left her lipstick on the vanity, next to her perfume bottle. Same color, different brand. Charlotte's was Revlon, Vittoria's Lancôme. I have verified both."

"The sales lady at Macy's happened to be my mother's distant cousin, and she gave me samples of both. So, which of the two women drank wine last with Jeb? It could have been either, right? I figured it was the first riddle we had to solve. Judging by the amount of the dried-up wine left on the bottom of the glass, it must have been within the last two days. Vittoria was not in Tennessee for the last month. Therefore, it only could have been Charlotte Kay," Corky was evidently proud of his logical summary.

"OK, call Charlotte Kay back for questioning again. And get Doug Bullock on the carpet, too. I think he might be the smoking gun." McCarthy rubbed his tired forehead and glanced at Corky from below his hand. He noted a doubting, half a smile on Corky's face, clearly indicating he did not believe what his boss said.

Corky already knew who the murderer was. It had to be Charlotte Kay Odum, Jeb's ex-wife. She had a motive, she had an opportunity, and she lied to the investigators. He recalled the poorly masked hatred she expressed when he met the newly widowed woman at her house. If Charlotte Kay only wanted a club and a spade, the solution of the case was right in front of them. She all but admitted the crime. By later being untruthful, it only became obvious she was covering up something. If McCarthy thought the killer was Doug Bullock, he was wrong. The criminal must have been Charlotte Kay. It was Corky's job to prove his chief wrong.

McCarthy, on the other hand, was not convinced of either Mrs. Odum's or Bullock's guilt. Neither Charlotte Kay nor Doug Bullock were coming across as innocent bystanders but somehow, he felt Doug Bullock was not a murderer. He might have been a small-town crook, a liar, or a user, but not a hard-core criminal. Doug really did not have a solid reason to commit the crime, either. Having an affair with Jeb's ex-wife should not have motivated him to stab Jeb to death. Especially not when they both were ready to break up and end their relationship.

Charlotte Kay recently got engaged to a businessman. She, surely, would not have dumped an established, well-to-do potential suitor for a 'handyman', no matter how hot he might have been in bed. McCarthy also learned Doug Bullock had a notion of his impending doom, and already dated a beautiful young girl from the apartment complex where he worked. He did not seem to be too heart-broken over Charlotte Kay, by any means.

McCarthy went over his notes once more, thinking he might have missed something. Who knows what he might have overlooked, unless he revisited the facts over and over. A good detective searches for answers until all puzzle pieces fall into place, creating a complete picture. So far, the cohesiveness eluded him. He felt, in his gut, the key was in finding the weapon. Damn, Dr. Johnson still owed him a return call, as he realized the coroner had failed to return his message.

Chapter 13

After Corky left, the sudden silence was deafening in McCarthy's office. He turned back to his notes once more. He forced himself to concentrate. He knew, if he just racked his brain more, at any moment he might recognize some previously missed little thing, something that could give a totally different direction to his search. He was reviewing all the interviews, when suddenly a light turned on in his mind, as a new insight: Mr. Wilson, Jeb's nearest neighbor, accounted for his dog's strange behavior. In the wee hours before Jeb Odum's murder, the Wilson's dog kept barking ferociously and tugged at his chain.

As a matter of fact, Earl Ray Wilson was rightfully alarmed, because his dog was usually quiet at night. Nobody came and went under the cloak of darkness, except an occasional deer. But even if it were a deer, the dog would not have created such havoc for so long. No, it must have been something or someone other than a wild animal.

Mr. Wilson said he went upstairs to get his rifle, but by the time he looked out, the dog was quiet and was only standing, with the chain pulled taut. He stared into the darkness, facing Jeb Odum's house. Mr. Wilson barely got back to bed, when the dog acted up again, first snarling, and then angrily barking as he fought the chain holding him at bay. The second time, Mr. Wilson caught a glimpse of a red taillight on a dark truck. He did not see the driver but noted the truck was speeding away toward the highway, spewing rocks behind from the gravel drive. Then all quieted down again. He almost ignored the incident, but two days later Jeb was found dead, and the unusual activities returned to his mind with crystal clear importance. He told about the events to the Sheriff, hoping he contributed to solving the puzzle.

Was the dark truck connected to Jeb's murder? Was it the night visitor who committed the crime? Did he come back the next day to complete his murderous plot? Although McCarthy had no answers, instinctively he knew this time he had stumbled onto something important. He felt he was a step closer to discovering the truth.

The rest of the day went uneventfully: Corky was out of the office somewhere, and McCarthy tested his theory by revisiting the crime scene. The big house was cordoned off by long strips of yellow crime-scene markers. The doors were all locked and sealed. *Not that anyone banged on the doors or wanted to force their way into the home,* he mused. The huge brick home looked serene and peaceful among the softly whispering pines.

In the backyard, a hummingbird feeder hung empty, and a disappointed little green jewel of a tiny bird waited on the bent iron holder for a refill. McCarthy vaguely registered the hummingbird's plight, but since he got involved with this tragic business, he could not help the hungry little bird. If only that hummingbird could talk!

He inspected the entrance, but there was nothing ominous on the lock or on the door itself. Certainly, there were no signs of forced entry on the wood frame, the door, or the lock itself. He concluded Jeb Odum must have known his attacker, and opened the door for him to let him into the house. Instantly, a nagging thought occurred to him: what if he was assaulted outside and not in the house? Maybe that's why there were no indoor tell-tale signs of crime anywhere.

He stepped outside and walked around, carefully observing the surroundings. All seemed to be in order; yet, something was amiss. He keenly felt something happened outside, but could not put his finger on the location. He only knew it was here, in front of the side entrance of the house, that Jeb must have been attacked.

He slowly walked with his eyes glued to the ground, when he finally spotted a track mark in the dirt. Three days ago, there was a torrential downpour, and the dirt road turned into a mud pond where the gravel had been washed away. In this bare spot, a truck left a mark with a visible imprint of the tire's brand. The dried sludge was definitely the detective's friend. Some letters on the tire were clearly imprinted, then caked into the clay when the hot sun baked it into a clump. Next to it was the partial print of a shoe. The pattern of the left forefoot was far more deeply printed than the hindfoot. *Aha, the assailant must have approached on tiptoes because his weight was on the front portion of his feet.* McCarthy smiled with satisfaction. A little farther, he detected a smaller footprint.

He leaned forward and looked for an awfully long time at the shoe print. He was careful not to go near or touch it. He placed a long stick nearby to mark the area before proceeding further. The shoe print had pointed toes, and the heel appeared narrower than expected. McCarthy thought it could have been made by either a lady's boot, or perhaps by a cowboy boot. Looking at the imprint for a long time, he concluded it could have been made by an above-average sized woman or a smaller man. No way to tell the gender from the indentation alone. The person must not have been too heavy; he judged by the relatively shallow mark. He or she slid a bit in the mud before landing in the final spot, just before stepping on the concrete driveway. The edge of the driveway was piled up with dried mud. This is where the aggressor must have entered Jeb's space. Obviously, the mud was carefully scraped off against the edge of the cement, because there was no continuation anywhere else. McCarthy was sure the assailant did not fly but walked. He just needed to find where the footsteps continued to piece the puzzle together.

"Hey, Mister," yelled a man from the neighboring yard. McCarthy looked up, a bit startled, and turned in the direction of the voice. Staring right into the setting sun, he only saw the silhouette of a man in the glaring rays. He was a tall black man with broad shoulders and wide chest. He must have been working hard his entire life; even now he had a rake in his hand.

"I spotted you coming and wanted to catch you," continued the man. "I am Mr. Odum's neighbor on the left, Wilson, Earl Ray Wilson. I tole' you about what my dog done the night before Jeb was found. D'you remember me?"

"I most certainly do, Mr. Wilson. I appreciate you coming forward with that information. I also found the markings left by the visitor, so your dog was right by barking up a storm. You have a good friend in that dog, I tell you," McCarthy laughed.

"Well, being in the woods, kind'a off the road, we need all the protection we can git," Mr. Wilson agreed. "Any progress on what happen'?"

"Some," the detective answered vaguely, "but we sure have a way to go."

"Ain't it simply awful, what people can do? Um, um, um," he shook his head. "There is no way to tell what's next. The wife and I sure were all shook up after we left the other day. I declare, this is just not expected in our community. We felt we is safe here, as safe as we could git. Maybe one heard about an occasional break-in, but murder? Why, it never, ever, happened here, and we have lived in this house for over forty years. Incredible. I shouldn't be wonderin' 'coz these are desperate times, and some godless people would do anything to git ahead in life, I reckon." Mr. Wilson shook his head so hard that the torn straw hat slid sideways and showed a patch of graying, short-cropped, curly, black hair.

"Oh, yes, in hard financial times the crime numbers increase, for sure. So you knew Mr. Odum well, did you?" McCarthy asked.

"Sure did, from the moment they broke ground and moved next to us. We was the first to live here, and it was me who named our street after my football team. I thought Jeb might object, but no, he jus' agreed without sayin' much. Jeb ain't much of a talker, if you know what I mean. He always worked, mowin' the lawn, cuttin' down trees, luggin' out trash to the landfill. We saw each other comin' or goin', but we ain't got much to say. I even sees his lady friend once. She sure was a looker, but she jus' was not cut out to work on a tractor. Even a blind man could sees that. That's for sure. And Jeb rodes that tractor day and night." Mr. Wilson turned sideways to spit a clump of chewed grass to the dirt. "Heck, as a matter of fact I hardly could imagine them together. They jus' did not seem to be cut from the same bit of cloth, if you knows what I mean. Like puttin' a fancy silk patch over old denim. No, Sir, that patch jus' don't make no improvement of the blue jean. Yep, that's it in a nutshell."

McCarthy let the man talk without interrupting him: after all, he wanted to learn all the things he could about Jeb. He watched Mr. Wilson with his comically sliding straw hat, his foot resting on the cross beam of the fence. McCarthy figured the more he talked, the more he revealed. So far, he learned Jeb Odum owned both a pickup truck and a tractor. On his first day of the investigation, he saw the truck had brand new Bridgestone tires; the white lettering sort of caught his attention in the dark garage. The tractor was stuck under a halfway broken cedar, next to a pile of branches. Apparently, that was the last task Jeb attacked before his end put a stop to all of it. The detective made a mental note to himself to investigate the tractor tires next.

"Yep, he was a good man. Took real good care of that big house and all them yard work. He could do everythin' hisself, but since he fancied this lady-friend of his, he don't have much time left for them repairs. No sir, he sure didn't. I guess it ain't much fun workin' around the house alone anymore, neither. I sawed lately he hired someone to put up his shutters. I thinks Jeb done paintin' them, but maybe he don't want to climb up that tall ladder to the second floor or somethin' 'coz this young man showed up to do it. But you know, he was a decent man, he never went into the house. He worked outside and ate his food sittin' on the steps. He was there the whole week before Jeb died. What a pity. Jeb never saw them nice shutters hangin' in place. Hm, I wonder if that kid got paid. You know, with Jeb's end and all. That sure would be a bummer, but that's the way it goes sometimes." Mr. Wilson was slowly running out of saying things.

McCarthy was all ears. Today he discovered a new truck mark which did not match the tires of Jeb's Ford. He knew at least two different people were visiting him, one tiptoeing in sneakers, and one wearing a low-heel boots or cowboy boots. Then there was a new person who worked on Jeb's house. He supposedly stayed outside, yet there were used glasses in the sink and the refrigerator. And one had been marked by lipstick. Then he recalled Jeb's neck showed the same color of lipstick. Surely, these marks were not left by the outdoor hired help; he smiled. There must have been other visitors, too, McCarthy concluded. If he could just get the owner of the lipstick and the weapon, he could roll up the whole story in no time.

"Well, I better go. I hears my son's revving up the tractor to mow the land." Mr. Wilson shook the McCarthy's hand and walked toward his house. The old man walked with a curious gait, bent forward from the hip, slightly limping to his left. He slowly chewed on the long stalk of grass hanging at the corner of his mouth.

When Mr. Wilson left, McCarthy supervised his help making imprints of the shoe and tire markings left in the mud. The lab guy knew his job well and did every step without McCarthy's direction. He had already poured silicone into the shoe prints and track marks, and lifted a fairly accurate positive. From this silicone positive McCarthy easily could read the tire brand was 'Dueler A/T'. Fancy and expensive, he concluded as he gave a short whistle with full appreciation. Whoever drove a truck on Dueler tires surely made much more money than a policeman or a sheriff. The lab technician interrupted his thoughts by promising to verify the marks comparing them against the computer database. Once the identification was completed, it was only a matter of time to get to the perpetrator.

Suddenly, McCarthy stopped dead in his tracks. He visualized Mr. Wilson as he was standing in the setting sun by the fence. He saw the man shaking his head, leaning over to tear off a long shoot of grass and slowly chewing its end. He saw him as his foot slid off of the fence, then turned and started back to his house. McCarthy saw almost as clearly as if it were in front of him again: Mr. Wilson wore a pair of cowboy boots.

By the end of the day, the investigator was worn out. As soon as he arrived home, he put his dinner on a tray, plopped down on his comfortable sofa, and turned on the TV. The first local news stunned him. Incredulously, he stared at the screen, forgetting about his food, and being hungry. The reporter was standing in front of an impressive Germantown mansion, reporting a vicious attack that left the homeowner in critical condition. The victim was a well-known local artist, a woman, who was transported by helicopter to the University Hospital. As the reporter spoke, she underwent emergency, life-saving, brain surgery. Before she was taken to the operating room, she regained consciousness long enough to name her husband Dr. James J. Johnson as her attacker.

Chapter 14

As the tragedy unfolded in front of all of Memphis on national television, McCarthy learned the shocking details of the Johnson's marriage. Although the drama was over in three short days, the memory lingered forever in the minds of acquaintances and millions who never met them, but were following the juicy news. After all, money, fame, betrayal, crime, and immediate punishment did not happen every day in their neighborhood.

Apparently, Dr. Johnson married his college sweetheart before he graduated from medical school, but the marriage was doomed from the beginning. He felt trapped by Mary's pregnancy, then found himself totally unprepared for fatherhood. He was a highly organized, neat, and predictably stoic person. His wife, on the other hand, was a few years younger, and a true Bohemian artist. She was loose and carefree, a real chatterbox. She and her friends were a world apart from her husband and his scientific world. No matter how hard she forced the two sides to be together in the beginning, Dr. Johnson and Mary's friends never developed any connection.

In the recent five or six years, the husband and wife barely spoke to each other. When their son was home, they dined together and carried out the perfunctory role of a family over an uncomfortable meal. He frequently had evening programs or was away for the night on business. She attended her art exhibitions alone. Eventually, both Dr. Johnson and his wife made private plans and lived their separate lives under the same roof. Year after year, time rolled away while they followed their own agendas, excluding the other, until they never even considered the possibility to be or to do anything together.

Mary was hot-tempered, and took the chilly relationship much more to her heart than her husband. Actually, the arrangement to live separate lives seemed to suit him far better than fitted his wife's personality. This discovery further aggravated her, and got on her nerves, until she burst into colorful verbal abuse, often throwing innocent decorations or plates to their demise. At the first sign of any confrontation, Dr. Johnson quietly retired into his bedroom and locked his door. No amount of screaming, tears, begging opened his door until the next morning when he silently left for work. By that time, Mary usually was in an alcohol-induced stupor, so he could leave without suffering from further scenes.

A few of her closest friends knew of their differences. After years of fireworks and drama, finally, a truce was achieved. The marriage continued unperturbed on paper and declined further in reality. Finally, Mary threatened her husband with a very public divorce as soon as their son graduated from high school. Once he was away in college, a divorce would have made the inevitable changes more palatable, she concluded. Dr. Johnson looked at her without any visible facial expression of dislike or surprise, before he turned to retreat to his sanctuary behind shut doors.

On the day Mary was attacked in her home, twilight was already setting, when a disheveled Dr. Johnson rang his neighbor's doorbell. He needed emergency help and an ambulance for his severely injured wife after an apparent burglary went wrong. He discovered the slumped body of Mary in the family room, a pool of blood around her head on the floor. He could not get her to respond to the resuscitation efforts he attempted. The phone lines were apparently cut, because there was no tone in the receiver. He was calm, but breathless from running the half a mile between his home and the nearest neighbor. Immediately he turned back and headed home to see what else could be done until the ambulance arrived. The shocked neighbors ran after him to help.

Indeed, Mary was in bad shape. The left side of her skull was bashed in, eyes bulging and bloody, face swollen, motionless, barely clinging to life. She sighed her last just about the same time the emergency technicians burst into the house. In the unfolding organized chaos, she was quickly intubated and resuscitated before being transferred to the ambulance. Sirens shrieked and breaks screeched as the ambulance sped away. Collierville's Baptist Hospital's emergency room was contacted *en route* to prepare for all heroic measures to be performed.

After being stabilized, the poor woman was helicopter lifted to Memphis, where a team of neurosurgeons were already scrubbed in and waiting for her arrival. The Collierville ER warned them in advance, and now they were ready to try the impossible, with hope of saving the victim's life. It looked like Mary needed either all the heroes she could get or an outright miracle to survive the trauma. Though Dr. Johnson was strangely calm, for him the stoic appearance was not unusual.

Mary regained transient consciousness just before surgery and named her husband as the attacker. Dr. Johnson was immediately taken into custody and kept overnight in jail.

Mr. McCarthy learned of the attack and the primary suspect in the evening news, along with the rest of Memphis and greater vicinity. He was so surprised that he dropped the bowl of ice cream on his lap and let it melt before he could get his thoughts together.

The emergency surgery spared Mary's life and she was placed on life-support in intensive care. According to the daily report, she was not out of the woods yet, but at least she had a fighting chance to recover. She suffered permanent damage to the brain, but the extent was not readily known this soon after the operation. Her bewildered son stayed by his mother's bed and vehemently defended his father by denying his involvement in the crime.

The day after Dr. Johnson was taken into custody, the Judge at the Shelby County's Court gave him back his limited freedom. He was released upon his own recognizance after posting a hundred-thousand-dollar bail and promising to remain in the area. He was barred from entering his home or approaching his wife. The Court took into consideration his immaculate records, prominent role in the community, and under oath denial to having anything to do with the crime.

However, the prosecutor already discovered Dr. Johnson's affair with his office nurse, his bad marriage, and pending divorce. Furthermore, he also found the bloody claw hammer used in the attack. No legal mind could possibly accept the doctor's delay in getting help due to his 'supposed' lack of phone lines. They reasoned, Dr. Johnson had a beeper and a cell phone on his belt, both could have been used before, or instead of, running the half a mile to the neighbors. Things were just way too fishy in the good doctor's defense.

By the evening following Mary's attack and surgery, Dr. Johnson was on the street, facing a mountain of legal problems. He had some money and credit cards in his wallet, but no home, family, reputation, or job. His girlfriend was nowhere to be found. He was ruined. The next morning, his lifeless body was discovered in the hotel bathroom, slumped into a tub of water mixed with darkened blood. He had three or four empty bottles of vodka nearby, and his vessels were slashed on both arms, groins, and neck.

Chapter 15

McCarthy requested Charlotte Kay Odum be formally interviewed as soon as Capt. Corky returned from the Collierville restaurant. The detective interrogated both the waitress and the manager of the restaurant where the divorced couple met two weeks before Jeb Odum's death. Both employees recalled them talking for a long time over dinner and ordering quite a few glasses of wine. They seemed particularly memorable because they frequented the restaurant for several years then, after a sudden hiatus, returned again.

The couple was welcomed by the staff, as if a long overdue friend were returning. The pleasantries, however, ended soon after they ordered their food. Charlotte Kay complained of her ribs being over-seasoned and dry and sent back the order. While she was in the ladies' room, Jeb apologized to the waitress on her behalf. The manager soothingly offered her plate to be on the house. Through his profound apologies, he cleverly interjected the cook's denial of any wrongdoing. At the end, Charlotte Kay calmed down and seemed satisfied with the manager's explanation while Jeb quietly paid for both dinners. All was solved in a pleasant way as far as the food was concerned.

In the beginning, the waitress returned a few times to check on them but, hearing their progressively heated discussion, she became uneasy and avoided their table. She recalled hearing the woman snapping at the man sitting across the table something to the effect of suing him. She was not sure why, but she heard her hissing at her partner, "If you did not live up to the Court orders, you force me to hire a lawyer. I will not hesitate to sue you, Jeb; you should know me by now."

The manager confirmed the same as he also overheard part of the argument. He thought it involved money and the sale of a house. He, in particular, was surprised to hear Mr. Odum referring about someone to Mrs. Odum as 'your man', because he did not know they had split up. Mrs. Odum's instant correction of 'my fiancée' made him realize they must have been divorced. Now he understood why they did not show up in the restaurant on their usual Friday evenings. Being a bit of a gossip himself, the manager pretended to work in the area. He also softened the music so he could listen better.

The restaurant was decorated to look like an alley flanked on both sides by brick houses. On one wall, there was a balcony with tables set for dinner, but only a life-size Elvis figure sat on a chair. He leaned on his right hand and with his famous crooked smile looked down at the diners. The music was all from the sixties, many of Elvis' immortal songs made famous by his crooning baritone. An occasional Ricky Nelson, Johnny Cash, and Patsy Kline added to create the perfect nostalgia for the rock-and-roll era.

The older generation genuinely seemed to enjoy the music and the atmosphere. They happily discovered the signatures of famous actors or less famous local politicians on the photographs decorating the walls. The food was always prepared to perfection and served without a hitch. The only time this excellence was marred was when someone arrived already upset and poured the frustration out on the innocent dish and harmless employees of the restaurant.

After serving three glasses of red wine to the couple and noting the increasingly agitated Mrs. Odum and the few responses in Mr. Odum's hushed voice, the manager heard the warning words before they parted: "I guarantee you, Jeb, you will regret this. If you play, you will pay. I will make sure that you will pay, and pay dearly. I will find someone to take care of it once and for all. You will see. You will not get away with it; I will make sure."

Detective Corky also discovered the manager knew the couple who sat behind the Odums in the next booth. Now armed with their names and address, he contacted the old couple. Unfortunately, they both were hard of hearing and could not add much more to his already gathered information. They confirmed, though, the fact that both the man and the woman seemed upset over a house or a property. They also added the woman was very vocal about not allowing the man to steal her share or something to that effect. Ah, yes, and they also overheard a few times she threatened the man with someone, although they denied hearing any names being mentioned.

When Corky reported his findings to his Chief, McCarthy requested Mrs. Odum to come to the station for questioning. He stayed outside of the one-way window and intensely watched Charlotte Kay's face, body language, and reactions to the interrogations.

Mrs. Odum sat comfortably on the plain wooden chair, her forearms resting on the table, hands holding each other with intertwined fingers. McCarthy noted her relaxed posture and inexpressive face. Yet, the comfortably natural position and seemingly calm demeanor had a dead give-away: her tightly clutched hands had pale, yellowish-white knuckles, and the fingertips almost busted with the congested blood. Neither this fact nor her staring without a single blink at Corky's stoic expression escaped McCarthy's expert eyes. Her high-heel shoes slowly swung under her tailored slacks, with their pointed toe aimed at Corky's shinbone under the table. One does not have to express feelings in words; they are far better depicted in the non-verbal communication.

"Just look at her and tell me what you know of her," turned McCarthy to the man standing next to him.

"Not much, I never saw her before, and did not talk with her, neither, when she came to the desk. Someone else took her to this room, not me," replied the young rookie defensively.

"I gathered that much. I only asked you to tell me simply what you see, and what it means to you."

"Well, I don't very well know what you mean. She is just sitting there, and I can't hear a thing." Kevin Cogan was a local farm boy and a recent, inexperienced addition to the Williston division of the sheriff's force.

McCarthy was getting frustrated. At first, when he became Williston's Sheriff, he was determined to improve work by raising awareness of detectable signs and thus better the interrogative skills of all his men. Now he realized some might never be good at detective work. It seemed that cruising streets and scaring speeding drivers were their call. Not the art of interviewing or probing, until the puzzle pieces fell into a complete picture.

He sighed and started to explain in a calm voice: "You learn a lot by observing people. The way they are dressed, walk into the room, greet you, how they sit, keep their hands calmly at rest or fidgeting, tapping with their feet or keeping them still, look at you or avoid meeting your eyes. These are all tell-tale signs of their make-up. Sometimes the signs speak the truth louder than their words, which could be an outright lie, anyway. Whether you will end up being a policeman or a detective in the sheriff department, you have to keep these in mind. Tell me, Kevin, what you see now?"

The young man was hesitant, but since the boss talked to him, he felt obligated to respond. "Gosh, Mr. McCarthy, I don't rightfully know. I ain't to try to find out nothing. But to tell you the God's honest truth, she looks OK to me. She sure looks purty with that black hair and them curls. My mama does not have that much hair and she probably is as old as her. Of course, my mama never would wear them pants and high-heel shoes, neither."

McCarthy was discouraged, but still did not give up teaching the man, "C'mon, Kevin, look, what do you see on her hands? Look at them. Do you see anything unusual?"

"You mean them fancy rings with the big bubble?"

"No, not the rings. Forget that. Look at her knuckles. Tell me what they say to you."

"Say?" Kevin wondered. "Should them say something? What d'you mean? I see she have a wide gold bracelet on her wrist, her hands is fine; she sure don't work with them hands in the sun or the fields. Even on her knuckles she ain't got no tan or no scar. And her nails is long and hot pink, too, she must goes to one of them places in town to get them done."

"Exactly. Now you are talking like a policeman, Kevin. Her hands are fine and manicured: she does not do any physical labor. She is well-to-do by that ring alone, which probably means someone cares for her or loves her enough to give her an expensive piece of jewelry. It looks like an engagement ring, doesn't it? Does she pamper herself? You bet, she does. Look at her hair, it's colored and styled. Her clothes are nice, too. I would bet they were quite expensive. And look at her hands, she gets her nails manicured. But she is nervous. She wiped her palms on the side of her slacks when she sat down, and she clutches them so tightly that they are white at the knuckles. Why do you think she does that?" McCarthy led the man further in his detective work.

"Nerves? Maybe she's just plain nervous," replied Kevin.

"That's it, Kevin: she is nervous. But why? Have you thought of that?"

"Well, everyone gets nervous when questioned by a policeman. That means nothing." Kevin slightly shrugged his shoulder. He sounded more self-assured than before.

"Oh, yes, it does." McCarthy sighed and, for the time being, he gave up teaching. He only hoped Kevin would remember the discussion later when it really mattered. No need to overwhelm him all at once. Teaching should be done slowly, steadily, consistently, just as the rain drops over the fields on a fall day. That's how the land absorbs the water, and that's how the mind soaks up new ideas. McCarthy turned back to the window and watched the silent interrogation of Mrs. Odum. Kevin disappeared behind a door as soon as he thought it was safe.

The pantomime slowly unfolded in front of McCarthy's eyes: he saw Corky leaning forward and asking questions to the woman, but could not hear his words. Yet, her reactions were interesting, to say the least. At one point she suddenly seemed upset for a second, then looked up to the ceiling and to the left before she answered. She rapidly talked, then abruptly stopped, and almost defiantly kept staring ahead. McCarthy instantly knew she lied. He picked up the microphone and spoke into the loudspeaker, calling Captain Corky to the phone. Corky apologized and left Mrs. Odum's room. He carefully shut the door behind himself. Now both Corky and McCarthy were standing by the one-way window and watched the woman sitting at the table, alone in the stark room.

Charlotte Kay Odum dropped her shoulders in obvious relief and leaned back on her seat. She looked around and saw no cameras or recording other than the one that was turned off by Corky before he stepped out. She picked up her handbag, and with both hands reached in the bag to search for something. Finally, her right hand emerged with a tube of lipstick in it. She looked at it for a second, then dropped it back into the purse. She picked up her iPhone but obviously changed her mind, and made no call. She continued the rummage, then took out an envelope and scribbled something on it. After the envelope disappeared in the bag again, she seemed more relaxed to wait for Corky's return.

Chapter 16

To Charlotte Kay Odum's greatest surprise, it was not Captain Corky, but a much taller and a bit older man who entered the room. He introduced himself as Sheriff McCarthy, and explained to her that Captain Corky was called away, so he came to replace him. Very politely, he asked her to summarize the discussion so far.

McCarthy listened without interrupting her until she said the words that she and Jeb 'remained good friends' after the divorce. The quotes from the restaurant meeting did not support Charlotte Kay's new version. McCarthy almost smiled at the thought that if Charlotte Kay wrote an autobiography, it best be displayed under 'fiction'. He did not miss her getting obviously annoyed with his repeated questions that seemed to focus on her relationship to Jeb. Finally, she admitted she had some difficulties with Jeb's dragging his feet in selling their house. After all, no one could blame her if she did not feel like conveniencing Jeb's girlfriend.

"Jeb had a girlfriend? Are you sure?" McCarthy struggled with the idea. Jeb was known to be a quiet man, who did everything in slow motion. Why would he have a close relationship with any woman shortly after his divorce? Did he completely misjudge the dead man or was Charlotte Kay wrong?

Before he could ask another question, Charlotte Kay blurted out with obvious sarcasm: "Really? Well, unless he became a cross-dresser, how do you explain all the clothes and high heels in his closet? Furthermore, how do you account for a girlfriend and an engaged fiancée? In case you didn't know, Jeb had a girlfriend in Tennessee and a fiancée in Alabama. Maybe the church-going, unobtrusive Jeb Odum was not exactly what he showed to the world. Maybe he was nothing but a cheater and a liar. Maybe I had a good reason to divorce him. What do you think?"

"It really does not matter what I think," replied McCarthy evenly. "What matters is the fact that he is dead, and we just learned of two new contacts who possibly could give us further information."

Charlotte Kay was visibly agitated. She usually would not let a subject drop, unless she got her total and absolute satisfaction of the topic being exhausted and broken down to its last atoms. She continued her bashing Jeb: "So you have no opinion. Men, you are all alike, you stick up for each other. You agree to have two women in your life, too, don't you? Boy, I feel sorry for your wife. My condolences to her."

McCarthy's face showed no emotions but slowly darkened as he held his breath and strained himself to remain calm. He stared for a long time at the cold and angry eyes of the woman across the table, then quietly said, "My wife is dead, Mrs. Odum."

Charlotte Kay instantly knew she not only missed a target but made no friend with her outburst. She was taken aback by the flat tone and factual response. All she could offer was her apologies, but she realized the damage has been done. It was not a good idea to insult the very man who was in charge of her interrogation.

"Mrs. Odum, do you live alone at your current residence?" McCarthy returned to the interrogation.

"Yes. I have no live-in boyfriend if that's what you are after," Charlotte Kay still sputtered the words but was more in control of her behavior than before.

"Hm. Then who is the young man staying with you most of the time? Do you have a son?" The seemingly innocent inquiry brought Charlotte Kay back to realization; it was she who was being grilled, and McCarthy probably knew more than what she thought was possible.

"No, I have stated I only have a daughter. The young man you refer to is only a casual friend."

"How casual, Mrs. Odum? Casual enough to have a vacation together?" McCarthy asked.

"What are you insinuating? That he is my lover? Please. I am engaged to a businessman. Please, give me a break, why would I go for a man without any money?" She quickly corrected herself: "I mean, without a profession or a good job. He is barely a friend, and an insignificant one at that, who helps out around the house. He is handy, and a new house always has some glitches that need to be repaired. I pay him, and he does what needs to be done. That's all.

There is no need for anyone to put a nose in my business and search for what's not there." Charlotte Kay looked like the pillar of righteousness and indignation. Indeed, she felt as if she successfully carried the entire weight of Solomon's Temple on her shoulders.

"Well, I only asked because you two seemed to share a cabin on the Caribbean cruise three months ago." McCarthy looked up from his papers, and his eyes remained focused on Charlotte Kay's face. He saw the sudden surprise, then fear passing over, before she flashed a false, but somewhat strained, coquettish smile at him, "I see you know more than I thought. OK, I admit, we had been together for a while. I realized it was a mistake I made. I ended the relationship by putting a stop to it. I slipped up since, but only once. You see, he begged me so much and was so persistent, I thought it was cute. Real cute. We made up for a while. This last flare-up of the affair lasted for that week only. Please keep it between us: if my fiancée learns about this, he would be mad enough to turn and run. He cannot ever find this out if I am to be married to him. Look at this ring," she stretched her well-manicured left hand in front of McCarthy's face, "Just look at this ring. Do you think I would give this up for a handy-man? It was a short-lived, little mistake that I already put behind me. I forgot it. Totally. After all, it meant nothing. It was nothing. Not even worth mentioning. Like it never existed. Why bother with it now? Look, Mr. McCarney, you do understand me, don't you?"

"McCarthy, Ma'am. And yes, I understand you. Completely." Neither his voice nor his expression showed any emotions. He easily continued: "Tell me, when were you at Jeb's house last? You said at least a year ago? Are you sure it was not more recently?"

Charlotte Kay quizzically searched for cues on the man's face but found none. She decided to change her last statement. "Well, about two months ago I stopped to pick up some of my things I left at the house. We never changed the security code or key, I still had access to the house. I warned Jeb he could not legally keep me out since half of the house was mine. Anyway, he was not home, and I don't think he ever discovered I was there. I did not stay long, just got what I needed and left. Honest, that's all I did."

"Did you do anything else then? Was that when you discovered he had a girlfriend?"

"Yes, that's when I realized he had a new woman in his life. He had her picture in the bedroom, his office, even on the bathroom counter. Which I don't mind, please understand me; as far as I am concerned, he can do whatever he wants. What I mind is his blatant disregard for the Court order. Evidently, he let her move in with him. Can you imagine what I felt when I saw her make-up on my vanity, her clothes hanging in my closet, her lingerie in my drawers?"

It was obvious that Charlotte Kay was offended by her discovery, but kept talking: "Nice stuff, by the way. But this does not negate the fact that this is my house, too."

"So that's how you discovered about the woman Jeb dated: you saw his new photos displayed in the house."

"That's right. And he had them all over, just as I said before. Should it matter to me? In a way, yes. I am not going to let her live in my house while Jeb, supposedly, is selling it. The divorce Decree specifically stated he must do that and pay me my share from the proceeds. According to the agreement, he could live there until it was sold, but he had to make an honest effort to sell it."

"What was the problem, he did not list the house to be sold?"

"In the beginning, right after the divorce, he did. Then he must have changed his mind, because he had to realize he has nowhere to go once it's sold. So, what did he do? He let the original contract expire, and never renewed it with the real estate firm. He thought he could lay low, live in my half of the house happily ever after, and I would forget about the contract. He didn't know me well enough. I called the real-estate office and uncovered his scheme. For the entire last year, he did not even re-list the home to sell. Obviously, he had no intentions of giving me my share."

"Mrs. Odum, you did not harm Jeb, did you?" McCarthy knew her answer was 'no', but had to ask her the question, anyway.

"Heavens, no! I am not a murderer. A poor little woman, like me, could not harm a fly," started Charlotte Kay with a coquettish flutter of her long eyelashes. Then a glance at McCarthy's stern face made her abandon her original act, and simply said, "No way. As I stated before, I did not even see him there. And that was about two months ago."

"But you talked to him since, didn't you?" asked McCarthy.

"Yes, I told you. I met him at Corky's. A restaurant. Hardly a place where I could have killed him, don't you think?" Charlotte Kay was getting more confident.

"Yes, I agree, Mrs. Odum. You could not kill him there. "

"So, if you don't think I murdered him, then why are you keeping me here?" She asked coolly, while secretly hoping to push McCarthy to admit her innocence and that there was no further need for her to be questioned.

"We do not have to keep you, Mrs. Odum. You are free to go. You just stay in town until we decide whether we may want to question you again. You were not planning another Caribbean cruise, were you?" McCarthy wanted to remind her of what she wished to keep a secret.

Charlotte Kay quickly glanced at McCarthy, "No, Mr. McCarthy. I do not plan any vacations in the near future. You can be assured of that. I stay at home, so feel free to call if you need me though I certainly hope you do your job quickly enough to apprehend the murderer and free me from your digging in my private life. We understand each other, I am sure."

McCarthy could not help but look at the woman with some awe as she picked up her fancy Michael Kors handbag and flashed her sparkling ring at him, then walked through the door. Her overtly sweet smell of cologne lingered on in the small room. The fragrance reminded McCarthy of funeral parlors, filled with wilting flowers. He sat motionless for a few minutes, staring at the notes he made. Then he called Captain Corky and asked him to contact Mrs. Odum's lover.

Chapter 17

After storming out of the dining room, Jake Odum disappeared in his workshop again. He was angry with the whole world. His rage was mainly first directed at himself, then at his youngest son, who provoked him to the level of madness and pushed him into an argument that was long overdue. Well, there were no further fights now. When he saw the tail lights of Billy's truck speeding down the dirt road, heading to the highway, Jake knew in his heart that Billy would not show up at home any time soon.

Then, a few months later, Jeb Odum was found dead. By the time the detectives started to snoop around to investigate the murder, Billy was far from home and he never learned of his uncle's fate. Yet, their destiny crossed each other once more at, of all places, the Williston Sheriff's office.

Jake had accepted the fact that he could never understand Billy. His youngest son's lack of motivation, but mainly his dislike of the land he so revered, alienated the father from his son. The young man's disrespect of the morals and values for what Jake stood for were just too far from his way of thinking. He realized each newer generation probably wanted different things, but couldn't they do it without clashing with the traditions? He would have never dreamed to talk back to his parents, no matter what he felt, or what they said.

In the beginning, he blamed Billy's big mouth on the ever-present, funny TV sitcoms. After all, he always watched Different Strokes and listened to the pert and precocious replies of the character played by the young black actor, Gary Coleman. Billy often laughed out loud at the character's quick comebacks and started to emulate him.

Jake did not find the remarks amusing, and quickly put a stop to them. If that was allowed in another family, it was their business. He just did not want it to occur in his household. He felt the whole thing was a TV show, and for getting a laugh only, not because it happened in real life. Either way, he was not tolerating such behavior in his home. Period. End of story.

He often said, "I would not even dream of saying that to my father. If I had said just half as much as this child did, my dad would have put his foot down my throat so deep that a surgeon would be called to remove it." He usually got disgusted soon, anyway, and returned to the barn or his workshop. His wife was working somewhere in the house and was only too glad to hear Billy's laughter. She did not see him doing anything wrong by watching the program. She left him alone as long as he was in the house.

Different Strokes was quickly followed by similar programs, though each seemed to be progressively more open in criticizing adults. The children kept bluntly blaming their parents, who in return apologized to them, instead of teaching them some manners. It seemed the whole society was fundamentally changing and embracing the new trend. When he realized a child's will regularly turned to be the determining factor over the adult's, Jake remarked with characteristic dryness, "Since when is the tail wagging the dog?"

Billy vehemently defended the recent changes in family dynamics and found nothing wrong with the style. As a matter of fact, he found the tendency refreshing and advocated abandoning the archaic, stiff parental roles. After all, young children had opinions too and also needed to be respected for their belief. He secretly also agreed with the newest ideas of reporting the parents to the police for 'parental brutality'. He probably would never had dared doing it himself, but he was awfully glad some kids had the gumption. He went only as far as turning the volume up on the TV news when such cases were reported. The older generation condemned the changing world while the younger one further pushed for dynamic transformation.

First the humor captured the TV audience, then they heard the same topic frequently enough in various real-life settings to get desensitized to it. Gentle Southern manners became an ever-thinning veneer over previously unheard of rudeness and disrespect. The older generation gradually lost the reverence given to age and wisdom, and a respected, wise, old man suddenly became just an old man or an old geezer. Billy first abandoned using the 'Mister' or 'Miss' from the names of people he talked about, then openly started to mock them. He laughingly referred to people slightly younger than his parents as 'GIT', which was his abbreviation for

'Geezer-in-Training'. Jake was dumbfounded to realize he was in the same age group, so his son must have put him also in the same category. He became an old geezer. At least, an 'old geezer' in Billy's eyes.

Jake Odum hoped that by the time his children reached a ripe age, they would also experience what he had to face. If the latest fad became a new standard of conducting relationships, they would get everything back with interest from their own children.

He smiled a bit at this thought and tried not to get offended by his sons. After all, they were like unrisen bread: not ready for the table, not fully baked, yet. True, Christopher and Michael were not bad; Michael, especially, was loving and respectful. Actually, Christopher became much better since he learned he was chosen to run the farm. The famous 'Land of Cotton' was to be his one day, being the first-born. Though he was to share it with Michael in equal shares, Jake made sure it was understood that Christopher would carry out the ultimate decisions. His only daughter, Grace, was always the apple of his eye, who never disagreed with Jake, but she was married and lived far away in Arizona. She would inherit some money, but not the land. Billy, on the other hand, was a predictably unpredictable individual. He continued to rebel against his father's authority and mainly ignored his mother. He was an irritating thorn in Jake's side.

Jake knew Kasia did not mind listening to criticism coming from her growing children as much as he did. His wife always played the role of a soothing, wiser parent, because she wanted to maintain a bridge between the different generations. Although she offered a sympathetic ear to listen to their 'presumed' injustices, she absolutely refused to hear them once they started to complain about Jake saying or doing something they did not like. The boys soon realized their mother stood by their father, and the two parents created an unbreakable unity. They grew up recognizing the fact that all complaints to Kasia against Jake were pointless. Grace was his only child who never clashed with him while growing up because she always adored and idolized her father. She was also the only one aware of how hard Kasia tried to soften the head of the family behind the scenes. The boys never knew that.

These thoughts calmed him down, and he was almost back to his stoic self when he heard the insistent call of the bell. This time it kept ringing with unmistakable urgency. Jake sighed and headed back to the house, thinking the room was finally cleaned up and they could finish the ruined dinner. Little did he expect the sight he found as soon as he entered the room.

Helen was still on all fours, cleaning the floor and the furniture. Zofia was in the kitchen with Krzysztof preparing another meal. Both Christopher and Michael were attending Kasia. Through the open double door, he immediately spotted the sofa where his wife rested, though Christopher and Michael partially obstructed his view.

Kasia softly cried and held her deformed and swollen right arm by her left hand. Jake instantly realized the arm was broken and understood her pain. He had suffered a similar fate while playing sports in school. He also tended animals with injuries. Yet, his wife seemed to be in more pain than what her arm should have caused. To his bewildered questioning, both boys gave the same consistent account of what had happened. Finally, Jake understood what happened after he left, and his anger knew no limits.

"Just where is that son-of-a-bitch? Get him here! Now!" Jake bellowed.

"I don't know. He left the room without a word. You don't want me to go after him, Dad, do you? I'd rather stay with Mother now," replied Christopher.

Michael was holding the cushion supporting Kasia's arm; he could not go. Jake decided the confrontation could wait. He had to take care of his wife first. "You wait, you bastard, you spawn of the devil, wait until I get back. If you had any brain, you would get lost, and never come in front of my eyes," muttered Jake, and the family knew his vengeance would have no end, not until he got it satisfied.

Ultimately, Kasia's injury shook Jake to the core, because his wife had never been ill before. Yet, what made him realize fully the extent of Billy's wrong-doing was Kasia's not protecting Billy. She just cried with a heart-wrenching sadness, almost as if she was a mother who was to bury her son. For the first time in her life, Kasia never uttered a word to stop her husband's ranting. Jake finally realized his wife was hurt way beyond the pain of the broken arm.

Jake helped Kasia into the truck and, with Michael supporting her on the other side, drove her to the emergency room. Collierville's Baptist Hospital was nearby. It was a nice facility. Being the only hospital in the vicinity, it also had an unchallenged and indisputably good reputation. Christopher and Helen remained home to clean up the house. Billy disappeared somewhere and was not seen, which was a blessing in itself because Jake knew he could really harm his son this time.

It did not take long to get the paperwork filled out and handed back to the smiling older lady behind the emergency room receptionist's window. The wait was prolonged and painful, especially when they realized before they were attended to, others were called in, though they arrived after them. Jake, in a strained voice, explained to Kasia and Michael that, "these were probably true emergencies, like a stroke or a heart attack. A broken arm might be painful, but no one would die of it." So, they waited patiently. Kasia quietly wiped big tear drops off of her face, which left dark wet spots on her blouse. When she suddenly moved her arm, the shooting pain forced her to yell out loud. This jolted Michael visibly and made Jake spring into action.

"OK, you are going in, whether they want it or not," announced Jake, and pushed the door open with enough force to unscrew the hinges. He brushed a short woman aside as she tried to stop them from entering.

"Sir, you have to wait. Please go back to the waiting room. You cannot just barge in," she pleaded to no avail.

Jake was a runaway locomotive. He controlled himself until a doctor arrived to assist Kasia. With the sense of getting relief for his wife's pain, his bottled-up anger and frustration poured out uncontrollably. The poor physician did not even know what triggered the avalanche of indignant complaints.

No matter how deep-toned and measured Jake's words were, the doctor seemed unperturbed and performed his exam at a steady pace, then ordered the X-rays. He acted as if he never heard a word. Finally, Kasia's arm was placed in a cast, and she was discharged home to Jake's care.

Once at home, things calmed down. Kasia secretly worried about the whereabouts of Billy, but the rest of the family accepted the fact that he was gone. Jake was too angry with him to think in any way about his absence. As a matter of fact, he thought that was the best solution. In his fury, he wished several times that he would not see Billy ever again.

Chapter 18

Billy, on the other hand, was not as calm as he hoped to be. He just left his home that gave him security, and he had no clear idea or goal which way he was to go. After he drove through Memphis, he decided to continue west until he either found a job or a place to stay. He had enough money to buy gas, and he had recently serviced his truck. He did not worry about driving. He calculated his money would last a good week if he did not stay in motels. Two nights he slept in his truck by the roadside. He ate fast food at rest stops. Finally, he pulled into Phoenix and eventually found Grace's house.

Grace was not at all surprised to see her baby brother. She already heard about her mother's accident and Billy's disappearance, so she sort of expected him. Where else would anyone go under the circumstances but to the safe place and shelter offered by a family?

Grace was in the middle of cooking while she watched and helped her children doing their homework. Half of the kitchen table was cleared to make room for their books and stacks of papers. The humming noise of the washer and the rhythmic clinking of a dryer signaled this was also a laundry day.

Grace was in a hurry. Her husband was to arrive at any minute, and he always stepped into the house claiming to be hungry. Without wasting time or movements, she set the table and sent the kids to the family room with their school work. "No TV, you hear? Just finish your work then we have dinner as soon as Daddy gets home. I will talk with Uncle Billy now, OK?" Grace was a woman who could juggle lots of chores simultaneously. She was definitely in charge of her home and family.

She let Billy talk first without interruption. Although her hands never stopped working, she did not miss a word of her brother's account of the recent events. If she was appalled at his act, she did not show it on her face. When Billy stopped talking, she remained hushed until the silence was unbearable. Billy broke the quiet by haltingly asking her in a pitiful voice, "Gracie, you tell me, what am I to do now?"

Grace sighed and replied firmly, "To begin with, you must apologize to Mother. And you must make peace with Dad. I reckon you can stay here for a while. We have an extra room and we don't mind. But you cannot live here the way you did at home. There are two teenagers in my house. There is no way you will grow or smoke pot here. No drugs. No alcohol. No girlfriends. And get a job. I don't care what work you do, as long as we don't have to support you financially. We are maxed on our credit cards, have a house payment, and we have two teenagers to raise. Jobs are not very secure here. I have to think of my family first. We cannot do more. But they still hire at the corner gas station, I saw a sign the last time I filled up my tank. You can apply there in the morning."

Billy agreed to everything Grace said, though he had no idea how to approach his parents. He was hoping Grace would make the initial contact. Still, his palms sweated with the sheer thought of facing them eventually.

The next few months were hard on Billy. He had to adjust to a new city, family, house, and job. Everything he knew before was suddenly gone. All these differences dragged along a set of new rules he was unfamiliar with, but which he had to observe and obey unless he wanted to hit the road again. So far, he had avoided contacting his parents. Grace did not push him too hard. She figured her brother would have to hit the bottom of the hole he dug first, before he could crawl out and stand up to be a man, before he would become the Prodigal Son. Once he had some insight into the gravity of his actions and the grave consequences, Grace could help him back to the family. By then he would be repentant enough to be molded more easily into a traditional filial role.

What Grace did not know was that Billy soon got involved with a rough crowd. He worked at the gas station as a general help, basically doing what he was told to do. He hated to get out of bed every day, just to be abused by some redneck who had enough money and luck to own the station with the little convenience store. He started to spend his evenings with his newly found buddies, which cost him a lot of money. As a newcomer, he was expected to treat everyone for drinks at a local dive. When this was not enough to break into their inner circle, Billy supplied them with pot. As usual, he continued the old habits to purchase goodwill and friendship. But those habits cost money, and money was scarce.

He began borrowing a few bucks here and there from Grace. He put on his most charming facial expression, a mixture of a humble and embarrassed little smile, and haltingly asked his sister: "Gracie, could you spare a little moolah for your freshly strained bro' again? Just a loan 'til Friday. When I get paid, I return the kindness. What d'you say?"

Although he promised to return the minor loans, he never repaid her. By the time his next paycheck arrived, he usually had nothing left, because he already spent it all. Grace decided the borrowed money was small enough not to make a fuss over. She did not want to alienate her brother over these trifling advances. Instead, after the first few weeks, she put her foot down firmly and did not lend him any more money. After all, Billy ate and lived free at her house. That was more than enough.

To top all that, her husband was increasingly uneasy with the new family member and complained to Grace a few times. Billy's deteriorating behavior, nervousness, and evasive answers made the head of the household feel apprehensive. He only saw Billy as a brat, the product of an overprotective and permissive mother and hard-working, but neglectful father.

The smoldering fire burst into a full-fledged bonfire when Grace's teenage son was caught smoking pot. He readily admitted he got the idea and the supplies from his uncle. He saw nothing wrong in doing it: Uncle Billy as an adult was smoking grass. Many of his young classmates also smoked a joint now and then. At the end of the big family meeting, Billy was summarily kicked out to the street by the head of the family. The teenager was grounded, his car keys and cell phone were taken away, and his privileges were drastically curbed. Grace was indignant and felt betrayed, but that did not prevent her secretly sliding a few ten-dollar bills into Billy's departing hands.

Billy spent the night in the gas station storage room, then moved in with Robby. Robert Falls, his new best bosom buddy, was a skinny, fairly well-kept young man. They were drinking acquaintances first, then became close friends when he offered the only helping hand to Billy in his need. Billy listened to Robby's stories with awe and acknowledged them without questioning anything. Robby seemed to be a man who enjoyed a good life, a life that had evaded Billy so far. Robby frequently boasted about his connections to the affluent South. He often crossed the border to Mexico, once even traveled to Colombia. Periodically, Robby disappeared for a few days, but he always returned with a full pocket from the visits. He claimed the extra cash came from his well-to-do contacts. Billy was convinced these connections supported Robby in his travels because he did not have any visible job.

"So, are you going to Laredo again? You know, Robby, I have never been to Texas, and would not mind going one day," Billy clearly begged to be taken along.

"You do, don't you?" Robby looked at him with new interest. "You know what? Why don't you come along and enjoy the ride. You might see things you never saw before." Robby seemed somewhat preoccupied but agreeable.

It did not take Billy much time to get his few things together. They tossed the two knapsacks in the back of the truck and headed for Laredo.

Chapter 19

The Fayette County Sheriff Department had always been housed in the same old building which originally seemed to be way too large for their needs. After they had spread out comfortably, and time passed, they filled every room in the building. The largest office became McCarthy's headquarters. His door was always open, not only to see what was going on among his men, but also allowing him to be observed working any time they looked. If they wanted to hear his phone calls, they did not need to tiptoe to his door and stand by the wall eavesdropping. Through the wide-open door, voices traveled, especially since McCarthy developed the habit to use a speakerphone.

When the new Democratic Presidential candidate promised a 'transparent government' in his 2008 election speech, the whole country was overtaken by the idea. Hope was not only budding but flourishing wildly in every section of the society, sparing a few dead-beats who most likely would not have been satisfied by a true saint or Mother Theresa, herself. Then the transparency quickly became obscured, and the sparkling clean ideas sank into the muddy water. It seemed the only man who turned the empty promises to reality was McCarthy. He governed his department with total transparency.

After completing his initial investigation of Mrs. Odum's ex-boyfriend, Captain Corky headed for McCarthy's office. Finishing all he discovered, he concluded with the self-assured statement: "So this guy is a definite 'person of interest'. What's your opinion?" Corky eagerly waited for an answer but, when the silence became uncomfortably prolonged, he added, "Don't you agree?"

McCarthy sat motionless behind the massive, old desk. He did not move a muscle, except his jaw was clenching and relaxing rhythmically. Corky knew the Chief was thinking hard, concentrating on what he had heard. If this chewing motion happened, he was usually racking his brain. When he first noted McCarthy's slightly tensing and relaxing jaw, he thought his new superior was chewing gum. By golly, he was about to tell him how rude and disrespectful that was, when McCarthy apologetically explained his habit. Corky was silently thankful to be saved by the moment before he sat out to teach his boss the basics of Southern politeness. Now he watched the jaw muscles tense and patiently waited for the response.

Suddenly McCarthy turned to him, "How long ago did you say Mrs. Odum broke up with this Doug Bullock? Over a year?"

"Yes, I assume that's what Bullock said."

"No, do not ever assume anything. Do not believe anything you hear, and only half of what you see. I assume nothing, and question everything."

"Right. Let me correct it: that's what Doug Bullock said."

"No, that's not what he said, that's what he lied. Remember, Mrs. Odum admitted to having had rekindled their relationship by having a brief affair with him recently. True, it only lasted for a week. That's when they went on the Royal Caribbean cruise, which was in December. It is April now. Bullock was covering something."

"I'll be darned. Then she lied, too, if she said it was only a week-long affair. I know for a fact that she left Jeb Odum for this man almost two years ago. How about that?"

"So they were both untruthful. They were concealing something. What else did this Doug Bullock say?"

"Not much. He insisted he only tried to help Mrs. Odum to get her just share from Jeb. When she cried to him over Jeb dragging his feet in selling their house, he felt sorry for her being short-changed. He realized she put her complete trust in him and asked for his help. He saw the poor, helpless woman had no one else to turn for protection but to him. Doug might have been a poor handyman, but he always thought of himself being the combination of a Southern gentleman and a Western cowboy. He was ready to act on a wronged lady's behalf. You know, a 'damsel in distress'. Now he rose to the occasion and promised Charlotte Kay to do whatever was needed to shake old Jeb up. He placed a few anonymous calls to him late at night. He pretended to be part of the Mafia. He saw the Godfather movie enough times to imitate Marlon Brando perfectly. By the way, I have heard him do it, he was real good. He swore that was all he did. Intimidate Jeb, that's all. He never stepped on Jeb's property, he said. Hey, Doug Bullock was nothing but a punk."

"I don't think so," said McCarthy slowly. "I think he also paid Jeb a visit. Maybe a day or two prior to his death."

"Where did you get this information? I have not heard anything indicating a personal contact, although I have known of his calls to Jeb," Corky defended his investigation.

"Where from? His phone records. After you told me about them, I looked them up, too. You were right: his number turned up repeatedly on Mrs. Odum's phone list. Here is a print-out of every call Bullock made. These are to Jeb, and those to Mrs. Odum. See? Jeb never called him back, but Mrs. Odum immediately returned Bullock's calls. See the pattern? Over the last two weeks the call frequency escalated. He called Jeb twice on the day before his death. And do you know where he was? The last two days he called from the same tower range that supplied Jeb's cell phones, too. He must have been nearby. I bet my last paycheck he finally confronted Jeb. Being ignored did not make him feel successful enough to please Mrs. Odum. I just don't think he killed Jeb. Bullock was a small-time crook, not Mafia material. He just fancied himself to be Mafia material. Besides the fact, he called Jeb's house even after Jeb was killed. Which proves he was not the killer, or he would have known Jeb could not answer the phone. Agree?"

Corky was quiet as if doused unexpectedly by cold water. Why didn't he think of this when he looked at the phone records first? He felt McCarthy got even with him now, and he received the payback for learning the autopsy findings before his chief. He would have to come up with something new and good to score again if he wanted to leave McCarthy in the dust.

"Do you want me to keep an eye on these two? Mrs. Odum and Bullock?" he asked.

"Absolutely. There is more between those two than what meets the eye. You warned them not to travel anywhere, and basically just stay in town, I hope?" McCarthy searched the eyes of his colleague. He knew Corky was a good detective, maybe not too experienced, but smart, eager, and honest. Corky would not have missed giving this warning; McCarthy was positive. With satisfaction, he acknowledged Corky's response before he switched the discussion to other potential suspects.

"Did you discover who Jeb's girlfriend was? Also, Mrs. Odum said something about a fiancée. These two might be the same gal as far as I know, but the devil does not sleep, and apparently slow Jeb Odum was not as slow as people thought."

"Oh, yeah, this is what I wanted to tell you about," started Corky in an excited voice. "Jeb had a fiancée who lived in Montgomery. Alabama, you know. She was a widow and still worked part-time as a nurse in the hospital. I believe she was a case manager or maybe a nurse practitioner there. I did not get all the information in, yet. Got a picture of her, can you believe she is sixty-eight? Looks good, doesn't she?" Corky put a few snapshots and a computer printout on McCarthy's desk.

McCarthy spread them out and studied each picture for a long time before he turned his attention to the printout. It was the woman's biography. When he finished reading it, he announced flatly, "This woman is not a murderer. Too honest, her eyes are too honest. But one never knows. Let's face it, Jeb was murdered. I have known nurses to kill people, but they usually kill with drugs and not stab anyone to death.

"You see, when you stab someone in the chest, you have to face the victim. You have to watch him get hurt, gasp for air, bleed onto your hand, collapse right onto your shoes, and eventually die. Right in front of you. It takes a lot of personal anger and unrelenting revenge to carry out a murder while looking into the eyes of a dying man. Drugs are more remote and much cleaner. Just the same, keep her in mind, and get her here as soon as you can. If not today, maybe tomorrow. I want to talk with her."

"Sure, that's not a problem. Now, do you want to hear of the local beauty? The girlfriend?" Corky barely could contain his excitement. He was afraid the news would poke a hole in his side if he could not tell it soon.

McCarthy looked up, awaiting the unusual. Unobtrusive Jeb Odum had two girlfriends, after all. Who the heck would have believed it? He muttered something about slow water that runs deep, and leaned back in his chair, listening to every word Corky uttered.

"Well, after Mrs. Odum sailed into the sunset, Jeb was left alone in that big barn of a house. He went to work as usual, and in the evenings, he mowed the lawn, bush-whacked, cut limbs off the trees, and the days passed. On Sundays, he went to church and attended Bible class. Every Sunday. He certainly wasn't waiting for a hearse to take him to church. He showed up as regularly as if he were a well-trained family ghost." Corky seemed very pleased with himself to be so witty that he even brought to McCarthy's serious face a fleeting, half-smile. This give him enough encouragement to continue his clever presentation.

"And if that was not enough, he started to attend every potluck and all social gatherings. Mind you, this might not be called a fun social outing where you came from, but it's quite the norm in our farm county. He might not have had much more excitement than playing a fierce domino game or a savage Monopoly. It's understandable because Baptists don't drink."

"Well, at least not in public," interjected McCarthy.

Corky chuckled in agreement, "Let me tell you, Baptists have only public morals. Privately they are just as sinful as anyone else."

"You might be right there," agreed McCarthy, "but go on with the girlfriend."

Corky eagerly continued, "As I said, Jeb started to get socially active. About a year after his divorce, he realized he might not meet a woman nearby, a woman who could be a partner in maintaining the lifestyle he got used to before his divorce. He had a beautiful, but empty house which needed to be furnished and turned into a home again. Maybe if the woman he met was well-to-do, he would marry her. Then they could buy out Charlotte Kay's half to keep the house and the twenty acres around it. See, Jeb had not much else to offer a woman but marriage. He certainly was not rich, did not look like a Hollywood heartthrob, though he was meticulously neat and clean. He had a steady job and a mundane life, but he also was on the brink of retirement. He was a nice enough man, but had his quirks, just like everyone."

"OK, so he had his faults. Maybe Charlotte Kay also discovered a few," McCarthy said dryly. "What else?"

"What else? When the first real-estate listing expired, he did not re-list the house. It was off market, as he said, 'only temporarily', until he could make up his mind whether to use the same agent or try another, perhaps a more aggressive one. Charlotte Kay was busy with her on-and-off relationship with Bullock, and then getting a face-lift and tummy-tuck, while planning to meet the ideal man. You know, the one whose age and looks were shadowed by his stack of money. Preferably a tall stack made by lots of money. So, she did not pay much attention to what her ex-husband was doing. She did not bother Jeb by insisting on getting the house on the market again. Slowly, they all fell into the routine of not contacting each other. Another half a year passed. That's when Jeb decided he needed a change. He got on the computer and listed himself on a dating service. Can you believe it? A dating service?"

"Yeah, desperate people do desperate things. So is that where he met the girlfriend?"

"No. The fiancée. The Montgomery girl knew him only from his emails, until he finally visited her. Apparently, he was plumb smitten by her looks and status. She also liked him, and they started a long-distance affair. Almost instantly, Jeb asked her to marry him and got her a ring. For me, the whole thing looks as if they both were at the end of their tethers. She wanted to marry a man, probably any decent man. He wanted to marry a well-to-do woman, probably one with a nice house. It sure was a match made in heaven."

"Oh, so the engaged fiancée was in Montgomery. Hm. Just how often did they see each other? Once a month?" McCarthy seemed to get interested.

"Probably only for long weekends. Usually, Jeb drove to Alabama. She only came to visit him for the first time last summer. But that was after the proverbial something hit the fan."

"What are you saying?"

"That's when he called and told her that their relationship was over. He admitted he found a woman locally, and he already started dating the new girl."

"You are kidding me. He was alone for years because he never found a girlfriend in Tennessee. Then he found one on the internet who offered everything he needed: looks, agility, money, and attraction. And that's when he went bonkers and dumped her for a local woman? What was she? Perhaps a Williston version of Miss America? A country temptress? Or a village tigress? Hard to believe. But I guess it's plausible. Even dogs get rabid when all goes well." McCarthy realized he just quoted his Irish grandmother's favorite saying.

"Let me continue, it gets better," said Corky. "As soon as the fiancée heard this, she stormed up to Williston. Whatever happened between them is not clear, so your guess is as good as mine. One thing was for sure: at the end Jeb called off the affair with the girlfriend, and returned to the Montgomery widow. You could bet your Christmas bonus that the girlfriend was not too happy."

"OK. So there were three women in Jeb's life: his ex-wife, who could not get her money because he dilly-dallied with the house sale. Then there was a long-distance fiancée who did not seem eager until he dumped her. At which point she went after him with full vengeance and yanked him back. And the third was the girlfriend who was probably promised the sun and the moon until she was unexpectedly dropped for the old girlfriend. I mean his fiancée or whatever. These relationships were getting a bit congested, don't you think?" McCarthy raised a finger each time as he counted Jeb's contacts.

"I guess each could have a motive to punish him. Or should I say 'enough motive' to punish him? Hm. There is no fury of Heaven and Hell to match the wrath of a passionate, discarded woman."

Chapter 20

McCarthy had to agree with Corky on his last remark. How many crimes did he manage to solve in Philadelphia which were committed by angry, hate-fueled lovers? He could not count them easily, there were just far too many. The most imaginative and vicious offenders usually turned out to be women. Yeah, Corky might have said the truth. It sure was Hell's fury.

Then his thoughts returned to the local murder and with controlled urgency he continued the routine steps of discovery.

"OK, so far so good. Let's get to the facts and the nitty-gritty now. I want names, addresses, phone numbers, and everything you can dig up on these three. Get them in for questioning. I could call my friend in Troy, Alabama, and ask him to interview the Montgomery widow there first. Boy, it's good to have friends! We are lucky to have a friend in need, aren't we? Depending on what he finds out, we might want her to get here."

Corky smiled with the self-satisfaction of scoring over his boss again: "No need to call your friend. Apparently, the widow was notified by someone, and she is on the plane to arrive in Memphis as we talk. A coincidence, I am sure."

"Do you know who informed this girl of Jeb's death?" McCarthy chose to ignore Corky's last remark. He did not forget it; he only stacked it away somewhere in his memory. When the proper time called for it, he would let the information surface. Then he would rely on the stored statement for a belated, yet, appropriate response. Instead, now he smoothly directed the topic back to the investigation.

"I could not say for sure," the slow response came. McCarthy suspected Corky himself was the culprit, but kept quiet. He continued the conversation in an even tone and noted Corky got relaxed again and breathed easier.

"Now, let's see. What do you know about these women? Anything?"

Corky was in his element once more. He knew something his boss did not. He proved his capabilities again. He was like Paul Drake, or at least a Paul Drake, Jr. Too bad McCarthy was no Perry Mason.

"Actually, I started to poke a bit around. The Montgomery widow is Mrs. Vittoria DelRosario. She was from Rome, or somewhere close to it. Hey, my tongue would tie up in knots trying to say the name of this weird place. Do you know how to pronounce it properly?" and he slipped his notes across the desk.

McCarthy easily said, "Citta di Castel Gandolfo, or the city of Castel Gandolfo. A pretty little place, maybe ten-twelve miles Southeast from Rome. That's where the Pope has his summer residence. Ah, they serve the best spaghetti alle vongole in the La Perla." McCarthy clicked his tongue at the recollection of his dream-like, heart-warming, wonderful honeymoon trip in Italy. Simultaneously, he realized he lost Corky altogether.

He apologetically smiled and added, "The La Perla was a true pearl of a restaurant, right on the shore of Lake Albano. Wonderful location and view, because through its white lattice-work one could see the whole lake. People swimming, children splashing in the water, pretty bikini-clad beauties baking bronze bodies on the sand. And the blue sky is broken only by the white triangles of the distant sailboats. I loved it there. The spaghetti dish was served with clams... one could lick all ten fingers afterward, not to waste a molecule of the tasty delicacy... Do you eat clams, Corky?"

"Not if I can help it," Corky replied instantly. "In seafood I go as far as a fried catfish. With hushpuppies. Always with hushpuppies, home-style fries, and iced tea," he grinned with hungry eyes.

"Anyway, to return to your question, here is what I have learned about Vittoria DelRosario. She is from this place originally. You know, whatever you called it. She married a debonair Delta Airline pilot who stopped in Rome and fell in love with her. Joe DelRosario. A second-generation American. They had two children, a good marriage for forty years, and then Joe's cancer made her a widow. He died six years ago. Vittoria bought a nice house in Montgomery, right by the Shakespeare Park, or whatever they call that place. I was told, this was a big park with special gardens, fountains, and theaters. It would be nice to see it once, don't you think?"

He waited for an answer, but McCarthy silently stared at him, so he continued. "Shortly after her husband's death, Vittoria sold their big home in Birmingham. I guess after her husband was gone, and the kids moved away, she did not need the mansion anymore. She took a job in Montgomery and worked as an intensive care nurse. After a few years she got tired of shift work and slowly resumed more and more administrative duties. In the last couple of years, she was semi-retired and worked only three days a week as a case manager. Lately she returned to the clinic to help out as a nurse practitioner. She was financially solid, so I gather she did it less for the money and more for the sake of doing something."

Corky turned the page of his notes but did not need to read the remaining report. "Jeb met her on the website and was dating her for three years. They got engaged in four months, but that changed very little of their arrangement. Not until one day Jeb announced he was finished with her. The new interest was local, convenient, and seemed to be more than willing to accommodate him. This is when Vittoria first came to Williston. In a hurry. Probably she did not want to lose her fiancée and her almost three-year involvement. It seemed to me, she felt like a losing poker player who was running after her investment."

"Well, one cannot blame her much if she came to check things out. I always felt once trust was lost, it might take a saint to restore faith."

"My mother always told me 'once a dog, always a dog'" agreed Corky. "Come to think of it, it's not likely that it was his first time to cheat. Maybe that's why his wife cooled off and eventually found a lover, too. Tit for tat. Maybe that was the real reason for the divorce. You know what? Now this explains why she became so revengeful. It always nagged me not to know why she hated Jeb so much. This could be the reason, don't you agree? I bet he did the same to her, too."

"I guess so. No one wakes up one morning and decides to cheat for the first time. Not at age sixty-seven," remarked McCarthy with conviction. "Quiet, unassuming Jeb Odum played a dangerous game between the two women. All he had to sell was his name and being a bachelor. He wanted to get the highest bidder to win the auction; that's all."

"Yeah, but he was not too smart. He prematurely told the fiancée about the new girlfriend. Before he was safely in with her, or before he secured her commitment. Then Vittoria put a screeching halt to this side-trip and swiftly eliminated the competition. At the end, all Jeb ended up was with both women becoming his enemy because you can be sure neither loved the situation he created for them."

"You couldn't blame them, could you?" asked McCarthy then he returned to business. "So what about this Williston beauty queen? What have you learned about her?"

"Her name is Lana Hadock. She goes to the same Mount Olive First Baptist Church where Jeb Odum is a member. They both attend the same Bible Study class, every Sunday before the regular service. Lana's husband was the choir director, but ran off with a soprano about four years ago. The whole church was shocked to learn he had a lover, especially after realizing that the woman of his interest was also a church member. They always considered him to be such a nice family man. By golly, no one ever thought he could do that. Everyone condemned the hussy soprano, and was saddened by the unexpected turn-out. They sided with poor Lana and consoled her in her loss.

"But Karma stepped in almost immediately. Imagine, shortly after leaving his wife, the man suddenly died. And what did Lana do? She instantly forgot the betrayal and the fact that he abandoned her before. She assumed the role of a lamenting widow. If her marital status was ever in question, she always corrected everyone to say that she was a widow. In the meantime, she looked for another man to marry. As far as I could see, Lana had no particular education or accomplishments. Her whole social entity depended on having a husband. She was paying maximum attention to herself, making absolutely sure she looked her very best at all times. As they say here 'she did the most with the least she had'."

"What 'least' were they referring to, when talking about Lana?" McCarthy wondered. "I was under the impression she was attractive."

"She was, no question about it. Beach-blonde hair, loads of make-up, brightly colored outfits, loud laughter—all geared to call for attention. Lana Hadock consciously programmed every part of her life gearing to land a husband. After all, the bees would gather sooner at a fragrant, bright, red wildflower than at a rare, but unscented orchid. Besides, a weed was always more tenacious and stronger than a cultivated, refined flower."

"And all this great effort was put out for a man like Jeb Odum?" McCarthy looked up from his notes.

"Looks like it. Don't forget, Lana only knew Jeb's best side. She saw him as a church-going, unassuming, single man, who was comfortably retired. She must have thought the divorce could not have been his fault because he was the one left by a vicious woman. After all, poor, dear Jeb Odum had an ungodly, immoral ex-wife, who did not attend their church and who immediately shacked up with another man. Who would not feel bad for him? I bet she only looked at Jeb as he appeared in church every Sunday, smartly dressed in a suit and tie, shoes polished, freshly shaven. She never saw him in his ragged, yellowed T-shirt and frayed old jeans, unshaven, dirty, and sweating on a tractor. Of course, knowing he lived in a huge house on twenty acres was not a hindrance, either. Mind you, this is only my opinion."

"I guess, Jeb never advertised that the bank still owned about one-third of that property, and his wife had half of the remaining two third. A minor inconvenience, right?"

"I guess so."

"Wait a second. How come Lana did not remember Jeb was formally engaged?" McCarthy questioned.

"She had to; everyone knew it in the Bible Class. Originally Jeb announced his engagement, they all were part of the excitement. Then periodically he excused himself for being absent because he was visiting his fiancée in Montgomery. I guess the problem was that no one ever saw Jeb's fiancée, so she was a non-existing figure for them. Not real. Like a fairy tale. All knew of her, yet no one knew her."

"I see. Since she was invisible, she could be ignored and then removed. Right?"

"Something like that." Corky nodded in agreement. "Anyway, Lana dug her ten well-manicured, long fingernails into Jeb, and hung onto him without him ever realizing who caught whom. Boy, he was a dope."

"Well, 'who runs after his tail, could lose his head'. Either Confucius said it, or I must have read it in a Chinese fortune cookie," laughed McCarthy.

"So, Jeb thought he must have had a winner. He wined and dined Lana after they got together on church pot-lucks and social outings. I discovered their favorite meeting place was the nearby Olympic Diner in Oakland. She sure played him for an old fiddle and, in return, he offered her the sweet music she wanted to hear.

"Apparently, Lana was more than willing to please Jeb when he asked to be invited to her house. She prepared a dinner and showed off with all her possessions. She proudly announced whatever he saw in her home was on her name. She was also a home-owner, just like he was. True, her house was much smaller, but at least it was all hers. With great satisfaction, Jeb acknowledged the fact that everything was debt-free because Lana paid off everything with her husband's life insurance. Jeb must have thought he hit the jackpot, if I may say so."

"Wow. I can imagine the shock Lana got after thinking all her ducks were lined up in a row when Jeb suddenly broke up with her."

"Well, I can't even imagine and, furthermore, would not want to," volunteered Corky. "Anyway, this is Jeb's harem as far as I know. So what do you want me to do next?"

"Just line up all of them for an interview as soon as you can. Let me know once you have the times, and I will be here, too. By the way, get the lie detector test ready for Mrs. Odum and Doug Bullock. They absolutely need one. No question. We might benefit a lot from what we learn from it, I believe. Are you OK with everything that's going on? You don't think we need help from an outside agency, do you?"

"Heavens, no! We can handle it. I already know who the culprit is, anyway. I know, I know, I will not tell you another word. You are the chief, and you have to do it your way. But I am the detective, and I do it my way. So, we'll see," Corky smiled self-assuredly. Paul Drake, his idol, whether in Heaven or on a library's dust-collecting bookshelf, would look at Corky with pride. No outsider was needed, as long as Captain Corky was on the case.

"Yep, we'll see, as the blind man said." McCarthy stood behind his desk to indicate the meeting was over. The afternoon was getting late, and he had other things planned before darkness set in. He was yet to meet the technician from the forensic laboratory, call the coroner's office, and check out the Odum's neighbor, Mr. Wilson, who wore the memorable cowboy boots.

Chapter 21

Webb County, Texas was suffering from an early heat wave. The April weather was usually warm, but never as much as this year. Even the oldest women were shaking their heads when searching their memory for a similar spring in the past. People closed the shades on all windows and gulped iced tea by the gallon to stay somewhat cool. Early morning, while there still was a tiny breeze, a few committed, exercise-crazy dog owners walked the shadier side of the streets. They bravely disregarded the hot air and let the cool sweat accumulate above the elastic waists of their shorts. Their stride was youthful and vigorous when they started out, but on the way back their steps became noticeably shorter and slower, and their feet dragged a bit closer to the pavement. The dogs, frankly, did not even want to leave the cool house, and only went for the walk as if doing a favor to the senseless human who was heading out the door. Panting older dogs hung their tongues out so much, that it was feared they may step on it and trip. No question, skipping spring, Webb County plunged into summer.

Business in downtown Laredo did not suffer too much from the heat. As a matter of fact, some stores almost thrived in the heat wave. Anyone caught in the scorching inferno outside for more than a few minutes, almost dived into the air-conditioned stores. Being embarrassed to admit the only reason was to get a respite from the baking sun, they purchased unnecessary umbrellas, duplicate sunglasses, even presents for non-existing or future grandchildren. Whatever a store offered, the salesman sold. After watching the customer taking his sweet time to look around, a little nudge from the salesman usually closed the deal. After the purchase had been finalized, the salesmen showed pity on the poor man by letting him talk for an extraordinary time. This way he was graciously spared for a few more minutes from re-entering the outside boiling air, as hot as Hades.

The nice old mansions with their shaded and manicured lawns fared better than the congested neighborhoods that made up shantytown. These houses desperately needed repair or at least a few cans of paint. Their grass was burnt to crackling hay, which was an insult even to the goats that were known to eat anything.

The small window units could barely cool a room though struggling at maximum power. Whether it was due to the excessive use of electricity or the faulty, old wiring, they often tripped the breaker and sometimes the entire block grew suddenly dark and silent. However, silence did not last long, because inevitably some irritated hot-head started to yell from his front step into the night. No one was targeted particularly, but the four-letter words were intended to affect everyone within earshot. Then the person who caused the shortage could take his share of the insults, and quickly fix the problem before he was singled out. Once peace was restored, everyone resumed doing whatever got interrupted by the mishap, until the same thing happened again.

The Ford truck was dust covered, but even under the thick gray-brown layer one could see it had a nice dark green base. It was not rusty, like the cars owned by most of the folks living here. It did not have a cracked windshield, and had no dents on its side, either. Obviously, its owner took pretty good care of it. He must have been well-to-do to buy a fancy truck with a double cabin, big enough to let two people sleep relatively comfortably in the back if caught on the road by the night.

People lazily raised their head hearing the passing truck, but were too hot to get to the window to take a better look. It did not matter much, because the stirred-up dust covered most of the cars and obscured the drivers, anyway. The dogs kept panting undisturbed under the porches, showing no desire to run after the truck, or bark a warning of never to return. The Ford entered an unfenced yard and came to a stop, almost hitting the tree trunk by the back steps. Nobody opened the doors or got out of the truck. The driver, obviously, was waiting for something or someone.

A few minutes later, two other trucks piled up behind him, close to the house. These were not as fancy as the Ford, though the blanket of dust did the best it could to cover the missing paint, lose grill, and sagging canvas top. The house door painfully squeaked to a crack, and part of a round, dark stick protruded from the opening. It resembled a broomstick, but the fading twilight reflected from an oily metal. A strongly accented male voice yelled from behind the door: "Get out and hold your hands up. Any monkey-business and you're done. Clear? Move."

Hearing this dubious invitation, the driver of the Ford stepped out and quickly approached the hidden man. After exchanging a few words, the door opened widely, and the rifle disappeared. Instead, a man in his late forties emerged, dressed in a worn pair of jeans and a loose green T-shirt. He was barefoot. His calloused feet with the deep, dark cracks at the heels and embedded dirt around the nails testified the fact that he liked to feel nature without any boundaries.

He went around the steps, and opened the basement trap-door, propping it up on a piece of wood. Then he signaled the drivers of the two old trucks to turn and back up. As soon as they came to a stop, from under the canvas silent, quickly moving figures jumped out, one after the other, and disappeared in the darkness. Once the truck bed was empty, the driver pulled away and without stopping drove onto the street and was gone. The same thing happened to the second truck.

Two young men and an older woman carried a huge aluminum pot and disposable plates and cups to the basement door. Another woman carried loaves of bread and a bucket of cool water. Neither spoke a word, they just carried out their tasks quickly. They made a few trips until all was delivered as planned. They pushed everything into the darkness, then closed and locked the trap door. The two young men from the truck were the only ones who were allowed into the house.

Billy and Robby got out of the fancy truck, happy to stretch their legs after they were cooped up in the car for a long time. No matter how comfortable the leather seats were, no matter how young and fit the two men were, the long drive still took a toll on them. Billy quietly followed Robby and imitated everything his friend did. He wiped his sweaty palms on his jeans before shaking the hand of the little man with the bushy mustache. At the introduction, he said something sounding like "Cockee" for a name. He did not seem to be too surprised seeing Billy in Robby's tow, but he was not overtly joyed getting a new visitor, either.

Inside the living room, a window air-conditioner noisily blew cold air to create a freezing strip of air in the middle, while the peripheries remained relatively warm. The man barely opened his mouth when a young girl in a white blouse and long colorful skirt entered the room, bringing cold bottles of beer on a big wooden tray. Corn chips and a big bowl of juicy, chopped tomato and emerald green, tiny squares of pepper were placed next to a mass of crushed, green avocado. Her straight black hair fell to cover her face when she bent to place the tray on the table. As she straightened up, with a snapping movement of her head, the whole rich, shiny, coal-colored mane got tossed back to cover her shoulders and back, all the way to her waistline.

"Do you need anything else?" Her voice was smooth and warm as velvet.

"Nah, get lost," barked the host without glancing at her. Billy was shocked. He never heard any man talk as disrespectfully as this man to a young lady before. His father might have been morose or short, but he would never have been rude to his wife. He was about to say something, when Robby's stern glance and a barely perceivable head shake made him change his mind. He remained silent, but eager and alert to catch every nuance of instructions from his friend, just as he promised him on the way to Laredo when they discussed the planned visit.

Robby smoothly remarked, "The best beer on this planet. Friend, you taste this King of Beers and I guarantee you, you never drink Busch or Michelob again." He slid a cold bottle toward Billy. Billy skillfully caught it at the edge of the table, and raised it to their host in a silent toast. The man's eyes were less fierce now, and overall, he seemed to be more at ease. He still sent an occasional unfriendly glance toward Billy, but he no longer had cold indifference and hot suspicion in his look. They clanked the bottles and Robby cheerfully shouted, "Salute! To friendship: new and old!"

Coqui replied quietly: "Salud!"

Robby put the half-empty bottle of Dos Equis back on the tray. He turned to Billy, "Now you see what I told you about. Coqui is a man to be appreciated, not only for his beer or for his pretty daughter, but also for his wisdom and business. He is one honest man; I guarantee you. You can trust him. And we sure thank him for the hospitality, don't we? He has the best house in the whole area, the biggest and the best. I can talk for both of us when I say we appreciate it tremendously, Coqui."

Billy quickly turned his eyes to their host, and saw a satisfied, small smile under his bushy mustache. Whether this or the second beer was responsible, he started to feel better about coming here. He was almost embarrassed for being scared in the beginning when he contemplated turning and taking off after the two beat-up trucks, the trucks that brought the faceless dark figures. Whatever happened to them locked up in the windowless basement? Billy did not dare to ask any questions. Coqui's voice interrupted the thoughts swirling in his mind about the men who were left in the dark, airless cellar.

"So, you are the new mule, huh?"

Robby laughed uncomfortably and seemed a bit ashamed, as if his swimming trunks unexpectedly had lost its string and slid to his knees. Billy could not make his mind up about whether he should be insulted or puzzled by the term 'mule'. He had never been called a 'mule' before, though he did plenty of asinine things. Seeing the two young men as two pawns on Coqui's chessboard, the master of ceremonies bellowed out a hearty laugh. He thought it was priceless to see the two gringos growing steadily confused.

"That's all right," he continued, more composed, "You should have seen Robby when I first met him. He was a nothing. A skinny nothing. And look at him now! He is still skinny, but it's clear he gets pretty good money to make his drive worth it, isn't it?"

"What drive do you refer to, Senor Coqui?" Billy was more than puzzled.

"Oh, don't fret, Coqui loves to kid you. He means us driving to Texas, that's all. And he does not like to be called Senor Coqui, he is just Coqui," Robby was quick to answer first.

Then he turned to their host, "You know, I don't even know your real name, I only know this 'Coqui'. I am sure it's just a nickname, am I right? Does it mean anything?" This was not the first occasion that Robby tried to get some personal information, but Coqui was more than a step ahead of him.

"When I was a businessman in Puerto Rico, they named me that. I have a deep voice, I am short, and I usually wear a green shirt. It was easy to see I resembled a Coqui. It is a tree-frog."

He looked at the tired faces of the two young men. "Shall we retire for the night? Hey, Alma, get the beds ready for the guys," he yelled toward the closed door. "And get them a bite so their stomach is quiet, or I would not sleep a wink from the rumble," he laughed again.

Although worn out from the heat and the long ride, Billy stretched himself to his impressive six-foot height, and produced his most charming smile. He instantly realized all efforts were wasted, because an old and heavy-set woman appeared in the doorway instead of the pretty Alma. She was laden with bed linen and a rolled-up cotton quilt. Without a word she started to push chairs and table aside to make beds on the floor for the house guests.

Coqui casually commented, "You can also sleep in beds, but there is no air conditioner in the bedroom. If I were you, I would stay here. You could not sleep in the heat, anyway." He bid them good night and followed the old women to another part of the house.

Robby and Billy fell in the beds made at their feet, and before their heads hit the pillow, they both were half asleep.

An early morning commotion and relentless dog barking woke them up. On the way out, they picked up two mugs of coffee in the kitchen. Alma was already busy preparing breakfast. She looked sweet and innocent in a white dress. She had a flaming red hibiscus in her hair, right over her ear. She silently chopped tomatoes and peppers into small cubes. The eggs were in a bowl next to the already chopped onions in front of her. Billy felt gnawing hunger in the pit of his stomach, and thought of the many breakfasts his mother made for him.

Coqui was quiet and seemed preoccupied, or perhaps the morning heat bothered him. He just returned to the house and was sweaty as if he had done heavy labor outside.

"How's it goin'?" asked Robby cheerfully.

"Goin'," the short answer surprised Billy.

"Hey, you, come with me," Coqui barked more of an order rather than asking him. Robby immediately disappeared, following him into the other room. They closed the door, but only their voices could be heard without enough clarity to understand what was discussed. It was not much of a dialogue, anyway, because Billy only heard Coqui's deep voice. When they returned, Robby went out to the backyard with Coqui. Billy heard some ruckus and slamming car doors, then Robby returned, as if nothing happened. With a barely noticeable shake of his head he stopped Billy from asking any questions. Instead, he ate the breakfast set on the big wooden kitchen table, thanked Alma and Coqui for the hospitality, and was ready to get going. Billy would not have minded lingering a bit more in the kitchen, but had no choice but to leave.

On the road he asked Robby, "What was this big hurry all about?" Robby drove silently for a while, then suddenly hit the steering wheel with his palm, as if in anger, and looked away for a long time before he answered. "Nothing. Coqui asked us to deliver a few packages for him, so we have to take a bit of a detour. You don't mind, do you?" Then he added, "He paid us in advance, so it's not like a freebie."

"Sure. At least we could repay him for the room and board, right?" Billy laughed good-naturedly.

Before they approached the border, Robby pulled off the road and rearranged the truck. Their luggage lay on top of Coqui's duffel bags on the cabin floor, and a carelessly tossed blanket hung halfway over everything. He seemed a bit anxious, so Billy offered to drive. "Just give me directions, I can do it".

The border patrolman was tired and sweating. He casually asked for identifications, looked at the driver's license, glanced at the empty truck bed, and in a friendly voice asked, "Is it already spring vacation? Must be, you are the tenth car going to camping this morning alone. If you hurry, you could catch up with the rest of your group, they are not far ahead. Watch out for the tequila and the girls, they could be dangerous." He smiled at the two young men as he took a fleeting look at the cabin, adding, "And camping might be also risky at places, be careful." He bid them farewell, and they drove on. Robby was visibly more relaxed and soon dozed off.

Billy drove on the dusty road, bouncing in and out of potholes. Robby gave him clear directions, which way to go and where to take the dirt road. Billy was ready to wake him up, thinking he got to a wrong turn when Robby opened his eyes. "Nah, you are OK, that's the way to a short-cut across the mountains." They drove another few miles until they seemed to be the only living creatures as far as the eyes could see. "I think this is it," said Robby, "stop here."

"This is it? What is it?" wondered Billy.

"The place where Coqui wanted us to leave the duffel bags. Someone would come to pick them up; I am sure. Give me a hand, would you?"

The duffel bags were heavy and awkwardly stuffed with something that bulged at places, but almost caved in on the top, at the middle. "What are we doing, smuggling gold or something? This is as heavy as salt," Billy was panting. On Robby's direction, they dropped the bags behind a huge rock. The yellowish boulder completely concealed the additions, hidden from anyone who happened by on the road. "How could anyone find this place?"

wondered Billy as he dropped the second, and heavier, bag next to the first.

"Don't worry, the coyotes will," Robby answered with a smirk. He did not look back but headed for the truck. He looked in both directions, but it was still lifeless all around them. Only parched groups of yucca and tall trees of cactus bearing pink fruit broke the horizon.

"Let's go, this is getting to be too creepy."

Billy turned to follow his friend, but his foot got caught in the handle of the duffel bag, and he tripped. Stumbling to his feet, angry for the embarrassing fall, he shook the dirt off his hands, and irately kicked the bag. The old zipper popped, and a dirty, shoeless, human foot slid out of the bag.

"Lord, almighty! Robby, look!" Billy gasped for air.

"OK, just get in the truck, won't you? We'll talk but for now let's just get going."

Robby took the wheel, spun the truck around, and left this God-forsaken wilderness in a big cloud of dust. He sighed with relief, knowing they were heading back to civilization.

Chapter 22

Miguel Antonio Esteban Vázquez y Colón left the holy city of Teotihuacán and headed for the Promise Land of America. Actually, he did not live in the ancient Aztec city, but in the desolate hills somewhere between Mexico City and the famous ruins. He, his wife Pilar, and their three small children lived not in a house built above the land, but in a home Miguel dug out of the barren mountain side with the help of his father and brothers. Every year he added a new room to the cave they called their own, because the growing family needed more space. They considered themselves lucky, compared to their neighbors: at least they had a little plateau in front of the entrance, which served as kitchen and gathering area. Here Pilar cooked over an open fire in the one skillet she owned. She arranged three flat-topped rocks in a triangle, leaving enough space between two of them for her small hand to gather the amber in a pile under the beat-up skillet. Miguel usually found enough wood and occasionally even some coal that was needed for cooking.

She also had a dented metal pitcher and two pots; the rest of the containers were cut off from plastic milk gallons, and an empty oil barrel which collected the precious and rare raindrops. Tlaloc, the God of Rain, blessed them with water in the rainy season. Pilar, being a good and industrious wife, caught and saved every drop. It might not have been pure rain, but tears which the Aztec jaguar-headed deity shed over their struggles. Pilar thanked with equal faith both Tlaloc and the Virgin Mary, not daring to omit either, in case the neglected one would take revenge on her. In the meantime, Miguel scrubbed the barrel with the rough sand until it was shining like the silver and copper trinkets he peddled to the tourists.

Finally, after two girls, Pilar gave birth to her third child, a boy. With a male offspring, the proud parents looked at life differently than before. Suddenly they realized their children deserved a better future than what the barren mountainside could offer. After all, they were humans and not barn-swallows to live in a nest made out of mud. They wanted to give them a real home, not only three or four beautiful sounding names to each child. What else can the dirt-poor give to their off-springs but fancy names, love, and dreams of a better life? Pilar wanted a home, however small or old it was, but a house with running water and a toilet. For the sake of a house, she even would compromise and gladly accept an outhouse instead of an indoor toilet. An outhouse still would have been a great improvement on the conditions they suffered as cave-dwellers.

"Oh, if I could just have my children sleep on a bed made of wood!" she often said while repairing with wet mud the bed they made from hard dirt. "And I would have a stove in my kitchen," she sighed with hope. A stove, where she could cook without squatting on her numb legs. She wanted to stand up straight like a real Doña should. Pilar had dreams of a better life while Miguel fiercely hungered for the changes to realize these dreams. These were not highly improbable, but somewhat unrealistic hopes, which ultimately forced Miguel to leave Pilar and venture to uncharted roads, pursuing nameless opportunities for an unknown and indefinite time.

On the day Miguel left, Pilar took off of her neck the tiny silver medallion of Virgin Mary she always wore, and placed it on Miguel's neck. She whispered: "The Mother of God will take care of you until we see each other again." Her dark eyes burnt from unshed teardrops. Yet, all the fear and sadness were well-hid behind her silky, long eyelashes. Miguel watched her face glowing with gentle love. He did not see the deepening wrinkles around her tired eyes, but had a glimpse of the fresh, young Pilar again, the girl who promised him everything a man could ever want. At this moment, Miguel felt the throbbing fear of the uncertainty waiting for him. He already felt lonely, knowing he had to go; yet, he could not tear himself away from Pilar's clinging body. He knew he never would forget the way his wife had looked at him before he headed for his undefined journey.

About thirty Mexican, Nicaraguan, and Guatemalan men and women crossed the unprotected border to the US. Most were looking for jobs, any job, that paid money to support their families. Once they got a steady income, and saved a few dollars, they intended to get the rest of their loved ones to join them. A couple of menacing-faced men came along, too, but they did not talk to anyone. They silently eyed the group, especially the women, but made no attempt to even remotely appear friendly. They just hung onto their guns and stared ahead as if on a mission.

The Rio Grande, also known as the Rio Bravo del Norte, carried mud from south-central Colorado to the Gulf of Mexico. The river also carried dark soil from San Luis Valley, red clay from New Mexico, and soft yellow sand from Texas. It washed away, picked up, and mixed up everything from the American and Mexican shores alike. It was a true American waterway.

Between El Paso, Texas and Ciudad Juarez, Chihuahua, the Rio Grande served as a border between the US and Mexico, her Southern neighbor. In spite of the greatness her name indicated, the river was barely navigable. The agricultural needs and recent heat wave claimed most of her water before it broke into a sandy delta and dumped into the Gulf the clean and good as well as the crime and filth.

In Nuevo Laredo, the group of hopefuls spent their last, quiet night on Mexican soil. They were only a speck in the colorful tapestry of people who strive to be different from each other, in spite of the common fate they shared. Each desired to be recognized and validated as a valuable individual, capable of doing any job, willing to use the last fiber of his muscles in order to fulfill commitments made to their families. They were determined to change the mere existence of those left at home. It did not matter what it took, or by what means.

America was the land of riches and the promise of a better life. This opportunity constantly loomed in front of their eyes. The new world represented an escape from a bare existence. Surely, hard work linked to willpower would make it possible to eke out if but a tiny niche of decent living. This hope gave them strength and stamina to endure the inhumane travel, the agonizing hunger, and the slow progress under the burning, tropical sun. The insatiable hunger to improve life empowered them even beyond their expectations. Ahead of Terra Caliente, the mirage of Terra Esperanza sparkled. Miguel Antonio Esteban Vázquez y Colón was one of these hopefuls.

Warm humidity covered the nighttime silhouettes of cacti, stunted palm trees, and short but thick clumps of undergrowth that led to the Rio Grande. Fast-moving clouds hid the moon. The stillness was broken only by the piercing hoot of an occasional screeching owl. Far away, somewhere in the distance, yelping coyotes sent invitations to a meal for the rest of their kin. The air was heavy to breathe, and the wildly beating hearts almost gave away the hiding places of the dark-clothed, dark-skinned men who patiently squatted in the prickly bushes. When the last lights went out on the distant opposite shore of the slowly flowing river, the shadows came to life and cautiously started to move toward the water. Crouching, almost on all fours, they ran on hardened bare feet as softly and silently as a stalking jaguar.

The water was cool and shallow, with unexpected pools swirling around the waders. They quickly sunk into the liquid darkness, their arms and legs furiously beating under the surface so as to avoid splashing and alerting anyone. In the middle of the river, there was a fast-flowing channel, which washed them downstream in spite of their efforts to resist it. Only an older, stocky peasant was carried away by the river because he lost grip on his son's hand and panicked, for he could not swim. When he slipped and hit his head on a rock, he did not get up again. They searched for him for a while but knew it was hopeless to find him in the pitch-dark night. It was probably too late anyway; they figured. His bloated body was fished out the following day, a nameless casualty of the unlawful migration into the land of opportunities.

Exhausted but victorious, they emerged on the Texas shore and hid under the low branches of trees on the water's edge. But there was no time to rest, yet; there was not a moment to waste if they wanted to remain undetected. Dripping in water, shivering from the cold in the warm and humid night, the men who just sneaked into Texas kept pushing forward. They almost crossed the wide clearing, when a mishap occurred.

Suddenly a loud yelp, followed by a wordless commotion and dull thuds, stopped the progress. They all froze. Holding their breath, they silently prayed that, against all odds, the scream would be attributed to a wounded animal. Quickly, they ran and barely managed to get out of the open field, when the lights of the arriving border patrol jeep started to scan the area. Face in the dirt, covered by hanging branches of trees, they did not dare to move even for the vicious bites of fire ants. Most of them remained undetected. Only a skinny teenager and his buddy were picked up.

The boy was in pain, frightened, and bled from two tiny puncture wounds on his ankle, where a snake bit him. Near a warm rock, a rattler curled up for the night and the unfortunate lad tripped over him in the dark. Now the remnants of the snake, beaten into the dirt by the startled men, were spread by the trail. One of the border patrol jeeps took the victims of the unintended attack to the city: the boy painfully limping on one leg, and the fragments of the snake carried in a bag. By that time, the maimed ankle was swollen to three times its original size and quickly blackened with dark blood seeping into the injured tissues. The terrified, shivering, young man alternately cried in pain and fervently prayed with diminishing hope. The snake already lost its life, and the boy knew he was next.

Those who survived the ordeal eventually found Coqui's safe-house. The lights remained turned off, but under the dark cloak of the night the infamous trap door opened and the basement swallowed the wet and exhausted men. They ate the left-over soup ladled from the bottom of the huge pot, and were fast asleep before they could finish the piece of bread in their hands. Those already asleep on the rugged and filthy mattresses strewn on the floor moved without fully waking up, to make room for the newcomers. In the corner, a motionless body was already stiff and cold. The body was left untouched, to be picked up in the morning in an old duffel bag. They all agreed the unfortunate man deserved to be laid to rest in his homeland and not disposed of in foreign soil. Finally, they were all asleep, no longer dreaming of going to America. They had arrived, and, for the first time, they had their dream turned into a reality. They had achieved the enviable state of being 'illegal aliens'.

Chapter 23

The next morning, the new arrivals left Coqui's basement and headed north. Miguel went with the loudest mouth, who promised unbelievable jobs and incredible amounts of money at the end of the trip. There were others too, who led groups to various cities and states, but since all were the same to most newcomers, they went where the most reimbursements could be made. They squeezed into the bed of the truck and had to sit so close to one another that no one could stretch out a leg. Jorge, the leader, warned them not to talk, insisted on being called George, and sat in the cabin with the driver, Ramón.

Miguel figured there must have been bad blood between these two because they barely said a word to each other. Their dark eyes frequently shot threatening glances, but their mouths remained pressed into a thin line. When Jorge had to give directions, he barked the orders. If Ramón questioned him, he snapped at Ramón to question not him, but El Condor, himself. Ramón ended the discussion by spitting in the dust and clamming up. Eventually, Miguel figured the mysterious El Condor was a man who must have had an army to order around. El Condor, himself, was on top of this secret army, never seen by anyone, except his closest, most trusted people. Although he was not seen, he apparently saw everything. He commanded everyone, and he demanded total loyalty from each. If there was a fearless nonbeliever, El Condor did not allow him to last for long. The man soon disappeared, never to be heard again. This barely shrouded cruelty instilled fear and blind obedience by the simple mention of his name. El Condor, or as he was known by his other name El Padre, was not someone to be ignored.

The beat-up truck stopped somewhere deep in Texas. They all stretched their numb legs and aching backs, while curiously looking around. There was not much to speak about, because as far as the eyes could see the land was flat, and only herds of cattle rested under the trees. They excitedly discussed how Jorge managed to feed them all.

"Hey, man, you were cool," one turned to Jorge, "that kid at McDonald's did not even question you. I can only imagine how wide he opened his eyes in surprise hearing the number of hamburgers, French fries, and cokes you ordered. By the way, thanks, man. I was truly starving by now."

Jorge contentedly smiled, "Well, you have to know how to talk to Americans. You must be humble and modest, as if you were looking for a helping hand. Once they feel sorry for you, they help you. They are nothing but a bunch of sentimental idiots. But who cares what these gringos are, as long as they do what you want, huh?"

"So how did you get so much food without alerting anyone?" the first man pressed further.

"Simple. I told them it was for the construction workers. I was the unlucky one they sent today for lunch in this heat. He even gave me ice water, seeing my sweaty face. Told you, all Americans are stupid. They really fall for anything. There is no construction within miles around here. Did you see any?"

"No," they all mumbled in agreement. The food quickly disappeared, and they silently watched Ramón and Jorge getting into a fight. They were pretty far from the group, so Miguel did not hear what was said, or why they fought. He realized, though, they were fighting over something important, just by watching their growing agitation and increasing gestures. Then Ramón turned and spat to end the discussion. Except this time, the spit landed on Jorge's boot. Without a word, Jorge pulled out a handgun and shot Ramón in the neck. The second shot lodged in Ramón's brain, but by that time he was already half dead and did not feel anything. Miguel pulled his old straw hat down to cover his eyes, and his back pressed against a tree, he pretended to sleep.

Jorge ordered them back in the truck, and they left in a hurry. Their short rest was over. He reminded them they were in Texas illegally and with a warning, "You better keep your mouth shut if you know what's good for you," he looked deep into each man's eyes. They looked down at their feet, silently. No one responded. Jorge continued, "As long as no one saw a thing, nothing has happened. But mention it once," he warned them, "anywhere, to anyone, and you'll see how fast you get your own payment." In his own crude way, Jorge made them realize they were beyond the law, unprotected in a new reality, which no longer resembled the idealistic picture they had. He flatly announced their only protection came by the order of the El Condor. He, Jorge, only carried out the wishes of his boss.

The area was soon abandoned, littered with empty paper cups, hamburger wrappers, straws nervously bent or idly chewed at the ends. Soiled napkins were re-used as toilet papers and were signaling piles of excrement deposited under the bushes. Some of the paper was caught on the branches, adding to the already weathered old trash. As they looked back, the entire site resembled a landfill. The speeding truck left a tangled-up, trash-littered field, which quickly melted into the dusty distance. After a while, the nasty details dissipated into the vastness of the green Texas countryside. The view only showed endless emerald pastures, thirsty trees, and peaceful herds of cattle. Ramón's body was left where he fell. Someone surely would discover and take care of it eventually.

On the road approaching Abilene, Texas, Jorge doused the truck with gasoline and it went up in flames like a torch. They arrived in groups of three or four in Abilene, taking the last couple of miles on foot. Each group was given an address by Jorge, where they were to meet. By the time they approached the Mesquite Golf Course, they were sitting among uprooted palms and various potted plants in the back of the truck. The two new trucks proudly announced they were all part of the "Elite Greenery and Lawn Care" business. They cheerfully waved at people who hesitated a bit, but smilingly returned the greetings. Yes, Americans were a bunch of fools, just like Jorge said.

At each city, the group became smaller, as some people stayed because they were offered jobs. During their last stop, Jorge insisted on three young women remaining under the protection of José and his partner. In the beginning, José was not sure about also taking the little girl. But the kid and the prettiest young woman were hanging onto each other, and neither would let the other go. The woman's huge eyes filled with tears, thinking she would lose the promised factory job. She insisted her kid could do just as much hard work as she would. José greedily agreed, though first he seemed nervous having an almost ten-year-old in his business. He excitedly spoke in rapid Spanish, while eyeing the little girl up and down. He even told her to turn around, so he could assess her better. Finally, he smiled and gruffly pointed at the door, "Shoo. Get in and we'll see what you two can do. You'll have to prove it to me first." The woman almost fell to her knees in gratitude and wanted to kiss José's hand, but he snapped it away and playfully hit her on the rump as he pushed her through the door. The young girl calmly followed her mother, but her eyes were opened wide in sheer wonder and excitement.

José's partner was a big-muscled, very dark-skinned fellow with gold caps on his front teeth. Evidently, he liked to show his shiny gold teeth because he often pulled his mouth into a weird smile that made him somehow threatening. He resembled a merciless, hungry hyena, ready to pounce on fresh meat.

The place itself was interesting, as it looked more like a secluded house than the factory Jorge promised. There were no windows facing the street, and the door had a square panel, which only opened when someone rang the bell. As the door was pushed wide open, people got a glimpse of the lavish decoration. From the sidewalk, all they saw was the luxurious red color of shiny silk and rich gold tassels on the edge of folded, heavy drapes and table covers. Then the women disappeared, and the big black man flashed a smile of his gold-capped teeth at them as he shut the door. The sea of red vanished and instead, there stood a mundane, drab house again.

Miguel was sickened by what he saw because he realized the appalling job waiting for these unfortunate women. It was not enough that the kid's pretty mom was gang-raped during the night, on her way crossing the border. That was only the prelude to what waited for her at José's house. Being without any legal rights in a country that had no records of her existence, she was at the mercy of her brutal keepers. She was soon beaten to submission. Being young and desirable, her little girl was assigned to an extra number of well-paying customers, who preferred a child to a grown woman. When not willing, she shared severe punishments with the mother.

José was ingenious in dishing out penalty. Regardless of who was the rebellious party, both the mother and her kid got kicked, beaten up, or branded with burning cigars equally. His belt left wide, red, swollen marks on their backs, and the twisted electric cords broke their skin with stinging pain. To protect her mom, the child soon learned to cooperate with José and his helper. They both got José's initials tattooed on their right thigh, indicating they were his property; they belonged to him.

Eventually, the mother and her little girl accepted their hopelessly cruel life with apathy. Both realized they had neither power nor luck to make any change. Their dream of freedom had turned into slavery; their nightmare would only end with the last breath they took. In the meantime, Jorge stuck a thick envelope into his shirt, then kept driving the rest of the newcomers toward Arizona.

At the city of Pecos, Jorge took Route 10. He skirted the border until he eventually passed Ciudad Juarez. For a second, Miguel had to force himself not to jump off the truck and run across the border, risking pain and hardship again. He felt he could run until he got home. Then he remembered the three hungry children and his wife in the cave that he clawed out from dirt, and she turned into a home. He saw the lovely face of Pilar almost clear enough to touch. He recalled her trustful eyes, and he knew he must stay on the truck. He had to continue what he started; he could not disappoint her. He needed to get a job, so he could send her some money soon, or they could not survive on the little reserve he left. His palms were wet and his knuckles white as he hung onto the edge of his bench, but he remained seated in the fast-moving truck. Finally, they arrived at Green Valley, Arizona, just South of Tucson.

It was in this town that Miguel had the misfortune of meeting Robert Falls and William Odum.

Chapter 24

The Fayette County Sheriff's phone line was busy. It seemed to ring non-stop every five minutes. Curiosity or perceived knowledge prompted people to call with information sought or given in the hope to solve Jeb Odum's murder. The woman at the front desk dutifully registered all incoming calls with name and return number and passed them along with the anonymous calls to Captain Corky. Corky, in return, discussed all promising leads with McCarthy.

McCarthy was waiting for Corky's return from Memphis. When he learned about Vittoria DelRosario's hasty trip to Memphis, he sent Corky to meet her at the airport. Corky gladly complied with the assignment, thinking he would get heads up on her story. One of these days he knew he would surpass McCarthy, and get the coveted position of Chief Investigator, Homicide Division, himself.

Vittoria was a small woman. When she was a young girl, people referred to her as being a 'pretty petite'. After two children and a busy life, studded with much sadness lately, she still remained attractively youthful. Corky thought she could have been a liar, considering her age. She surely looked much younger than sixty-eight. Of course, she was one of the well-to-do, big-city women who always had the means to look better than the country folks. These women never worked as hard or as long, and never had as few amenities, as a farmer's wife. The big cities also had lots of beauty salons with their magic tricks, from hair coloring to relaxing facial massage. Then there were the rich folks' spas and fitness centers at their fingertips, to slim down. Their neighborhood was probably peppered by fancy department stores. Corky concluded Vittoria surely took advantage of all of these to belie her age.

He also enjoyed watching Vittoria's quick movements and rapid walk. He certainly did not need to slow down for her to keep up with his long steps. Maybe the way she carried herself was what made her appear young, he concluded. He liked the subdued elegance and self-assurance that radiated from every move Vittoria made.

"I am pleased to meet you, Captain Corky," smiled Vittoria, extending her hand to a firm handshake. "I must thank you for your call though I must also admit, it was probably the biggest shock I have had. And you were absolutely correct; it was totally unexpected. Poor Jeb, I would have never thought that would be his end. Did you learn who did it? Did you discover anything yet?"

Corky felt important to be asked these questions. He also felt comfortable enough with this friendly woman to reveal what the investigation unearthed so far. "Well, we have lots of leads and a few strong suspects, but no definite cause or person yet. We hope you can shed some light on the circumstances that would help us. We, and I personally, very much appreciate your cooperation."

"Of course, I want to help you in everything I can. I want to know who did this hideous act just as much, if not more, than you do. I will answer any questions you have, and tell you anything I know. I have nothing to hide." Corky noted she seemed sincere.

Vittoria continued: "I have a little dilemma, though. I have been in Williston only a few times. Whenever I visited, it was always Jeb who drove me around. I did not need to rent a car, and now I do not know the area enough to drive around. Not that I have many places to go, but at least to his house and perhaps to the church. Also, I have always stayed at his home, and I assume now I cannot. Am I correct?"

Corky quickly responded: "We had to secure the house, it was a crime scene. You're right, you cannot stay there. As a matter of fact, you cannot even go there, except with us. But the driving is no problem, if you don't mind riding in a police car."

Vittoria smiled, "What a gentleman you are, Captain Corky. You have no idea how much I appreciate your kindness."

Corky was pleased, and, in a wave of generosity, he offered Vittoria his guest room. "You see, there are no hotels or motels in Williston. The only one we used to have, right by the Post Office, closed about a year ago. There was not enough business to keep it open. As you have probably gathered by now, we are a small community, Ma'am; visitors usually came to stay with their families. Perhaps you could get a hotel in Collierville or Somerville, though, but then you would need a car with a good GPS, for sure."

"I could not impose upon you, Captain Corky," Vittoria replied, "but just the same, I thank you for the offer. "

In a bolt of lightning, Corky realized what Vittoria must have thought and quickly added, "I beg your pardon for not telling you, Ma'am, but I do not live alone. I live with my mother. Ever since I can recall, my mom always talked about making a bed-and-breakfast out of the house. You see, she is at home all day long in a big old house. An 'antebellum house', she calls it. I guess she is bored and this would give her something to do. I always discouraged her from the fear of getting a stranger in the house, but this would be different. You don't look like you could harm an old lady, could you? Besides, I already know you. So, what do you say?"

"I am speechless," replied Vittoria. "I am so thankful because, frankly, I did not even give a thought to where I would stay, or how I would get around. When you called me, and the shock wore off, my first thought was to get here fast. Of course, I would reimburse your mother for her home and work. I could not accept it in any other way."

"Well, the offer stands, Ma'am, and you discuss the details with Mom." Corky carried Vittoria's overnight bag to his car and politely opened the door for her.

It took a good hour to get to distant Williston from Memphis International Airport. The warm spring weather opened azaleas and irises in front of the homes, and the trees unfolded light-green, almost transparent leaves, to cover the barren branches. Patches of locust trees spread scents of sweet honey from their clustered white flowers. The flowers were buzzing with bees. Tennessee came to life with the promise of another glorious summer.

Passing a large cotton field, Vittoria recalled how Jeb stopped by the road, so she could get a branch of cotton covered by zigzagged dark green leaves and spilling fluffy cotton from where the white flowers used to be. Those were the happy times. And that was in last August, only eight months ago. Who would have thought that in a few months she would be questioned in a murder? In the murder of the smiling man who patiently waited for her to avoid the thorns of the cotton while she searched for the perfect branch.

Vittoria looked bitterly at nature rejuvenating in such splendor. It was hard for her to accept that life did not come to a halt even for a second with Jeb's death. She reached into her purse and clutched in her palm the key to his house. At least she had something tangible with her, not only her memories. Captain Corky did not notice anything when she rummaged in her purse, and her secret remained well-hidden in the side pocket of her handbag. A man suspected very little and knew even less, if anything, of what a woman carried in her purse.

They drove to Williston, chatting idly about the weather, seasonal change, and the neighboring attractions Vittoria visited in Memphis. Yes, indeed, she spent a whole day in Graceland, and she became a real Elvis fan since she learned about the entertainer's well-guarded, private personality. She was surprised by his generosity of giving and donating, which was kept in the background, not smeared all over across newspapers or displayed on a stage. She was touched by his trusting naiveté that was targeted by the unscrupulous people who surrounded him. Vittoria felt that was Elvis' real tragedy, and she pitied the abused man. And, yes, she saw the Pink Palace inside and out, thanks for the reminder. She was even in the adjoining IMAX-theater and saw a National Geographic documentary on the huge screen. And yes, indeed, she ate BBQ ribs at both the Rendezvous and Corky's, and she preferred Corky's food. Of course, she walked along Beale Street, too, saw the display in the Sun Record, and even listened to a band playing in the park one summer evening. And no, she did not miss visiting the Peabody Hotel and its famous ducks. Unfortunately, she could not get all the way down to the Mississippi water, although she really would have loved to step in the river once.

Captain Corky was impressed by listening to Vittoria's obvious love for Tennessee. He soon realized, in the beginning, Vittoria projected the deep feelings she had for Jeb Odum to his surroundings. Later she grew a true appreciation of the Southern state and its people. Corky knew, whether Vittoria remained connected to Tennessee or not, the affinity she developed would have remained unchanged.

Corky was cautious not to antagonize or alert Vittoria unnecessarily. He had a difficult time to appear open, yet, not to reveal what they have learned from Jeb's ex-wife, from the ex-wife's boyfriend, or about Jeb's lady friend. That was one topic that bothered Corky the most. He did not know how much Vittoria knew of Lana Hadock. She probably only learned as little as what Jeb told her, he decided, and nothing else.

"We have great weather now, not like when you were here last. You should have seen some of the snow we got in February. We sure did not have a white Christmas but got a blanket of snow for Valentine's Day. When did you say you were here last, in December?" He talked about neutral topics like the weather and asked seemingly innocent questions almost as an after-thought. He was a good detective, for he always started his investigations by establishing basic facts and a timeline. Even as a child Corky was a curious kid by nature, and as he grew up, he chose the job of a detective that fitted him perfectly to satisfy this trait.

Corky could not help but be an investigator, even when not in uniform or out of the office. Now he worked not only to gather information ahead of McCarthy, but to quench his thirst for the details. He always agreed with his idol, Paul Drake, often quoting him: "The solution was in the details." Besides, it was justified to ask questions, because this trip, for all intents and purposes, was an official duty. After all, McCarthy himself sent his assistant to the airport to pick up Mrs. DelRosario with the instruction to bring her right to the office of the Fayette County Sheriff, Homicide Division.

Chapter 25

Once in the office of the Chief Investigator, Vittoria asked what had happened, and heard in detail what the detectives discovered so far. Then it was McCarthy's turn to ask the questions. After a few minutes of discussion, he openly asked Vittoria, "Did you harm Jeb Odum?" and was relieved to hear her sincere response, though a bit tainted by self-righteous indignation.

"No. Never. Though at one point I thought I should, but that was only figuratively speaking. Or rather, figuratively thinking," she corrected herself.

"And when was that?" inquired McCarthy.

"At the end of last August. That's when Jeb told me he had been interested in another woman and, as a matter of fact, was already dating her."

"Another woman? And who was that woman?"

"Lana Hadock. She was from his church. They attended the same Sunday school and Bible studies."

The two detectives quickly glanced at each other, before McCarthy asked, "Sunday school, huh? I bet they did more than just pray, wouldn't you agree? And Jeb just told you that point-blank, openly, with details and all?" Ron McCarthy did not know Jeb closely, but found it peculiar to imagine any man flatly announcing he was going to ditch his fiancée, unless he already made up his mind to cease the relationship. It just did not make any sense otherwise. Then, once he did, why did he change his mind again and why did he return to Vittoria? He had to have a reason which escaped the investigator, yet.

It seemed to McCarthy Jeb had already terminated his affair with his fiancée, and was pursuing a new potential interest with full conviction. Perhaps it was difficult for the ditched woman to admit Jeb walked out on her. Perhaps she kept her eyes closed, so she didn't see what was coming. Maybe she relied on her ears a bit too much, and not enough on her eyes, by only believing what Jeb was telling her. She sure should have kept her eyes peeled not to miss the truth. Yes, this denial could have resulted in her total surprise when Jeb revealed to her his interest in Lana Hadock. Perhaps Vittoria only eased the blow later by claiming she was caught off guard. McCarthy looked into her eyes "I ask you again, did you harm or arrange in any way to get Jeb harmed?"

"No, of course not. As a matter of fact, we made up, and everything between us seemed to be even better than before."

"Can you tell me what he said? I mean, describe all the circumstances, what was said and how he told it to you. Then tell me what happened afterward." McCarthy kept his steady gaze on Vittoria, noting her comfortable posture as she sat on the chair and sipped her coffee.

In the meantime, as if out of boredom or being absent-minded, he started to make one-word notes for himself on a yellow legal pad. His right hand did not need his visual guidance. He trained himself to do fairly legible scribbles in a straight line even if he did not look at the writing. The video recorder silently registered every word, anyway.

"Where should I start?" Vittoria asked. "We saw each other every four to six weeks, usually for long weekends, plus a few days here and there. We went on vacation and spent another ten-twelve days together during the holidays. It was not easy because Jeb worked, and so did I. He had his house, and I had mine, so we had our hands full with obligations. Yes, we discussed one of us selling our house, but Jeb really was not too keen on doing it, and I could not. With the poor economy and the even worse real-estate market, the value of my house dropped about forty percent, and no one would have paid the price it was worth.

"In reality, no one was looking for any houses either, except investors. These unscrupulous people picked up foreclosures, short sales, and houses sold by desperate owners. Learning of the dire circumstances, they shamelessly offered a price that was ridiculously low, really on the brim of an outright insult. The unfortunate owner had no choice but to go bankrupt unless he accepted the offer. The ruthless crooks picked up a good house for a song and a dance. I could not afford to lose my house like that. Thank heavens, I was not desperate to do it, either. This is why we kept on traveling every so often; otherwise, we could not be with each other."

She sighed then continued in an even tone, "In May, Jeb spent a week with me. I surprised him with a birthday party to celebrate his special day. I invited a few friends, and we had a lovely time. We went to see a movie, walked in the park, did some shopping. Basically, we lived the mundane life of a married couple. That was the first time I felt comfortable bringing up finances to Jeb. You see, he was due to retire at the end of August, and he planned to move in with me. Of course, he assured me he was not a freeloader and was planning to pay half of the household expenses.

"Two days before he drove home to Tennessee, we were sitting on my screened porch and had a calm, logical discussion. That's when we decided how we would divide the expenses to make it even for both of us. He was rather generous in his offers. It felt good, and it truly touched me, to realize how considerate he was. I remember thinking how lucky I was to meet such a decent guy. We already liked similar little things, like having our early morning coffee while watching the sunrise. And now I had learned he already planned out a comfortable future for me. At my age, what more could I expect, right? He left on the best terms, assured me of his unending affection and love. He repeated often he barely could wait to begin retirement. He promised that the very next day after he left his work at St. Jude, at the crack of dawn, he would start driving to Montgomery. He wanted to start a new life with me as soon as he was free of his work. For the first time, I felt truly comfortable and positive about the future with him.

"We continued the daily phone contact. Since the very beginning of our relationship, we called each other twice a day, morning and before bedtime. That is, I called him. At least in the beginning I did, but lately he changed when he started to call me. It surprised me, because originally Jeb said if I make the calls then he did not disturb me or interrupt my work. He convinced me this way I could talk to him whenever it was convenient for me. Jeb reasoned he was always at home every evening, anyway, so it did not matter for him what time I called. The new calling pattern just did not fit his previous formula, but I did not pay much attention or, rather, did not attribute any significance to his changed routine. Anyway, that summer it was he who made the calls.

"As the summer progressed, he had more and more work with the approaching retirement, and the planned move to Montgomery. First, he could not come to visit me in June, and he delayed it to July. Then he postponed the July trip, too, because of his cataract surgery.

"Immediately, I offered to fly to Memphis and take care of him, but Jeb said he already made arrangements with his sister. He said he did not want to inconvenience me. His sister did not work, and she lived nearby. She could take good care of him, so he saw no reason why I should come to Tennessee. It only would mean an extra expense which we could save for the time when we would be together. Eventually, he convinced me not to be there as he did not need my help. He had his valid reasons and I accepted the hold-off without second thoughts."

"Let me see. All these changes took place after the financial talk you two had in May, am I correct? When you told him he had no free ride, but had to share the household expenses equally. After this reality sunk in, he decided for the first time not to come to see you. Then his sister was to take care of him, not you. As a matter of fact, he did not even want you to come to visit him. Right? Did you question yourself why? Perhaps because he already told his sister you were being phased out and replaced? Maybe the unexpected show up would collapse his concocted cover for his plans? Didn't it seem strange, all of a sudden, to see him distancing himself?" McCarthy's eyes did not miss Vittoria's obviously shocked expression.

"Well, it was not that clear. You see, whatever he did, it was subtle and gradual. And all along he was apologetic and gave me time to accept the new developments. I could also find my own explanation and excuse for each," replied Vittoria with a small self-deprecating smile.

"I figured starting September first he would be with me permanently, anyway. He wanted to marry me. So, what would a couple of months delay mean? Nothing. Right? Boy, was I ever wrong!"

She shook her head in disbelief. McCarthy remained quiet. He just concentrated on what was said and intensely kept watching the speaker to detect her emotions hidden behind the spoken words.

Vittoria picked up the story again. "This also gave me a good opportunity to rearrange my home to make room for him. Then I gave an overall good scrub to everything in anticipation of his arrival." She appeared calm and almost matter-of-fact. McCarthy suspected it was not as easy for her as she portrayed.

"In the third week of August, he called me on a Sunday, just as he got home from the church service. In retrospect, I realized he must have received the needed push to confront me while at church, that's why he had this timing.

"You see, Jeb became really eager and actually looked forward to participate in his Bible school, attend the church service, visit the prayer group, be present at every potluck, and social gathering they had. I even remarked to him, sort of jokingly, that he probably was a corpse at every funeral, and a bride at every wedding. He laughed it off, but was not bothered by it enough to make a change. As the summer advanced, it occurred to me that he kept delaying every planned trip to Montgomery. Yet, he talked with so much enthusiasm about soon starting our combined lives that I could not remain disappointed for too long. I brushed away all the negative thoughts. Toward the end of the summer, I could not explain why I had the fleeting, nagging thoughts return over his subtle change. Now I was to find out."

Vittoria smiled dryly, then continued in an even tone. "That's when he said, 'We have to talk.' But it was only he who talked, I was stunned speechless. He started out by telling me point-blank that neither could he move away from Williston nor could he ever live in Montgomery. He realized he promised it to me over and over, and decided to do so as soon as he began his retirement; however, he could not do it, after all. Since he lived his whole life within a hundred miles of Memphis, he felt he was not ready or able to leave it for anything or anyone. I asked him, 'Not even for me?' and hoped this would knock him back to his senses. He did not hesitate or seemed to be in any discomfort in replying, 'No, not even for you'."

Vittoria lowered her voice, "Then he dropped the second shoe by saying 'I think it would be for the best to call our engagement off. As a matter of fact, I have already started to date a woman from my Bible class. It was nothing special, yet, we just wanted to see where it would lead.' Then he added, 'It just happened: one day we saw each other in a different light. I did not really mean for it to happen.'

"I was speechless, not only at the totally unexpected turn, but at how easily he was able to tell me what he did. He never seemed to comprehend that he betrayed my trust."

"Yes, he revealed his change of mind and heart with ease, and also chose an easy way out, over the phone. You should know by now that he was not man enough to face you in person," McCarthy quietly remarked.

Chapter 26

Vittoria DelRosario first blushed with embarrassment, then turned ashen gray as she realized her fiancée's character fault. A stranger could instantly see it, yet, she did not. Or maybe she just did not want to see it.

Although McCarthy saw the changes on her face and could recognize the underlying emotional turmoil, he had to continue the uncomfortable discussion. Because he liked Vittoria, he wanted her to understand that whatever happened was not all her fault. She was not to hold herself guilty over another person's transgression. Her blunder was to endure and tolerate it, not to commit it. She could not have been over it and see clearly if even now she was trying to find excuses for her Jeb.

McCarthy doggedly remained on track and continued the investigation with a noticeably doubtful skepticism, "What did he say? Did I hear you right? That 'it just happened'? Like walking down a street and saying, 'Man, I just hate when this happens to me?' I don't think so. It did not just happen. He made a conscious decision to pursue, date, kiss, and fondle another woman. He was not an innocent bystander; he was an active participant. It did not just happen," McCarthy shook his head and, though his voice sounded calm and controlled, he clearly was outraged.

"Well, that's what he said," continued Vittoria. "I told him an 'exclusive engagement' referred to two people and no other person was included. If he did not observe this rule or did not understand the meaning of exclusivity, he should have started to look for a good psychiatrist who enjoyed a challenge."

McCarthy could not help but smile. Vittoria continued, "At the end, he begged me not to hate him, after all, it was hard and painful on him what happened. I could not believe my own ears. Did he expect me to feel sorry for him? Perhaps even console him? No, that was overkill. I told him that although I am a Christian, the time was long gone when the condemned forgave the lions for devouring them.

"Oh, yes, he also wanted to remain friends and projected, 'We can call each other from time to time, honey'. This is where I started to recover from my stunned state and got angry for the first time. Friends? Friends did not double-cross each other. Calling me 'honey' after all this betrayal? No, we should not call each other. I was not an 'also runneth', a substitute, in case the first choice did not turn out as planned, just to be placed on the back burner as a secure, reserved, left-over, ready to be pulled forward when his whim dictated. As if he had no horse, then he would settle for a mule. No, I was better than that. I deserved more than that."

McCarthy started to look at her with gradually increasing respect.

Vittoria continued, "All along I remained mainly stunned. Who? When? How did he meet her? His answers left no doubt in me that he already made up his mind. He only presented me with a *fait accompli*, as the French say. In essence, this woman was Lana Hadock, the Merry Widow, from his Bible class. For the entire summer, Jeb's behavior was undeniably more than suspicious: clearly, something was fishy."

McCarthy gave a small smile as he repeated Vittoria's last words, "Something was fishy. You could say that. Actually, it was stinking fishy, and not only because her name was Lana Hadock. Am I correct?"

"Yes. According to Jeb, she was the pillar of the church, a pious woman. What he liked in her was her constant, thrilling laughter and the great smile, no matter what was going on in her life. He described her as a little bird because she always seemed to be happy. Then he gave me the *coup-de-grace*, the last stab to kill my feelings. My heart sank into my knees when he revealed his whole family, his daughter, his sister and her husband, everybody already knew of her and knew about our purported break-up for at least the last two months. Everybody knew we supposedly broke up, but me. I was kept in a world of lies by his daily phone calls and incessant promises. He kept lying to me every day. Sometimes twice a day. Whenever he called, that is. Actually, he had to lie to Lana and his family as well as to everyone else. In the interim, of course, he had to keep lying to me, too."

"I knew there was something missing," McCarthy interrupted her. "Now I can see how Jeb already padded his new seat with a bunch of tales so his sister and daughter would not question him about the new girlfriend. This is why he didn't want you to come to help him after his cataract surgery. His tower of lies would have crumbled with your arrival, wouldn't it? He already prepared his family for the change by inventing the break-up with you, didn't he? Can you see how pre-meditated it all was? It was not as impulsively rash as he tried to convince you. No, my dear, he was not unexpectedly caught off-guard. He knew very well what he was doing, trust me. I would not be surprised to learn how much time he spent on planning the whole scenario out to the last detail."

"Looking back, I have to agree with you, but at that time I had difficulty just comprehending what I heard. It was especially difficult to accept it because Jeb was such a church-going, religious man. After what I saw in him, I truly did not even dream that he would be a liar and a cheat." Vittoria shook her head in disbelief. Simple, decent, and honest Jeb Odum planned to the last detail smearing her with vicious lies to exonerate himself from any wrongdoing. And all along he kept misleading her. And all along she kept believing him. That still blew her mind. What a nightmare!

"Oh, yes, but he was going to church every Sunday to get an absolution, don't you agree?"

"Well, at least he probably prayed for forgiveness."

"In a way you could be right. Imagine how bad and hurtful a person would be if there were no church morals to guide him. Or her." It was hard to miss the sarcasm in McCarthy's voice.

"Did you ever tell his family how he misled them? That you two never did break up, and he only justified his cheating by these so-called explanations? Giving them some tall tales as a reason for his actions, if only for what could not be avoided. Did he ever tell you what excuses he gave them for breaking up with you?"

"No, not really. He only told them that we did not get along and he could not continue."

"Ahem. That's why he called you twice a day and assured you of his love, right? Did you ever tell his sister that?"

"No, I could not. I kept quiet. You see, if I did, he would have lost his face or whatever was left of it. I am sure his entire family already knew him enough to suspect him lying again. After all, they went through his divorce and years of various contacts. There is no doubt in my mind they all knew him enough to know he habitually hid some and colored or misrepresented other facts. But blood is blood and not water, and loyalty belongs to the family member and not to an outsider. So I didn't say anything. I also instinctively realized that if he lost his face, he would have held me responsible for it and never forgiven me. It would have made him nothing but a two-timing liar."

"It's not who you lay with, but who you lie to," McCarthy interrupted her dryly.

Vittoria looked up and her eyes met McCarthy's, "I guess a man is a man, and it is hard for a man not to step astray if tempted, am I correct?"

"If you truly love someone, being faithful is easy," McCarthy replied shortly.

For a second, Vittoria's dark eyes piercingly glared at him, but almost instantly the fire dissipated and she added with some trepidation, "You are right, it should be easy. I was approached by one of the internists at the hospital not long ago. He said he watched me for a while and liked me. He complimented my looks, my work, then he asked me for a date. I was completely floored; his words were so unexpected. I never paid attention to him before, I just did my work there and left. I did not look for any side affairs or cheap thrills, trust me. Do you know what I told him? I responded with a charming smile and the warmest 'thank you' I could manage and added that since I was engaged, I did not think my fiancée would have liked it. I could not go. At the end, the poor doctor got embarrassed and apologized. He very respectfully greeted me from a distance whenever he spotted me in the hospital ever since."

"See? This is exactly what I meant: it is easy if you love a person. You could do it, why couldn't he?" replied McCarthy.

Vittoria looked at him with painful eye and paused in silence before she could continue calmly, "Needless to say, I was terribly upset. I truly did not expect this. Jeb was neither a dashing Casanova nor a heart-skipping Adonis. He did not look like or act like a stereotypical cheater. I never would have fathomed he could blatantly lie and mislead me. I settled for him because I thought he was a simple, honest, country boy. I thought he was an honorable man whose word spoke his true feelings and whose 'yes' meant a 'yes' and whose 'no' meant a 'no'."

"Ah, yes, an honorable man," replied McCarthy. "Well, my dear, he was far from it. About as far as the moon from a barking dog."

Vittoria raised an eyebrow, but did not reply. Silence grew between them and became uncomfortable. After a long pause, when she felt in control of her emotions again, she continued.

"Although I felt he could offer me far less than what I expected or was accustomed to, I compromised enough for him not to be betrayed in return. I fell hard from the imaginary pedestal I was perched on, and I fell right onto my face. After a few days of non-stop crying, I got angry. I guess we all go a little mad sometimes. It looked to me Jeb got off easy, with one phone call. At first, I was shocked then disappointed in him. I was devastated, but mainly incredulous that a man could do this to me. I would have never done it to him. I was working to prepare my house and rearrange my life to accommodate him while all along he fabricated stories about me, lied to me, and lusted after someone else.

"That's when I decided to come see this famous Williston he clung to so much. Most of all, I wanted to confront him and not let him get off scot-free. He chose the easy way out with a short phone call. I was determined to make him see me in person, and say everything right into my face. The following weekend I came to Memphis."

McCarthy looked at his scribbles. Words of 'disappointment', 'humiliation', 'pain', 'frustration', and 'betrayal' were hooked together, then arrowed to the single word 'retaliation', followed by three question marks.

Vittoria picked up the story again. "We had a very emotional, huge discussion. I cried. He felt sorry for seeing me sobbing. I reasoned with him. He became less and less convinced that he made the right decision by abandoning me and choosing Lana. I told him, I was willing to move to Tennessee, if he could not leave the area. I had a terrific job offer in Memphis, with a hefty sign-up bonus, an all paid relocation, and full benefits for the entire family. He was surprised to hear what the projected salary was. He even asked me twice, as if he did not understand or believe it for the first time. That's when he suddenly turned around. He asked me in a haste, 'Can we reconsider this? This situation? What we talked about?' He asked for the smallest details in my job offer. He seemed very interested.

"This was after three hours into the discussion. That's when he said he fully realized how he wronged me. He seemed a bit ashamed and embarrassed when he told me, 'You would be shocked to meet Lana: she is not someone you would expect me to date. She is sort of chunky and definitely country. Secretly I named her BB for 'big butt'. I only tell it to you so you can imagine her.'

"Instantly, his remark took me back to almost staggering, it made me feel so uneasy. After all, he was bad-mouthing to me the very person for whom he deserted me. A couple of hours prior he claimed to be in love with her, and now he just divulged his ugliest disrespect by calling her a 'big butt'? It created a rancid taste in my mouth. Yet, I brushed it away, knowing he returned to me. I might have even felt a bit of satisfaction realizing if that was his opinion of her then he never would return to her. Maybe I even found his honesty sort of refreshing.

"He called up Lana. They talked for a long time. Jeb told her something which I could not hear, because he talked very quietly. When he put the phone down, he told me, 'It's all over. I am back.' I thought, he meant the affair was over."

"Let me understand this. So as soon as he heard about your job offer, he was willing to dump the church woman whom he 'suddenly saw in a different light', wasn't he? She must have meant an awful lot for him to dump her all of a sudden. Dump the love interest for the promise of future money. Nice. A true gentleman. Sincere love. Did it ever occur you, where did it put him? Or you? Or Lana? Apparently, your fiancée could easily pick and choose norms, rules, and commandments as his mood or interest dictated it," McCarthy summarized Jeb's change of heart.

Vittoria did not look up, but continued staring at her hands. "I was exhausted physically and mentally, but also was relieved. I no longer tried to make sense or find a rational cause for his irrational act. I forgave him. Just to be on the safe side, at the end I warned him that another such mistake would establish a pattern, and then I could no longer excuse it to be an exception, or call it a blunder. In that case, I guaranteed him I could never find a reason to forgive him or forget his dishonesty."

"Now, wait a second. Did he actually admit he was wrong? No. Did he take responsibility for his affair? No. Did he own his act? Not at all. Did he ever say to you he knew he has made a terrible mistake? I have not heard that, either. Did he ask for your forgiveness? Maybe in a round-about, vague way. Not really. Did he promise to reassure you to make up for it every day of the rest of his life? Not at all." McCarthy summarized the long accounting. The shocked Vittoria just stared hearing him putting into words her own hidden and unspoken feelings which gnawed at her ever since that day.

Her face was clearly puzzled as McCarthy's assessment and her memories started to jive. At the end she hesitantly admitted, "No, he never did any of these. He only said he was sorry to see me hurt. Then we sort of swept everything under the rug and decided to continue our engagement, as if this affair never has happened, or as if there were never any interruption."

While Vittoria talked, McCarthy slowly crossed out 'revenge', and above it he wrote 'dumb' in bold, capital letters.

Chapter 27

The Reverend Babcock was caught off guard by the incoming call from the Sheriff's Office. Ron McCarthy wanted to meet the Reverend to discuss something of a mutual interest, he said.

Kenneth Babcock, Doctor of Theology and Scholar of Divine Studies, could not imagine what common concern they might have, but politely agreed to the meeting. He was more than a bit curious, thinking of various recent events that possibly clashed with the law. Was it maybe old Mrs. Pearl Lutz who streaked naked again? Ever since the poor soul lost her mind and imagined being a hooker, at times she ventured into the street without a stitch. Or was it Evan Morris being spotted drunk again? He occasionally attended service, but the Mount Olive Southern Baptist Church never acknowledged him, whether drunk or sober. No, it must have been Charlie Croft, that young whippersnapper, who probably was picked up for loitering while necking on lover's lane one too many times. The Reverend warned him about the Devil's temptations and not to turn 'lover's lane' to 'sex drive' but Charlie continued anyway, except he changed his partners ever so often.

For a fleeting second, he thought about poor Jeb Odum. The news of Jeb's death already spread like wildfire. He was a steady contributor to the church, attended every service and function, but never stirred up a controversy. He discarded the thought that unobtrusive Jeb and his quiet death could have been on McCarthy's mind. Then his thoughts shifted to the finances of the church and the upcoming big Easter service. He was convinced a good attendance surely would raise the funds to repair at least the parking lot. Maybe McCarthy was about to tell him something about the contractor from nearby Oakland. Reverend Babcock recently got wind of a shady business dealing of the contractor. Good-willed church members already warned him to be careful of the proposed repair job.

McCarthy arrived at the church office on time, only to find a cordial Reverend, who already thought he figured out what prompted this meeting. Hearing the upcoming visit of the Sheriff, his secretary alerted Reverend Babcock of the Somerville Police Department's Spring Fund Raiser. It seemed entirely logical that as one branch of law enforcement supported the other, the Sheriff acted on behalf of the local police, and only wanted to ensure the Reverend's participation.

Since Mount Olive Southern Baptist Church was in the heart of Somerville, and since Mr. Babcock relied on the friendly relationship with the local police, he decided to donate a modest sum from the Easter collection. This way he secured the presence of a uniformed man in front of the church exit to direct the wave of heavy traffic after the Sunday services. After all, the neighboring little towns like Williston, Macon, Oakland, and even Cordova were represented among the faithful who filled the pews in every Sunday. He was totally unprepared for the questions circling around the Bible school teacher Lana Hadock.

The Reverend Babcock was a sincere man. He also was the leader of his church and zealously guarded his reputation. He skillfully avoided all blemishes that might have put him or his flock in a bad light. Now he would pay full attention to the Sheriff, waiting to hear the reason of this unusual visit to be revealed, be it a fundraiser or a church member.

"You heard, two days ago Jeb Odum was found dead in his house, didn't you?" started McCarthy.

"Yes, I have heard. Bad news travels fast. It was quite a shock, because three days prior he was here, right on time, both at Sunday school and service. During service, he sat in the back pew. Before the sermon, he attended Bible class. He looked well; no one would have ever guessed this to be his last time. Death sneaks in like a thief, no one ever knows when the end comes, does one?"

He stared at his hands and slightly shook his head in disbelief before he continued. "We knew Jeb well, he was a member of this church and, if I may say so, an impeccable member. Quiet, faithful, reliable. A real honest, good Christian man. We were all saddened to hear about his untimely end. May he rest in peace." The reverend's words trailed off, clearly waiting for a response or some input from McCarthy.

McCarthy did not hesitate. "I would like to hear more about him. As you know, every little bit of information could be significant. Who knows what shred of news would shed light on his death, right?"

"Yes, I agree, the key to every dilemma is hidden somewhere in its components. Though I did not hear there was any riddle in his death, was there?" McCarthy detected surprise, apprehension, and curiosity in Reverend Babcock's voice.

His words were smoothly assuring, "No, we know what happened. Not much riddle in that. We just don't know Mr. Odum much; that's all. Perhaps hearing from you and his friends, we might learn something to help us put things in order. Was he close to anyone in church? Did anyone know him well?"

"No, he basically was a loner. He was a man of good standards but was very low-key. If anyone talked to him, he readily smiled and even joked. He just never initiated much talk. Come to think of it, no one was really close to him. I have not heard him inviting anyone, nor did I hear anyone inviting him for a visit, ever. Not that I know of, anyway."

"Not a single person? Are you telling me that he came to Bible School and service every Sunday and made not a single friend? Now that's interesting," interjected McCarthy. "He was a member of this church before his divorce, am I correct?"

"Oh, yes, he was a member over fifteen years. I knew him since I was placed here, for a bit over eight years."

"Then you must have known his ex-wife, too, am I correct?"

"No, I could not say that. I met her once; that's all. Jeb always arrived and left alone. His wife did not like our church, and did not attend with Jeb. I have heard she made a remark that this was nothing but a country church and was not sophisticated enough for her. Now, mind you, that was hearsay only, but it sure rang true when we never saw her, not even at Christmas or Easter. I think she went to the big church in Germantown, which had more well-to-do folks. She was sort of ritzy, anyway, she fit among those people better, I am sure."

"Hm. That does not say much for her faith or their marriage, does it?" McCarthy realized the Odum's marriage must have been over way before the seed of the idea of divorce was planted. "How about Jeb Odum? Did he have any relationships? I mean a relationship either before or after his divorce? Any time?"

"Jeb? No. He was not a player. At first, he did not because he was married. Then he did not because he was engaged. I even met his fiancée, a nice woman, from Alabama. She attended a couple of times with Jeb while visiting him. In the beginning I thought they seemed to be suited for each other. Later I was not that convinced."

"You met his fiancée? Did you think she looked as if she fit in the congregation? Obviously, this was important to Jeb, wouldn't you say so?"

"Well, she was nice and rather charming, but clearly she was an outsider, if you know what I mean. People thought she talked funny, because she had an accent. And she dressed a bit too elegant, too different, some women said. Personally, I did not note that, but as a man I was not aware of the fine nuances like the women were. My wife mentioned them to me, and then I paid more attention. After a few occasions, we got a bit familiar with her. The more we talked to her, the more we all came to the conclusion that Jeb was way above his head in this relationship. As if he tried to swim in deep waters, when in reality he could barely float, and needed to touch the bottom with his toes. But one never knows what is in another person's mind or heart, right?"

"Both love and infatuation sure could be blind," agreed McCarthy, barely able to conceal his satisfaction at the turn the conversation took.

"I don't know if it was such blind love," started the Reverend slowly, "After all, Jeb suddenly broke up with her last year. He apparently fancied his Sunday school teacher, Lana Hadock, more. They talked a lot, always sat by each other, showed up at potluck dinners and domino nights together. It was nice to see he found a very good match, right here in our church. Too bad, it did not last long. One Sunday the fiancée showed up, and that ended the romance with Lana. Everyone felt disappointed because we all rooted for Lana. She went through a tough time with her divorce before, and it was nice to see she finally found a good man who seemed to be smitten by her. I have heard from many people how upset Lana was when her new relationship came to a screeching halt."

"Really? Did she talk about it with others? Did she confide in you, too?" McCarthy kept his unwavering eyes on the face of Reverend Babcock.

"I cannot say much more, but she was disheartened for sure. She put on a great show, smiled as if nothing bothered her, and went on as usual. But see this shoulder?" Mr. Babcock patted his left shoulder, "That's where she cried. And she cried quite a bit, I would say."

"I guess, she must have been pretty disillusioned," McCarthy agreed.

"More like hurt and frustrated, she was. The way I understood, it was Lana who approached Jeb first, because he seemed to be too quiet and deep in thoughts. Lana had a cheerful personality. She always seemed upbeat and laughing, as if nothing ever bothered her. Mainly, she had the advantage of being here, present, and seen every time. Furthermore, she was understanding and supportive of Jeb. She openly said many times, it was not fair to poor Jeb to be so neglected by his fiancée and 'by letting him be alone, that shameless woman, Victoria, really proved she did not love Jeb much'. Lana assured Jeb, and we all heard that she told him repeatedly, he was a good man who deserved much better."

"Ah, the plot thickens! I guess the 'better' which Jeb really deserved, was Lana, herself."

"Well, after several discussions that's what Jeb must have thought, too. You know how it is. If we want to believe something, we can readily accept it. Lana always told him she was there to listen to him if he wanted to talk more. They met for lunch. Eventually went for dinner. Slowly, the topic changed from the fiancée to their interest in each other. Lana instantly saw a good opportunity to hook up with a man who had a similar background. You know, small town, local, same religion, not much demand to make a change. And Jeb felt comfortable in the caring kindness Lana offered and asked her for more. They kept seeing each other."

"How about Jeb's engagement? Didn't Lana know he was formally engaged to be married to Vittoria?" McCarthy inquired.

"Oh, yes, we all knew about it. I remember how surprised we all were, on the day when Jeb announced his engagement. Periodically, afterward he missed church on a few weekends because he went to see his fiancée. No, the engagement was not over, I understood he regularly kept in contact with Victoria."

McCarthy noted, with slight annoyance, that Vittoria was being called by the Americanized form of Victoria. Surely, the Reverend Babcock was not that ignorant, he should have used her name properly. It was only that country folks did not adapt to new forms and alien ideas too readily.

Maybe, just maybe, there lurked here an even bigger problem than what it first seemed: the Southern country folks could not truly accept people who were not born and raised in Dixie Land.

Chapter 28

The stained-glass windows of the rectory fractured the afternoon sun into brilliant colors. McCarthy enjoyed the playful colors change the Reverend's solemn appearance: half of his face was pink, the other yellow, and his hands were soft blue. Well, art always reflected on people, though it did not necessarily compliment them.

McCarthy was familiar with Somerton and knew it might have been a small town, but was one of the richest farmland community of the Tennessee rolling hills. This wealth also showed on every aspect of the church. Many members were large land owners, some had hundreds of cattle or herds of sheep. They talked with a Southern slow speech and used words perhaps heard nowhere else, but here. A visitor from the Northeast might have called them rednecks. Yet, they were good-hearted and freely gave to their center of the community. The Mount Olive Southern Baptist Church kept them together, and gave them a sense of belonging. Through the church, they could prove to the strange Presbyterians and even weirder Catholics how wrong they were by saying 'Southern Baptists ain't got no morals'. After all, they did not consume spirits in public and what went on behind closed doors was nobody's business.

Hearing Reverend Babcock's strong voice, McCarthy shifted his thoughts and earnestly listened to every word the preacher said.

"Jeb and Victoria called each other, as usual, but his heart probably was not in it anymore. Even if it were, it did not last long. How could it, with Lana constantly being around him, talking to him, being in front of his eyes? I was not privileged to know whether Victoria felt anything changed or not, but over the summer Jeb certainly transformed. He discovered he liked Lana. After Lana coyly remarked a few times, 'Why, Jeb Odum, it sure sounds you are in love with me,' Jeb started to think maybe he really was in love with her. He certainly was attracted to her, but it took the words of Lana to open his eyes enough to realize he also must have loved her."

Mr. Babcock looked straight into McCarthy's eyes as he continued. "And what was there not to like in her? To start with, she had the same background, both being country folks. She lived a few miles from the church, not far from Jeb. She had a nice house which was all paid for. She settled in the community. No affairs or gossip about her. At least I have never heard any. She paid attention to herself, maybe a bit too much, but an aging woman who wants to catch a husband would have to do that. My wife said that was sort of a given.

"She even started to pay attention to her weight, and started to lose some. Not that she was very obese, but I would say she was rather overweight. You know, on the chunky side. Some men like that, like a little meat on a woman. Her waist, hips, and legs were always her worst features. That's why she usually wore long skirts. She tried to cover them. Now she began to wear more fashionable outfits. Some were outright trendy, like what teenagers wear. That was a bit too much; I had to agree with the folks. To summon it, obviously, lately she was in a different mood, ready to convert herself, because it became clear that in Jeb she saw a good possibility to change her future."

"Didn't others note what was going on? And nobody ever questioned it? After all, you all knew Jeb was spoken for, right? I always thought marriage and engagement were taboo, sort of off limits." McCarthy disliked deceit, and he was too straight to hide his conviction.

"Yes, of course, it should have been off limits. But Lana and Jeb kept carrying on until people noticed they were up to something and approached Lana by asking what happened. She just looked at them with an innocent face then turned to Jeb with a big smile, nudging him to tell them what happened. Lana felt it should be Jeb, the strong and leading party in the relationship, who should let everyone know the good news. After all, he was a man, or should she say, 'her man'. No, it was Jeb's responsibility to tell the good news to everyone.

"Jeb was caught off guard, and found himself in a very uncomfortable situation because, so far, he had made no decision. He sweated the questioning silently until finally Lana commanded him to reveal the choice they supposedly have made: the engagement was off, and now Jeb and Lana were a couple. Actually, at the end, it was Lana who made the announcement. Jeb just stood there. People hugged Lana and congratulated Jeb. Although he remained speechless all along, everyone got the impression from Lana that evidently Jeb was in agreement with her."

"So when did Jeb tell Vittoria the surprise ending of their engagement? I bet it must have been quite a shock."

"Well, he kept delaying and delaying the talk with his fiancée, until one Sunday I spotted Jeb and Lana in a heated discussion in the parking lot, right after church. She called me over and asked me if I could advise Jeb on how to straighten out his affairs. Jeb was quiet as usual, but I saw that he was rather uncomfortable, with a crying woman and his preacher talking to him about very private matters in the open. I did not say much, except that I was happy to see two lonely people from my church joining forces. I quoted them the Bible, and encouraged Jeb to reveal the truth because the truth would set him free." Here the Reverend Babcock unobtrusively placed his hand on the nearby Bible, as if making a reference to his quoted source.

"I understood later that Lana ended up winning, because after that big scene Jeb called up Victoria as soon as he got home, and finally announced to her that they were done. He told her he found someone else, and he wanted to be with the other woman. I believe he tried to soften the blow by telling his fiancée that they still could remain friends, and call each other periodically. I have heard later from Lana that she and Victoria both rejected this idea.

"The very next weekend Lana, in all smiles and radiant in her happiness, immediately announced to the entire Sunday school that she and Jeb were seriously dating. She hinted, under the greatest secrecy, that she would not be surprised if Jeb was heading toward marriage in the near future. As a matter of fact, she asked the ladies if they knew which store carried the best bridal gown for a late-in-life ceremony.

"A self-assured, victorious Lana also thanked me for pushing Jeb into making a final decision, as now they were free from the ex-fiancée. I was quite speechless hearing my participation had been construed as a 'push', instead of being considered to be a 'help', but Lana's lively, incessant chatting prevented me defending my limited involvement. I have not seen Lana that strong or convicted ever before. She truly surprised me."

"A typical Southern Belle, wasn't she? Just like an attractive, fragile-looking butterfly, which was resilient enough to be made of steel: an iron butterfly. It seemed to me she only cared about her wants. She appeared as a meek and mild, helplessly fragile, little bird; yet, she was as unstoppable as a tidal wave in pursuing her fervent desires. Yes, she was as forceful as a tidal wave that relentlessly gained strength as it attacked and erased all that got in her way. In the meantime, she kept smiling as if she were normal. Reverend Babcock, have you ever seen a person forever in a total bliss of happiness? I have not. Have you ever met a person who always seemed to be on Cloud Nine, never needed a moment to reflect or quietly meditate…? Such a person exists maybe in a fairy tale, but not in real life. And surely could not be found in our neck of the woods in Tennessee."

McCarthy shook his head incredulously. He waited for Reverend Babcock to say something, but the man of the cloth remained silent, so he continued to wrap up his evaluation.

"Lana was bending, but not breaking. She was coyly playing with Jeb and barely covered her leading. He certainly did not recognize she had the force of a deadly hurricane. She was expertly manipulating and skillfully leading the wishy-washy Jeb until he changed and her will was done. Reverend Babcock, didn't you find it unusual that a Sunday school teacher, a devout and faithful Baptist woman would break up a man's relationship? After knowing what happened, don't you think she should fall to her knees and beg for forgiveness for destroying two people's happiness and eventually ruining their lives? Look at the results of her capricious meddling! Would this immorality be consistent with her dedication to the Ten Commandments? Was not this just a trifle hypocritical? What kind of faith did she have, that allowed her to do this? I am not a Baptist, but I believe we use the same book, don't we? My Bible teaches me not to covet what others already have. Or is it different in your church and instead of the 'Thy will be done' you teach 'my will be done'?" laughed McCarthy.

The Reverend uncomfortably shifted in his seat. "We are only human, and we can only do so much. And to be honest, let me say this in Lana's defense: she did not do it alone. After all, Jeb participated in it, too. Lana may have started it, but Jeb did nothing to discourage or stop her. Maybe she kept going after Jeb, but he must have liked it, or he would not have allowed her to continue. He could have, and should have, reminded Lana of his engagement. And if that was not enough to stop Lana's advances, he could have kept talking about his fiancée. But he did not. He allowed Lana to chase him, until he was caught and could not get out of the mess without hurting someone. So, he was not totally innocent, either."

"True", McCarthy agreed, "it takes two, the 'beggar' and the 'beggee', to beg. Adam was just as much blamed and punished for falling for Eve's temptation, because he willingly ate the apple. History repeats itself if we don't learn from it."

"Well, things rapidly shifted, anyway. In two weeks Jeb showed up in church with Victoria, introduced her as her fiancée, and we all looked at each other incredulously. We sure were confused. Did not Lana announce she and Jeb were seriously involved? Nevertheless, nobody said a word to either Jeb or Victoria.

"Lana left her chair vacant for Victoria next to Jeb's, and sat by the wall alone. She looked mighty sore and not smiling for the first time. True, it would have been impossible under so much make-up, anyway. Victoria charmingly kept talking with everyone and waved at Lana when their eyes met. Apparently, she had no idea who the blond woman was." The Reverend smiled with a hint of ready-made absolution before he continued his thought. "It made no difference, anyway, because as soon as the last words of the sermon were spoken, Lana disappeared."

"What happened after that? Did you talk with her afterward?" McCarthy was all business again.

"Yes. She was very hurt. You see, she was convinced it was all smooth sailing after Jeb supposedly broke off the engagement. Then Victoria showed up on the following Sunday. Frankly, Victoria was a more accomplished and much more of a refined woman than Lana. What I meant to say was sophisticated, not a country-girl like Lana. She also was much trimmer than Lana. All good reasons to be disliked, don't you think?" chuckled the Reverend Babcock then continued seriously "I guess as long as Lana did not meet, but only heard about her, Victoria was really a non-existing entity to her. For her, Jeb's fiancée was a faceless, distant figure who was to dissolve into the Alabama void. Lana already had Jeb in her hand, just about clutching him tight in her grasp, when the ghost of his past appeared and claimed him once more. You can understand her aggravation, can't you? She was an aging woman who lost the future she planned in her mind all the way to a forthcoming marriage. To top all that, she, Lana Hadock, the Sunday school teacher and strong supporter of the church, was ditched for and by an outsider. That was more than just embarrassing in front of the members, who all knew her and knew of her plans with Jeb."

The Reverend thoughtfully continued. "Look, nobody would want to be in Lana's shoes. Frankly, she must have felt people were snickering at her, and she was ridiculed by all for being twice the loser. I can honestly say nobody did that. We were way too surprised by the developments to even think. We just tried to digest the news. Some women might have whispered with false sympathy 'too bad, when she worked so hard to get him', but that was about all."

"Do you think Lana was angry enough to harm Jeb?" asked McCarthy.

"I don't know," Mr. Babcock said slowly, "I hope she would not. But then, Jeb has died, so it is immaterial to speculate, isn't it?"

"Not really, Reverend Babcock. You see, Jeb Odum was murdered."

Chapter 29

Charlotte Kay was tired. She felt every bone in her feet was poking through the sole, making it hard to walk. Each step got progressively more painful, until she finally kicked her high heels off and walked into her house, swinging them in her hand. On the way home, she stopped at her daughter's house but just enough to drop her off, she did not even get out of the car. They both were exhausted, rushing from the coroner's office to a funeral parlor, from there to the cemetery office, then to get a casket, order flowers, talk with his preacher, notify distant relatives, and the good Lord knows what else for Jeb's last day on earth.

Charlotte Kay was a bit annoyed with her unexpected role in making the final arrangements. Knowing that Mary Beth could not do everything alone, she had no choice but to step up to the plate. When she left Jeb, she surely did not bargain for this or plan to ever do anything for him. She sighed and muttered, "Oh, well, that needed to be done, but thank heavens, the day is over."

All she wanted was to get into her fuzzy slippers and warm robe. As soon as she changed her clothes, she planned to turn on one of the many reruns of the Golden Girls, or something similar, that required neither thinking nor did it create any emotional upheaval. She had enough turmoil for a day. Charlotte Kay was convinced she could not handle any more disasters without making an error she might regret later.

The moment she opened her door, she saw two big feet in dirty white socks hanging over the arm rest of the living room sofa. Then a man raised his head, showing a sweaty and sleep-tousled mop of hair and rows of healthy white teeth gleaming in an ear-to-ear smile. "It's about time you got home, honey."

"Doug! What the devil are you doing here? How did you get in? You scared the living daylights out of me."

"Is that a way to greet your man? C'mon, baby, give me a kiss." Doug was obviously blind not to see her shoeless feet that were testifying to the fact that a worn-out body was not far behind the tired face.

"C'mon, baby, c'mon baby. That's all you know. I told you before, never to come here unless I invited you. You absolutely should not show up in my house whenever you want. I told you that, too. Was I talking to you or to the wall? You must first call me. Did you get it?" Doug heard the irritation in her voice, but ignored it.

"Baby, I have a key; I can come when I want to, don't you think so?"

"No. Give me the key. This has gone too far. We have to put an end to this. I have had enough." She held her hand out, ready to grab the key. Doug realized Charlotte Kay was in no loving mood and he better tread waters carefully. It happened before that they had fights, usually when she had other problems. So far, he always managed to change her mind enough to get her in the bedroom before the brawl escalated out of control. After spending an hour in bed, everything calmed down and went smoothly for a while.

"What's the matter? Are you continuing the 'get-rid-of-Doug' treatment? Charlotte, be careful, one day you might just push me too far. A man has his breaking point, too."

"Oh, yeah? Then let me tell you something. So does a woman," Charlotte Kay snapped. "And I have just reached my breaking point."

"Why? What did I do now? I did nothing. It is you who have changed. I have noted how cold and irritable you have become lately. I just don't know why. Do you have someone else?"

"Don't change the subject, and don't start looking for reasons that would make me be the culprit. Instead, look into a mirror. Or, just stop talking to me and get out," snapped Charlotte. She saw Doug's eyes darken, but his mouth curled into a false smile.

"Is my baby tired? I bet you are, and you did not stop to eat, neither. D'you wanna grab something? My treat, OK?"

"I am tired and hungry, but I don't want to go anywhere. And I most certainly don't want to go with you. I was planning to have a quiet evening, and I was planning to spend it alone. You were not supposed to be here, especially not supposed to surprise me by showing up whenever you wished. This has to end, Doug, and I am not joking now. You are not going to come and go to and from my house as you please, not anymore. I have had more than enough of your crazy ideas to knock the wind out of me. Are you getting up or not?" Charlotte Kay's voice barely changed, but her eyes were hard, and the lines of her face were taut. Doug felt the tension was mounting.

"Why can't I just keep the key? Look, I promise I won't use it unless you know I am coming around. OK?"

"No, it's not OK. I told you what you were to do, and I did not change my mind."

"Oh, honey, you know I am just a simple country boy, and don't understand big words. You have to use short words with me, and give me easy directions that I can follow." Doug was obviously getting angry. His outrage poured into caustic barbs, all aimed at Charlotte Kay and her haughty attitude.

"Do not get sarcastic with me, Doug Bullock. Simple country boy! You knew very well what I said. How short does a word have to be for you? 'No' is too long to comprehend? Which part of 'no' did you not get? The 'n' or the 'o'? I clearly said I want the house key, and I want it now. And get off that sofa. Your socks are dirty, and you mess up the armrest."

"What's the matter with you? Did something happen?" Doug realized Charlotte Kay rejected his attempts to change her mood, no matter what or how he tried. It also finally dawned on him that her wrath was aimed directly at him. He was hopelessly sinking in her anger as if he stepped into quicksand. He started to straighten up slowly into a sitting position, putting his dirty socks-covered feet on the floor. He certainly had no fun so far, though he hoped an evening with Charlotte Kay could rekindle her affection enough to at least get into bed once more, if nothing else. Furthermore, even that projected poor mood was quickly deteriorating.

At last Doug realized everything went astray, into the wrong direction, not at all as he planned or expected. Deep down he knew they were through, and only the final show-down was left to be encountered. At the end, he hoped to have a little enjoyment from repaying Charlotte Kay for kicking him out. For the last two months, the woman was acting like a witch that lost control of her broomstick and was going all over without any direction. She made Doug's life miserable. She had not a morsel of love or kindness left in her. Doug felt he was used, and he hated the feeling of being dumped and laughed at by a woman.

When he discovered Charlotte Kay had a new boyfriend, he started to stalk her. He stayed nearby on her street in a parked car and watched her taking the man into her house. The man seemed much older than Doug. He was dressed in a smart business suit and, as they walked to the door, he held the woman's waist with casual familiarity. They disappeared, and he did not emerge again for a while.

Doug had to fight the urge to use his key and surprise them. Instead, the next day he invited Charlotte Kay for dinner, but before he could confront her, he spotted a new ring on her hand. He only saw it for a second because she put her hand on her lap and, when she placed it back on the table, the ring was no longer on her finger. Doug instantly realized the older man was someone he could not compete with because the man promised Charlotte Kay the life Doug could never offer. He felt bitter with burning jealousy and maddening anger. He managed to remain calm through the dinner and kept his mouth shut. It was during this dinner that he decided to hurt her back just as much, if not more, as she had hurt him.

The strife between Charlotte Kay and her ex-husband came at a perfect timing to serve Doug's compelling urge in getting revenge for being rejected. He did not have a clear idea yet, what he could or should do to pay her back. He only knew, should an opportune moment show up, he wanted to have access to her for a final retaliation. That's why he willingly accepted Charlotte Kay's idea to shake up her mealy-mouthed ex-husband and harass him until he sold the house which was the last remaining connection between her and her ex, Jeb Odum.

Doug detected a rising irritation in Charlotte Kay's voice. "Nothing happened. Nothing. Got it? Why should you think anything happened, just because I asked you to respect my privacy? How dare you question me, anyway? And just what makes you think I owe you any explanation? I owe you nothing, certainly not to give you any reason why I say or don't say something."

"Why? Because you act strange, not at all the way you used to talk to me. Look, I would have done anything for you. As a matter of fact, I probably already did. I always protected and helped you. I deserved at least a 'thanks'. But did you ever acknowledge what I did? No, not at all. Did you ever see anything good in what I did for you so far? No. Did you ever appreciate a single thing I did? No.

Never. All I hear is you, you, you. Everything has to be on your terms. You never, ever have considered me or my feelings."

"Really? And just what was the great sacrifice you did for me? Since you told me you were my protector and savior, I guess you have expected apologies for not seeing you as my knight on a mission of rescue. Let me tell you, buddy that dog won't hunt. I can take care of myself, I do not need your protection. But since you mentioned it, at least tell me what it was, so I could know it too."

"C'mon, baby, you know it was I who got your house listed. Without me, your ex would be still sitting in it without lifting a finger. He would be entertaining his girlfriend in your half of the house, too, don't you forget that."

Charlotte Kay swallowed hard but felt way too far gone in the discussion to back up. "OK, you did that much. I said 'thank you' already; what more was I to do? Pay with my body?"

"That's a great idea," Doug smirked and stood up to get close to Charlotte. He was ready to have a roll in bed with this witch for the last time before it was over. At the end, he decided, it would be him who would tell her he dumped her. What a revenge that would be. To see her shocked face, to make her realize the unexpected turn, maybe to see a few of her tears; now that would be worth forcing himself to make love to her once more. "Now you are talking," he said as he tried to put his arms around her. But Charlotte Kay smoothly stepped back and was out of his reach again.

"What's the matter? You don't love me anymore? After all what was said and done between us, this is not what I expected. This is not how you should treat your man," Doug was indignant, and rightfully so. He recognized he was losing the battle and may never have the imagined opportunity to dump Charlotte Kay.

Suddenly he saw the woman, standing defiantly in front of him as a tough old bird, and not a dainty little lady. Like a New York Yankee woman, and not a delicate Southern sweetheart. She was made out of stone. Doug realized his role as a lover disappeared altogether, and could never be resurrected again.

"Don't you ever teach me how to treat men. First of all, you were never my man. Push me a bit more, and you will see how fast you can find yourself on the street. I have no idea what you were referring to by saying 'what was said and done between us'. Though you were right in one thing: 'it was said and it was done', the rest was pure garbage." Charlotte Kay put extra emphasis on the word 'was'.

"You don't remember anymore, do you?" Doug felt the stinging words hitting him like a swirling nest of wasps. "Then let me spell it out for you. First, you cried about how much Jeb ignored you. So I gave you all the attention you needed. Then you complained about him being passive and boringly predictable. I kept you on your toes. Should you care to recall, you stated it. You disliked him because he was stoic, non-communicative, and cold. To contrast him, I gave you love, more than you ever had from Jeb. Then you discovered he was not even faithful, because he cheated on you with someone at work. He wounded you beyond ever having a chance to be healed. Instead of your cold fish of a husband, I gave you passion and all the loving emotions you could handle." He kept his eyes on Charlotte Kay, but the tight lines of her sullen face remained as deep as before. The stone-like hardened expression never softened, no matter what he said.

Doug continued in bitter desperation. "I was never lazy, I did all the work in your house, painted, repaired, and replaced whatever you wanted on a whim of your fancy. You said how great it was to have a man's man finally, and not a piece of wood like Jeb. All he did was mow the lawn and the rest was up to you to find someone to do everything else. Did you forget that?"

Doug barely inhaled long enough to continue his tirade. "Frankly, in my wildest dreams I couldn't figure out why you ever married him. Perhaps you thought he was hot or handy? You may find it highly peculiar, but I believe he never was hot, only handy. He might have set high expectations, but I bet even his Viagra let him down," he grinned.

"Oh, and this judgment comes from who? You? Just who do you think you are? Certainly no winner. But, then, how could I expect a Kentucky Derby winning racehorse from two plow horses?"

Doug stepped forward, ready to slap Charlotte Kay across the mouth. She backed up instantly without allowing him to act and quickly continued in a changed tone, "Whatever. You can say whatever you want," Charlotte shrugged a shoulder, then impatiently returned to her main concern, "The key, Doug, I want my key." She kept standing in front of the sofa with her outstretched hand to get the house key. She seemed to be unmoved by Doug's hurt feelings.

"That's all you want, because you have decided 'Doug, you done your job well, now you are out, you are not needed anymore', is that it? 'Hit the road, Jack, and don't come back no more, no more, no more.' You could even sing it, Charlotte Kay, couldn't you? I am to be discarded because this is what you have decided. I do not matter, as usual. Why? Just tell me what happened?" Doug's resentment was hard to miss. Charlotte Kay's face remained stone-hard. It was obvious she was determined to get her way.

Chapter 30

Doug realized he was not winning. He was no match for Charlotte Kay's quick mind and iron will which also combined a far better vocabulary and bigger mouth then his own. He quickly changed his tune to be sweet again, and smiled at the woman, "Babe, you had a rough day. Let me massage your back and get those knots out of your muscles." He started to get closer to her again, but she took a step back, clearly indicating there was an invisible wall between them.

"You don't get it, Doug, do you? It's over. It would have never worked between us, anyway. Just be honest, what did we have in common? Nothing," she continued, ignoring his gesture, bordering on the obscene that was supposed to remind her of shared pleasures in the past.

"Nothing. Let's face it, you were kinda limited. We could never discuss anything because of your narrow background and your interests that were completely different from mine. You could not take part in a higher level of entertainment. We could not go to a theater because you didn't understand or enjoy it. I was tired of going to every action movie. I did not want to sneak in the dark and leave before they turned on the lights. Did you ever try to figure out why did I have to do that? Because I did not want people to see you with me, Doug. That's why.

"For a woman of my caliber it was embarrassing to be seen with you. I have never enjoyed NASCAR races or every damn college football game they played on the entire East Coast. I could not talk to you, no matter what I said or did, because you were glued to watch TV when any of these were on. These differences aside, just tell me, what could you give me that I did not already have? Nothing. I already have a house. I already have a car. You didn't have either. That old, beat-up truck did not matter. What I truly needed, you could not give me."

"Amazing, Charlotte, I could not give you what you needed, you said. Yet, everything you needed, I did for you. I kept you happy in the bedroom. We had fun, didn't we? Now you cannot remember anything, can you? I guess by now you have conveniently forgotten the cruise we took, too, right?"

"No, I did not. As a matter of fact, the Sheriff reminded me of it today. In case you wonder, he knew all about that cruise. No question in my mind, he kept an eye on you for a while. Do you have any idea why? Why would an investigator be interested in a simple, blue-collar worker, in a man without any political affiliation, any religious conviction, or any ambition other than doing menial home repairs? You tell me, Doug."

"Thanks, now I am clear on what you think of me. Thanks a lot. OK, Charlotte, let this lowly handyman tell you a thing or two. It was you who cried on my shoulder that you lost your money or house, or whatever you still shared with your ex. It was you who asked me to ruffle him up a bit. After I did what you wanted, he was found dead. And now you wonder why am I being investigated? Really, I thought you were smarter than that."

"Doug, let me tell you one thing. It is hard to deal with a stupid man, and you are really close to being one. I have never asked you to 'ruffle him up'. Did you ever hear me using this term? First of all, this is your expression, not mine. It is low-class verbiage. I do not use expressions of that sort because I have an educated vocabulary. Second, I would never ask anyone to hurt another person for me or on my behalf." Charlotte was clearly indignant and easily rose to a higher level of dignity as she spoke.

"Right, you would not ask another person to hurt your ex-husband, because you could do it yourself better than anyone else could," Doug interrupted her. "I know you better than what you think. Don't push me, Charlotte Kay Odum. Once I put all the details on the table, the police would know you, too."

"So that's what it is, the truth finally has come out. Good to know. You are just overflowing with deep love, aren't you?" Charlotte Kay retorted. "At the end you showed your true colors. Do you want to terrorize me? Are you threatening me? Watch it, because I could reveal about you as much as you could lie about me. Every man has two sides, Doug, an inside and an outside. I know your inside better than you think. If I were you, I would not be talking from such a high horse. Trust me, I would be really careful.

Before I go any further, just tell me what you did with poor Jeb. He was found dead. What did you do?"

"What did I do? I did not kill him if that's what you are trying to insinuate. I am not a murderer though you might consider me one, Charlotte. You had much more ground to finish him off than I did. I only gave him a reason to get moving with the idea of selling your house again. Shall I say to get 'motivated'? Yeah, you should consider me a 'motivational speaker' and not a 'killer'," Doug chuckled.

"You don't get it Doug, do you? The Sheriff interrogated me for hours. The Chief of the Homicide Investigation. This is serious. They know you and they know of you. They will question you, too. This is no longer a joke."

"So what if they question me? I did not do anything. I called him a couple of times, that's all." Doug sounded unperturbed; yet, Charlotte Kay knew him way too well to recognize his mounting nervousness.

"OK, tell me what you have said. Tell me as if I were the investigator himself, questioning you."

"I called his house and asked him why he delayed the house sale, that's all. Nothing more."

"Oh, for crying out loud, Doug, you are not seriously expecting me to believe you? If you think I buy your lame story, you are severely insulting my intelligence." Charlotte Kay decided to change her tune. Suddenly she appeared to be kinder and more interested in him. She calculated, in this way she might hear more details. "Please, Doug, I know you have tried to defend my interests, and also know you don't take rejections well. But if you want me to help you, you have to tell me exactly what you said and how Jeb responded."

"He did not respond at all. He asked me twice who I was, but when I only repeated to him 'to sell that house was in his best interest because he might regret a delay,' he hung up the phone. He did not believe me. Actually, he was quite cocky, wasn't he, to dare to hang up on me? The least I expected him to do was to question me why, or say something. But he just hung up without a word."

Charlotte Kay searched his face but decided to continue using her understanding, defenseless-little-woman's voice once more. "Oh, Douggie, you were doing it all for me."

"You better believe it, I did it for you. I was fixing him to give you your money. I told him so. I also warned him about keeping my eyes on him. I knew where he lived, when he came and went, and what distance he lived from anyone who could hear him. When I asked him, 'Now wouldn't it be tragic if you were not to be found for days, if anything happened to you?' That's when he finally lost it and he questioned who I was."

"What did he say? Remember his words, Doug, and tell me exactly what he said."

"Just 'Who is this?' then before he hung up, 'Who the hell are you?', that's all he said."

"Are you sure? How did he sound? Do you think he suspected you?"

"No, I am sure he did not. He only sounded sleepy."

"Sleepy? What time did you call him? Midnight?" For a second, Charlotte Kay slipped out of her role of the understanding and concerned loving woman, then easily continued in her previous sweet tone, "You had to stay up late, Douggie, to make that call, didn't you?"

"You better believe it. It was way after my bedtime. Way after midnight," he smirked, "but it was worth it because I figured he finally paid me attention."

"I bet he did. Jeb usually went to sleep at the same time the chickens did, and got up before the cock crowed. Did you call him back after he hung up on you?"

"Yeah. Every night. We even had a good little chat at the end." Doug was obviously satisfied with his effectiveness and the fact that he finally got Charlotte Kay's full attention. It was a mistake to brag, though.

"You did what? What chat? When? Think, Doug, think! I need to hear every word that was said. It might be more important than you imagine." Charlotte Kay was evidently more anxious than Doug thought she should have been. Concerned? Maybe. Nervous? Nah, she should have known Doug Bullock was smart, and could handle an old pemby-bemby like Jeb Odum.

"He asked me where I was calling from. So I told him from Williston. He did not believe me until I described to him where the street was freshly blocked by the old post office building. He realized I was not bluffing. On the next call, I told him I just passed his entrance and admired the nice job he did on the lawn earlier that day. I did not think he got that message fully, so next I said I did not care for him cutting down a tree and leaving a tall trunk, it should have been cut closer to the ground. Now that should have alerted him, don't you think?"

"What tree did he cut down, the big one by the left entrance?" Charlotte Kay inquired.

"No, the one on his driveway, halfway up to the house. You know, where the road curved and the tree leaned in, kinda falling onto the road."

"You mean you got onto his private property? Were you crazy? Anyone could have spotted you driving up to the house." Charlotte Kay got alarmed. "Did you see any lights anywhere? Didn't you remember he shared the first part of the driveway with the two neighbors? You had to be plum mad to go closer and closer until you just about ended up in his house. Lord, what a cattywampus you made!"

"Cattywampus? I never heard you say that before."

"Well, now you did. You made a mess, a total disaster,"

"Oh, please, Charlotte, nobody saw me. No, of course not. I told you, it was after midnight. They were all asleep, only that black man's dog was barking a bit, that's all."

"Wait a second. Stop piddling around, Doug, and tell me straight what you did. You had to go up all the way to the carport, otherwise you could not turn around from the trees to get back to the highway. Did you?"

"Sure. But I did not really stop, just made a quick U-turn and drove out again. He might have spotted my truck because there was suddenly light in one of the windows. But I was way too fast for him to get a good look. And I was way too smart for him, because I smeared my license plate with mud before, so he could not possibly read it."

He was looking at the woman expecting a well-deserved accolade. Instead, Charlotte Kay raised her voice and almost yelled at him, "God, Almighty! You are nuts! Don't you know he could have taken a picture of your truck? Then you could have done whatever you wanted with the obscured license plate; that big dent on your right door would have been enough identification for anyone. Even for Jeb. And he had rifles in the house! If he shot you, he could have been jailed. Please tell me, you never went closer to him, ever again, only once, only at that time!"

Doug eyed her for a long minute as if seeing the woman for the first time. Charlotte Kay was worried about Jeb getting in jail if he shot the intruder. Charlotte Kay did not care if Jeb killed Doug Bullock, she only cared about her ex-husband not being imprisoned. He thought hard before he slowly said, "No, I did not." Charlotte Kay visibly sighed, though with little conviction.

"This is all, am I right, Doug? Nothing more? You have told me everything and left nothing out?"

"Yeah, that's it. The Sheriff has nothing on me. No way could he tan my hide. They could question me until the cows got home, what could they say? That I made a few anonymous calls? Big deal, kids could have done that. That I was on his driveway? So what? If I made a wrong turn in the dark, I had no choice but to continue until I could turn around to get out. Don't you worry; I always knew what I was doing."

"I thought it was you who had the worries. Or the one who should have the worries. I told you, the investigator at the Sheriff's Office already questioned me. It was only a matter of time before he got to you. I am positive you are next to be investigated. And you should be, by all means. I bet my life when you get home his request will be hanging on your door." Her face showed hatred, almost as if she abhorred the sheer sight of the suddenly speechless man standing in front of her.

"As for me, I don't know whether I could believe you or not. I mean if I ever could believe you after what you had done. I only know you harassed an innocent man, you stalked my ex-husband, and now he is dead. Then you tried to blame me for your actions, but I absolutely refuse to be part of the mess you created. Now give me my key and get out of here. You disgust me. I never want to see you again."

Once the door slammed after Doug, Charlotte Kay slumped into an overstuffed armchair. She felt deflated like a balloon that suddenly lost all its air. She looked aged and exhausted. She sat motionless for a long time, staring at the pale metal house key in front of her. The key landed on the table next to the phone, where Doug tossed it before he angrily stormed out of her house and life.

Charlotte Kay slowly reached out for the phone and dialed the Fayette County Sheriff Department. She hesitated a bit, but, before she could change her mind, a man's voice jolted her into talking. Charlotte Kay took a deep breath and started to say the sentence she rehearsed in her mind. She asked for Chief Investigator McCarthy. She had important information for him which he surely wanted to hear.

Chapter 31

Before he joined law enforcement, Wade Hands was considered a 'good old boy' by everyone. Once in uniform, the handsome Texan looked even more dashing. Many ladies called for sudden car trouble when seeing him on the road. He always had his window rolled down, his elbow hanging out a bit, and a big smile accompanied the genuine happiness he felt every day on the job. He was truly blessed with a good nature, not merely a physique that was not too hard on the eyes.

Today the Sheriff's car was not cruising leisurely the dusty streets. The closed windows signaled an official business and a clear warning not to be side-tracked. The Chief chuckled when he said, "We sure need a 'Hands-on Sheriff', today, Wade. By default, it is your assignment." It was an insider-joke; Wade got used to his assignments being announced this way. Early morning, Sheriff Hands got the news of a dead body found under some bushes, two bullet holes in the head, and not a person in the vicinity to be the suspect. Only truck wheel marks in the yellow dust, a make-shift but abandoned campsite, couple of empty shells of a 9-mm handgun, and some discarded trash signaled a possible relationship to the unknown victim.

The crime site was as deserted as any other country site, void of humans, and stirring with wildlife. Wade Hands wondered why animals were called 'wildlife', when it was the humans who broke peace and life most of the time. Animals killed when they were hungry or rabid, humans when dark emotions compelled them to commit the crime. They were many times wilder than the animals.

He stood in front of the bushes and kept observing the scene. He was etching every little detail into his mind, the dead body's position, his simple clothing, the location of the bushes and trees, and the surrounding abandoned trash. He noted that the murderer or murderers had been in a hurry because nobody tried to bury or cover the dead man. He was simply rolled out of the way and discarded in the scanty shadow of a thirsty bush. The lack of leaves barely provided coverage or protection from the scorching sun. The man was probably in his forties; his dark hair, hanging mustache, high cheekbones indicated some Indian blood, perhaps of long forgotten Aztec ancestry. Well, his ancient Gods may have protected him from being a sacrificial offer, but surely did not save him from the evils of a modern era. Most certainly they did not prevent lead being pumped into his brain.

Wade pushed the sheriff's hat higher on his forehead with his right thumb as he looked around. The sun was beating down on him mercilessly. The peacefully grazing cattle in the distance were not helpful enough to tell what they might have seen. The dead man did not talk, either. Or did he?

Wade reached in the man's pocket and found a part of a crumbled McDonald receipt, a few coins, and a switch blade. No wallet, no personal identification, nothing to indicate whether he was coming or going, or what business he had in the area. He gave no indication to whether he was from Texas or from somewhere else. Wade removed his hat to wipe the sweat off of his forehead.

The limited clues indicated a transient group, which certainly created a dilemma to find out who the murdered man was. The sheriff knew too well the destruction these groups usually left behind. Border-related crimes started to crop up with regular recurrence a few years back, and their numbers steadily climbed. In the year 2015 alone, Texas had over seven-hundred-thousand crimes committed against the legal residents. These included fourteen-hundred murders and almost nine-thousand rapes, over hundred-fifty-thousand burglaries, and innumerable trespassing and car thefts. The rest were aggravated body attacks, insults resulting in various injuries, and other crimes. Crime rate increase accounted for the escalation of the population/crime index from 3 in 2010 to 16 five years later. The trashed countryside was another story.

Although most assaults were listed in detail, the criminals who committed them were either not discovered or could not be detained. The border was just as free for crossing from the US to Mexico and then back, and the suspects jumped the line of jurisdiction as soon as the investigation targeted them. Residents felt unprotected and vulnerable, at the mercy of the outlaws. Since the government failed to protect them, they started to take defense into their own hands, which only escalated the number of deaths. Eventually, it seemed laws did not apply as they once did, no matter what the police force said, no matter what the news media neglected to report.

The border was not secured, and the border patrol was overwhelmed. In addition, the enforcing agents had not been issued ammunition, while the oncoming foreign invasion was well equipped with firearms. The most amazing fact was that most of these weapons were made in the US.

Wade was convinced that first somebody had to smuggle the guns South, in order to find their way into the hands of criminals and across the border again. Somebody got paid big bucks doing it, whether as rogue individuals or organized groups. Some people gossiped the government itself supported the weapon sale to the Mexican drug cartel. Names of high ranking politicians were linked to the million dollar deals. Surely, there had to be some truth to the rumors, otherwise how could the politicians explain getting filthy rich on a fixed salary? As far as Wade knew, there were no elected officials or big businessmen involved, at least not directly. Either way, they must have been well paid not to consider the consequences.

Wade Hands knew that every form of government punished criminals, regardless who was in power either as an individual leader or as a ruling group. If a crook wanted to avoid punishment and justified incarceration, he had enough sense to be the first to escape from that country. The unsecured border between Mexico and the Southern states of America was an open invitation to any felon seeking asylum. Every day, throngs of poverty driven hopefuls mixed with fanatic terrorists crossed the border. Every day loads of illicit drugs, weapons, and big money exchanged hands, seemingly without any hold up over the divider.

Unfortunately, the destitute and decent individuals met and unavoidably clashed with these mercenary offenders and hardened criminals. The penniless indigents instantly were viewed as insignificant and unaccountable. They were at the mercy of the vicious and deplorable outlaws and attacked just as much as the legal residents of Texas and Arizona. Furthermore, being in the same shoes of breaking the law when stepping on US soil without permission, they all were smeared with the same derogatory generalization. They were all categorized as unwanted, undesired, no-good, or low-class enemy that struck fear in the families living near and far.

The world surely was a big witches' brew, boiling and spewing, retching and sputtering without foreseeable end. The expelled foreigners coming from various countries formed an oncoming horde that entered the US, and their drive was unstoppable and uncontrollable. Today's incident was just one of the routine daily occurrences, nothing more and not at all unusual in Sheriff Hand's work.

He looked around, visibly wincing at the site of trash scattered around. Burrito and hamburger wraps, greasy paper containers of French fries, and Coke cups with the straw still left in them were rolling in the wind until trapped on bushes. Human excrement in piles was covered by hordes of flies. "Man sure has no respect for God's Earth, to keep it as pristine as He created," muttered Wade. He waited until the car disappeared with the body bag, then finished his notes, and finally headed to the nearest McDonald's.

During this time, Ramón waited for justice, in a morgue, for his life being extinguished.

Jorge, on the other hand, could not wait to put enough distance between his truck and the place where he left Ramón's body. He already got over the murder, it did not bother him. He never even gave it a second thought. Death was part of life. Death was ordered by El Condor and he, Jorge, only carried out an order. If anyone was responsible for Ramón's death, it was El Condor. Or maybe Ramón himself.

After all, the death was justified, Jorge reasoned, because Ramon practically asked for it. It was Ramon who quarreled with him, who questioned everything Jorge was doing, wasn't it?

Jorge easily convinced himself being free from any blame. How could he be guilty when he only reacted to Ramón's provocation? No, shooting Ramon was clearly justified. Jorge did nothing wrong or unpredicted. Indeed, at the end, Jorge decided the death was Ramón's own fault, and quickly forgot about the whole incident.

If you have no conscience, it cannot bother you.

Chapter 32

The yellow double arch announced to Wade he was approaching the turn to McDonald's. He parked the car in the shade and entered the over-cooled restaurant. Only two customers were eating at a table and one man was waiting at the counter for his food. They were certainly outnumbered by the cashiers and cooks. Of course, it was after breakfast, but way before lunch when a throng of people was expected.

His food and cup on a tray, Wade sat at the corner table, where he could watch the serving counter and the soda fountain, yet keep an eye on the parking lot, too. His keen ears almost immediately picked up the conversation. The idle employees excitedly discussed the recent news of the local murder. Each seemed to know something interesting to add which the others had not heard on the radio or seen on the TV. Neither of the two customers got involved in the discussion: one read the daily local newspaper, and the other stared at his food in between biting off huge chunks of the double cheeseburger.

Wade casually looked up and scrutinized the speakers one by one. He had no peculiar interest in them, they were just killing time while slowly initiating a needed clean-up of the place. He heard the cook yelling at a young kid to get out of his way, he was not to bother him again; Wade glanced at the young man. He had red hair, lots of freckles, and almost blond eyelashes barely covering his childlike stare. Wade realized the boy was a bit slow in thinking and simple in his speech, but he worked the sponge and an old rag furiously. As soon as their eyes met, the boy opened his mouth, then changed his mind, and only flashed a shy smile at him. Wade called him over.

"Hey, son, do you think you could get me a refill of my soda with plenty of ice? I would appreciate it."

"Sure, sure, Rusty could do it gladly," the boy agreed readily. Wade smiled hearing the kid referred to himself in third person. In no time, he rushed back with the over-filled cup splashing the soda at each step.

"You were really good," started Wade, giving a compliment to the eager young man, "you would go far if you keep it up. Have you worked here long?"

"About three months," came the proud answer. "It is my first real job. I get paid real money now, and can eat a sandwich for free if I am hungry. And I can drink as much Coke as I want to," he beamed.

"You deserve that," agreed Wade and slowly directed the conversation toward his interest. The boy was pleased to talk to a sheriff. He felt elevated from his lowly rank, being the one chosen among all the others, though most of the time they were either yelling or laughing at him. He looked back with pride to the counter, but no one seemed to care about him enough to notice his sense of satisfaction. Wade continued in a smooth, deep voice to praise him until he saw the boy was ready to do practically anything he would ask.

"So, what is your job here, Rusty? Do you ever work the window or mainly inside?"

"Inside, but yesterday we were short, so they allowed me to take orders, too. I got the biggest order in the entire place, maybe the biggerest, since this joint opened," he boasted," and I made no mistake."

"No kidding. The biggest order, huh? How big was it? I bet you would recall it for a long time," smiled Wade.

"Sure, sure. Rusty would always recall it." He stopped for a second then quickly recited in a monotonous voice as if he were placing the order again, "15 burritos, 18 chipotle fried chicken wraps, 12 double cheeseburgers, 3 with extra bacon, one fish sandwich, 31 large fries, 2 apple pies, and 31 large sodas, and double the napkins." He looked back at Wade. "Now that was something, wasn't it?"

"Boy, you must be the smartest man in this whole joint," said the sheriff with conviction. "You have the memory of an elephant. I bet you could even remember who ordered it," and expectantly looked at the beaming boy.

"Sure, sure. But it was not one man, there were three of them. One man could not carry all that food alone, you know. Hey, they had a hungry construction crew; they were delivering the orders to them."

"Construction? What construction?" Wade asked.

"I don't know, they did not say. But I tell you, they were not from no construction, neither. Because they had none of them tool belts or paint splashed on their clothes or shoes." He smiled triumphantly. Then he added almost as an after-thought, "It was funny. Last night, before I fell asleep, I thought how far they had to take that food because I know no construction here. Do you? That food probably got cold by the time they got back to their work."

"Hey, you are brilliant! I don't know any construction nearby, either." Wade felt his muscles tighten suddenly, and he was ready to pounce on the naïve young man like a crouching leopard on an ignorant gazelle. He deliberately slowed himself, so as not to spook the boy. The professional took control over the private man's impatient curiosity. He did not want to scare Rusty because Wade knew that would likely clam the boy up. The sheriff was sure there was more to learn from this young man if he kept the conversation light and continued carefully.

"Three people, you don't say. I guess they needed the muscles, for you loaded them up with all that food. They must have been young, like you, to have the strength, wouldn't you say?" he asked.

"No, they were old; two were more like your age. One was a bit younger. But that one never opened his mouth. He just played a mute." The answer was instant, and the voice sounded innocent.

Wade was slightly taken aback. He was being considered old? By golly, this boy must have been really slow and maybe even a bit retarded to say that straight to his face. Then he realized that for an eighteen or nineteen-year-old, anyone over forty was old. He easily continued, "My age, huh? Both of them?"

"No, the one who paid me, the George guy, was the oldest. But the other took the receipt. Although they almost fought over it, and even tore it apart, I saw him putting it in his pocket, not in his wallet. And he put the return money in his billfold although it was the George fellow who gave me the money. It was a nice wallet, too. Colorful, printed leather, the kind they make in Mexico. And I tell you a secret," Rusty leaned across the table and lowered his voice, "I know for a fact they were from Mexico. When they got to the exit, the man with the nice wallet told the other 'hold the door for me, Jorge, my hands are full'. Jorge is in Spanish, you know. And the other hissed at him 'Shut up, Ramón'. So, what do you think now? I was right, wasn't I? Wasn't I?"

"Absolutely. You were absolutely right." Wade knew he had struck gold. "So what time was this, do you remember?" Wade asked casually.

"Sure, sure. Rusty knows. I have a memory of an elephant. You said it. Let's see now. I took the number two cashier five minutes after two when the regular cashier got sick. They were my first customers. The first for me, but the last for the lunch rush. And it took the three cooks almost half an hour to fill that big order. I had to check out everything, but they did OK. No mistake."

Wade calculated quickly it must have been around three when the silent young man, Jorge, and Ramón reached their group. No, they were not delivering lunch for a hungry construction crew. Not at three in the afternoon. He turned to the blushing young kid with a grin.

"Man, I tell you, McDonald's was lucky to hire you. I predict you will be the manager here one day, you just watch. I will come back and eat here at least once a week then. Deal?" he smiled.

Rusty's face flushed almost dark enough to hide the horde of freckles. No matter how slow the boy was, this time he turned out to be the smartest help. His mild autism registered every tiny detail. His insignificant job and low profile allowed him to observe inconspicuously, and his idiot savant nature later recalled minuscule particulars. He impressed and surprised the sheriff by presenting a matter-of-fact, logical deduction. Maybe he truly was underestimated and was not as slow as everyone thought. Maybe he would make it and be the manager one day. Wade smiled with satisfaction as he started the engine.

The sheriff already learned the two names to get the investigation rolling. He knew the dead man must have been Ramón. It was he who had the wrinkled partial receipt in his pocket. But the colorful leather wallet was missing. His murderer must have taken it. On his way to the office, he kept turning in his mind what he heard and wondered whether it was Jorge or the silent young man who put the bullets in Ramón's head.

What Sheriff Wade Hands did not know, yet, was how far this investigation would lead him. He knew it was not only his duty and job to find the murderer. His honor, integrity, and reputation depended on his success. He was prepared single-mindedly to follow the scent as a bloodhound, no matter where the footsteps took him.

Sheriff Wade Hands would have been surprised to learn that, eventually, he was to trail the tracks to Green Valley, Arizona, where he would finally run into the unlikely trio of Miguel, Billy Odum, and Robert Falls.

Chapter 33

In the Southwest desert, water is scarce and considered just as valuable as gold or silver. During long, dry months, when no rain falls and all living creatures pant in hope for rain, water is rated above and beyond these metals. After all, water sustains life, which cannot be said of either gold or silver.

In the Upper Santa Cruz Valley, over 90 million cubic meters of water were pumped from the aquifer, mainly for agriculture. The household and commercial use got only about fifteen percent, and that included the maintenance of the golf courses. At the end of the line were the private homes; the smaller a house was on the outskirts of the community, the less water trickled from its faucets.

Arizona allowed any amount of water to be pumped from the aquifer, though they periodically warned the population of the ever-dropping water table and projected drastic drought in the future. Finally, they worked out a plan with the US Bureau of Reclamation for a Central Arizona Project Canal, in which they would transport the Colorado River water to Arizona. As the plans were put to construction, people became more hopeful of avoiding the looming disaster.

Green Valley had been surrounded by copper mines that paid the employees well, but the city goods were not necessarily keeping up with the demand. About twenty miles north was Tucson, frequented by ladies who shopped for special occasions. True, the Hispanic families rather traveled south even if they had to double the distance to Nogales, Sonora, Mexico. Although Nogales offered specialty bits and pieces, one would find more sophisticated items in a big city such as Tucson. After spending their hard-earned money in this Mecca of department stores, they returned to Green Valley to tell friends and foes alike why their garment deserved rich praise. Ah, Tucson was cultured and refined, they were all in agreement, and this showed in everything that came from there...

With the arrival of spring days and the multitude of birdwatchers, the nearby quiet and majestic Santa Rita Mountain burst into action. Famous for the variety of rare birds, the area invited hikers, who tiptoed through the woods to avoid scaring off an occasional cactus wren. Although neither interested nor knowledgeable, Billy Odum also followed the well-worn trails. He was surprised to learn, the night before, that his friend Robert suddenly decided to hike in the morning. Billy never knew Robert was a nature buff, but he tagged along without asking a thing. By now, Billy had learned Robert never liked to be questioned. Just the same, Billy was simply happy to have new excitement. Life with Robert Falls was unpredictable and exhilarating.

As Billy was treading the soft spring mud behind his friend, he was thinking about the changes he experienced since he left the cotton fields of Tennessee. Without Robert, he would have probably never visited Mexico or met Coqui and his pretty daughter. Too bad, they could not stay longer. True, he would have never been involved in smuggling dead bodies either, but that incident was forgotten, never to be mentioned again. He got fancy, modern clothes from Robert, which suited the new image he wanted to project. No sir, he was no longer a country bumpkin, a 'Billy Bob' as his father called him. Billy quickly shifted his thoughts from his old home and his stern father to his current company. Now he was on his first birdwatch; something he heard about, but had never done.

Spring burst open the early flowers and the light-green, new leaves slowly stretched out in the warm sunshine. Above, the sky was brilliantly blue with small tufts of playful, fluffy clouds. Somewhere on the trail they were to meet Robert's friends later. Billy had the promise of another good day ahead.

Lately he discovered life had so many unexpected and amazing twists, it had so much fun, it surely was not as monotonous or dull as the one he knew in his country home of Williston. How far that old life seemed to be by now! It seemed unreal that he used to live in a township, population three-hundred-ninety, if one did not count the dogs and horses. Now he lived near Tucson, traveled and discovered the Southwest, saw places and people he never knew existed. His new life was everything he ever dreamed it could be. One thing was sure, it was never boring.

His new partner, Robert, probably was the most sophisticated man and truly the most generous friend he ever encountered. He patiently listened to Billy's sad saga about his cold and uncaring father and his simple and unsophisticated mother, who at least showed some love toward him. Robert also heard an earful about Billy's brothers, who did everything to please the Dad and cheat Billy out of his rightful inheritance. At last Billy thought he found a person who understood and loved him like no one else. He considered himself lucky to have met Robert.

He also silently blessed the day when he was brave enough to leave the stale family that never understood or cared for him. Billy quickly brushed away the nagging thoughts that questioned his mother's health, or the still existing, deeply buried fear of his father's anger. He never contacted them so far, no matter what he promised to his sister. As time passed, it seemed less and less easy to make the needed call. No, that family life was in the past, and could not or should not be resurrected for Billy. He felt he did not need them anyway, since Robert replaced the closest people from his previous life.

The fleeting thoughts of his early years reminded him of his sister, and the money he borrowed from her, but Billy just as fast got over the bothersome thought of needed repayment. After all, his sister had a nice house, her husband worked, they had everything they wanted; surely, they did not need the money from him to feed the family or to pay the mortgage. As far as Billy was concerned, that loan was a sister's gift to help him start a new life. And what a life he had now! He got new clothes, traveled with Robert in either his fancy Cadillac or in his even fancier truck. He lived in style.

Billy heard daily that Robert loved him, he even said he would marry Billy if he could. In the beginning, this feeling was a bit uncomfortable to Billy, though he had had a male lover before. True, he kept it a secret, until he blurted it out in his anger just before he left Tennessee. He still liked to look at pretty girls, but Robby disliked them, so Billy abandoned the flirting too. Now they had no distractions between them. Oh, yes, he came as far from tiny, sleepy, rural Williston, Tennessee, as he possibly could.

"Hey, Robert, do you think they knew I was destined for a higher class of life?" Billy's voice broke the humdrum of the sloshing sounds of steps.

Robert did not slow down or turn back, but kept the speed even as he called back, "*They* meaning who? Dude, learn to communicate clearly and not in Tennessee riddles."

Billy got indignant. "Stop it, Robert. Stop constantly referring, in such a derogatory manner, to my past. Don't you think it is overdone by now? It's not funny. You got enough mileage out of it, Robert. I meant everyone by saying 'they'. Everyone who ever knew me."

For a second Robert turned his head to glance at his friend over his left shoulder, then easily responded in a carefree voice, "Yeah, whatever. Whatever you say. You know best. But don't get sore, and let's not be so formal, don't call me 'Robert' all the time. 'Robby' would do between us." After a moment he added nonchalantly, as if to soothe Billy's ruffled feathers, "They probably suspected something more of you. You might be right there. That's it, they suspected it. So what greatness are you planning to pull? Huh?"

"I don't know, yet," responded Billy slowly, "I have some ideas, but first I want to make sure they would work. I don't want to make a mistake and give my folks a good opportunity to laugh at me for being a failure. I can just hear my father telling the family 'So what else is new? He failed so far in everything he ever did, why not at this?' or I can see my brothers quietly look away and no one responding to Father for a long time. No, first I want to be dead-sure I will succeed before making a move."

They quietly walked for a few steps, each engulfed in his own thoughts. Billy was tossing and turning his ideas in his mind, unsure when to find the appropriate moment to reveal them to his friend. Robby smirked at his friend's indecisiveness. He instinctively felt the best response was silence, knowing Billy could not remain mute for any length of time, and the urge to break the stillness soon would make him talk again.

Robby was right, because in a few minutes Billy started, "I have decided to make some money. I mean serious money. When I have enough, I will go home and show them what I have accumulated: a nice, shiny, new car, fancy new clothes, a roll of greens in my pocket, and of course, my new friend, you. You would come with me, Robby, wouldn't you?"

"Sure. Just how do you propose to make that money? So far, I supported you. You have not made a penny."

"I could do what you do, couldn't I? Then we would be in business together. What do you say?"

Robby was careful not to show on his face how glad he was to hear this. He sure was pleased with the developments. So far, he secretly molded Billy to his own needs by first financially then emotionally controlling his friend. When he was in a good mood, he felt Billy was the love of his life. Perhaps Billy was the closest Robby ever allowed a person to get to him. Sure, he had other lovers before, but he did not feel as deeply for any of them as he did for Billy. But these good days did not last long.

When Robby was angry or morose for any reason, he instantly became convinced Billy was a no-good bum, at best slow-witted, and deserved to be used as needed. He believed Billy was simple, materialistic, and superficial who knew the price of everything, but the value of nothing. He knew that once Billy got involved in drug and people trafficking, he would lose the remaining control over his life. Then he, Robert Falls, would be his ruler and savior. He would tie Billy down, so he never would leave him. Then the two would make a family and stay together for good.

Billy Odum was weak and inexperienced; a good follower, not a leader or a go-getter. A lovable man, but feeble-minded; therefore, a perfect type to be used as needed. Eventually, Billy would have to delegate all power and command to the more sophisticated partner. *Easy-peasy*, Robby concluded with satisfaction as he watched the gradual changes taking place in Billy. His mastery in manipulation and skillfulness started to show the desired result, as Billy evolved to a good ally while totally relying on him for guidance and help. After he successfully broke Billy's budding interest in Coqui's pretty daughter, Alma, the two men became lovers. *Not too shabby an accomplishment within less than two months,* he smiled smugly. Robby definitely was more than encouraged with Billy's advancement.

"Well, well, well, look who is talking!" started Robby, feigning a pleased surprise. "So, you want to work with me. All right, it's a possibility, but we should discuss it seriously. Business should be treated as a business, seriously. So if you really are committed to work with me, you have to do a good job; after all, it is my reputation you use. Got it? I have a good name in business. I cannot risk losing it. You have to be sure and not only have it as one of your flighty ideas." After a moment silence, he slowly added, almost as an afterthought, "I guess I could show you the ropes."

Robby slowed a bit then suddenly stopped and looked around. He jovially announced, "Now this would be a perfect spot to rest and have a bite, what do you think?" and he started to unwrap his sandwich.

Billy was too excited to eat and decided to discover the ravine on the opposite side of the trail. He heard rushing water from the depth of the valley, obscured by bushes and huge rocks. He started to descend carefully, navigating around the boulders and soon disappeared from view.

By the time he breathlessly emerged, he saw Robby talking to a stocky man. He could only see part of the man's face and his bushy mustache, but even the limited view was enough to notice the man was jittery. As soon as the stranger heard footsteps behind him, his right hand instantly reached for his holster. Robby quickly told him something, which made the stranger relax his grip on his gun and pull it out from under his colorful poncho. He turned back to face Billy and they shook hands.

That's when Billy noticed another man sitting quietly on a rock nearby. This fellow did not seem to be interested in the discussion. As a matter-of-fact, he looked dead tired. His face was worn out. Billy noted by his face he was a young man, but he had eyes of a worn-out, age-old dog which belied his age. He looked like he would fall asleep as soon as his body would hit the ground, if he just tipped a bit more forward.

After the stranger had finished with Robby, he turned to the quiet young man. He rapidly said a few words in Spanish, then shoved a vibrant, multi-colored leather wallet in the man's hand, before he disappeared down on the winding road.

Robby casually remarked to Billy's questioning, "Oh, he was just a friend, who asked me to do him a favor. You see, he got a big contract out of town, and he does not know what to do with his cousin now. This is his cousin, sitting there on that rock. The guy just arrived unexpectedly from Mexico for a visit, and my friend cannot take him along to the job. It's a new job; you know how it is. So I offered that we take care of the dude for a while. You would be a great help by teaching him the ropes; I mean English and our customs. What do you think? By the way, his name is Miguel. Miguel Vázquez."

Billy smiled, "Sure, anything for you, Robby."

His friend was ready to turn back and head home. "Heck, there are no birds here to see. Maybe it's too early in the year yet, who knows. Let's get back, I am ready to kick these boots off and just chill a little. You don't want to stay, either, do you?"

"Ready whenever you are," Billy replied agreeably while indicating to the quiet young man to get up and follow him. Robby led them on the winding path back to the car in no time. In the interim, Billy wondered what more surprises this day would bring, and how he would communicate with someone who spoke no English, but whom he was supposed to teach everything that was American.

Chapter 34

Billy got his first job when Robby came down with fever and cough the next day, so severe that it seemed to wreck his skinny chest. He hacked and wheezed to a point that he barely could catch his breath. In spite of his illness, Robby drilled Billy over and over, playing out every scenario to prepare his friend for a safe trip and a successful return.

Billy was excited because all he was supposed to do was pick up some packages in Iguala, Mexico, and bring them back to Laredo. And for this little service he was to be paid rather well, considerably more than he expected. Thank heavens, Robby used his negotiating skills and made a far better deal for him than he, himself would have done. Although Billy did not mind Robby's involvement, especially seeing the results, he felt it was not necessary because it seemed like it was an easy job. After all, they were just packages, not a big deal. Robby said the trip had inherent, but concealed, danger and the price should go up, depending on the contents of the packages. This time it was a load of heroin, cut and proportioned in neat brick-like bags. Billy tried to reason with Robby that there were not too many packages and not heavy at all to justify the high dividend. His friend just shut him up and, at the end, Billy was thankful for the outcome. He felt this trip held the key to start a new life. He was also promised many more jobs once he successfully completed the transfer.

After a few hours, Billy was not even listening to his friend's raspy warnings. Hearing the same thing over and over, he already knew what was coming next. Instead of being bored with Robby's repetitions, Billy made mental notes about what to buy from his first earnings. He was convinced he could accomplish the assignment without being caught. What was so dangerous or impossible there? Nothing. Billy decided Robby only made a big deal out of an easy job because he was extremely protective of him, and not because of the possibly associated danger. Billy's barely voiced opinion did not stop Robby from carefully reviewing every step involved. As a matter of fact, it only increased his warnings. For an added, extra security, Robby ordered Miguel to go with him to Mexico, not as much for company, but rather as a guide and translator.

When the Texas Sheriff's car pulled up in front of Robby's house, Wade Hands found the slowly recuperating Robert Falls at home alone. Robby no longer had a fever, but still coughed a lot, and he barely had the strength to answer the door. Recently being sick, weak, and worried about his friends, he became easily irritated thinking Billy and Miguel forgot the house key in their hurry. After all, he found Miguel's wallet on the countertop, too, after they left.

When Wade Hands delivered the tragic news of Billy's death and Miguel's disappearance, Robby's blood drained from his face, and his knees lost all their strength. If the sheriff did not catch him, Robby probably would have fallen to the floor. The tall, muscular Wade practically carried him to a chair, then got a glass of water for him. His keen eyes did not miss Robby putting the empty glass on the counter, next to a colorful Mexican leather wallet.

Wade casually picked the wallet up and, while admiring the leather work, he asked Robby if that beautiful piece of art was his. Wade examined it with interest from every side, even opened it up, and nonchalantly looked into it. In the wallet, there were only a few coins and wrinkled paper money stuffed next to a torn McDonald's receipt. It looked like it was ripped in half, but the other part was missing. Sheriff Wade Hands knew where the other half was to be found. He also knew he just got only a few questions away from finding Ramón's murderer.

The sheriff's office got the information about Miguel and Billy from a drug agent who had infiltrated the underground smuggling society. He only knew the first names of the two victims and Robby as their contact. At Robby's place, Wade accidentally stumbled upon the unique wallet and discovered the ominous McDonald's receipt which connected Miguel to his investigation. Now he had only one suspect to chase, Jorge, the actual murderer. Billy was not part of his search. Although he felt sorry for another person being killed by the drug lords, he also knew this was part of the life Billy chose. The moment a man got involved with the illegal business of transporting or distributing any of the substances or any contraband, he took his life into his own hands. Yep. Karma has a habit of biting you in the butt the moment you turn your back to it.

Wade Hands was a welcome help in Arizona. He was readily extended all courtesy to continue his tracking of Ramón's murderer. Although they all thought he was quite a bit loony to sacrifice his vacation for chasing a criminal, but if that kept him 'ticking', that was fine with them.

Wade followed the trail all the way from Texas, and would have continued the chase as long and as far as it took to get the killer, even if it was all the way to the shores of the Pacific Ocean. He pursued the criminal as a bloodhound pursues the scent of blood. The overworked local agents were actually glad to have one less wild-goose chase by having the handsome Texas sheriff among them. They just waved their hands with a "Who cares, let him knock himself out, if that's what makes him happy," and did not interfere with his investigation. They had enough to do on their own, anyway.

All the way back to his office, Wade had the nagging thought of familiarity with Billy. He noticed the smiling young man on the snapshot in Robby's home and instantly recalled him as someone he had seen before. Robby said his name was Billy Odum and he was Robby's partner. Billy's name did not mean anything to Wade Hands, but his face somehow struck him as someone he should recognize. He knew he never arrested Billy or ran into him during his work, he was sure. He could not have known him as a child, either, because Robby said his friend has never lived in Texas, and he originally came from Tennessee. Yet, Wade was certain he had seen him before. If only he could shake off the dust clouding his memory! But no matter how hard he racked his brain, he could not figure it out.

The secretary was busy and barely greeted him when he returned to the office. Wade liked the voluptuous young woman. She seemed to reciprocate his budding feelings before, so Wade dared to lean over her shoulder to whisper some sweet endearments to her. Suddenly, he spotted a flyer on her desk. "That's it!" he yelled, and the startled Martiza Salazar almost jumped out of her chair. "Jesus, Mary, and Joseph, Wade, what's the matter with you? What is it? What did I do now?" she asked.

"Not you, silly, it has nothing to do with you." He reached to grab the flyer off of her desk. He shook it in front of her eyes, while repeating himself, "That's it! I knew I had seen this guy somewhere. This is the man on the snapshot I could not place. Holy catfish, look at that! Next to him is a pretty good composition drawing of Robby.

Or someone who easily could be Robert Falls. Dog dang, I should have brought him in for questioning."

Learning Wade had nothing against her, Martiza relaxed. "This picture? Yeah, I got the flyer like a few days ago, but did not have time like to post it, yet. It was like all along on my desk, maybe you saw it there. Sorry for the delay, but I was like just about to put it up on the board, though."

"Never mind, just make me a copy, quick". He grabbed the copy and yelled back from the door, "I'll be back soon". He was heading straight back to Robby's place.

Robby lived clear across town, a good hour's drive from the sheriff's station. In the after-work traffic, it could take even longer. As he turned into Robby's street, he almost collided with a speeding truck. This was a vehicle hard to miss: it was raised high above the oversized tires, it surely looked like quite an expensive, new, custom-made truck. The shiny black paint was decorated with flaming red stripes. No, it was hard to miss.

Under normal circumstances, Wade would have stopped the man behind the steering wheel, if for nothing else, but to question what his big hurry was and to give him a warning. But he was not in Texas, and he had no jurisdiction in Arizona. Besides, this time he was on a mission. He had to let him get away. He was sure some of the local cops would soon spot him and probably would give him a hefty ticket instead of a simple warning. He continued to Robby's house.

The house looked deserted. All the shades were pulled and no one answered the door. A neighbor picking up her mail yelled over, "You just missed him, Sheriff. He sure was in a hurry when he left. Look at those thick marks his burned rubber made on the pavement," she laughed.

Sheriff Wade Hands barely missed his target. In retrospect, he was convinced Robby was spooked by his previous visit and the tragic news he delivered. Maybe Robby was guilty, too, somehow. Maybe he also was involved in drugs. Maybe he was kidnapping Billy, or in some way he played a part in Billy's disappearance. The flyer clearly connected him to the missing person that turned out to be William Robert Odum of Tennessee. Whatever else he might have done, Wade did not know, but he was certain it was nothing safe or legal.

All the way back to the office, Wade blamed himself and Martiza Salazar's curves for the delay that gave Robby just enough time to escape.

Chapter 35

Fright spread like a plague through Williston. Every member of the small community lived in fear. The killer was nameless, faceless, unknown to all, but they all realized someone lurked in the darkness of the night and was on the loose to blend into the crowd in daylight. Nobody knew who the murderer was, but suspected everyone else. Suspicion found any place to land on, just like a seagull landing on any post. The nightmare deepened with each day that failed to name the criminal.

The nearby police stations and sheriff departments had a handful of false calls, misleading or irrelevant information, voiced suspicions, and unfounded accusations every day since Jeb Odum's death was revealed as a homicide.

Because houses were far apart, and large pieces of empty land separated most of them, people started to lock their doors. Before the news of the murder became public knowledge, house keys were hung almost as if they were decorations. Keys were rarely used unless the family was away for a few days. Now they got full use. In addition to locking up, some jittery housewives jammed the entrance doors with a piece of furniture for the night. The men took their guns and rifles out of the locked gun rack and kept them loaded near the bed. At the only security company who serviced the area the phone rang off the hook with demands of immediate installation of home alarms. These were unprecedented steps, but the cause necessitating them was also unprecedented.

Ron McCarthy was frustrated with the recurrent blocks that hampered the investigation. Being the Chief of Homicide Investigation, he well knew the ultimate responsibility laid heavily on his shoulders. Furthermore, solving this murder could attest not only to his preparedness and abilities, but also it would mean his ultimate acceptance by Williston and its surroundings, and of course, that meant Fayette County, too.

The new coroner, who temporarily replaced the disgraced and now dead Dr. Johnson, had no idea what instrument could have caused the deadly wound. He was more of a bookworm than a practical person, and his lack of experience only added to his scholarly but vague answers. McCarthy soon realized he had no further questions for the young doctor, because he did not want to hear lengthy dissertations which meant nothing to him. What he wanted to hear, the substitute coroner did not know.

On top of this frustration, Corky greeted him at the station with a poorly masked sarcastic smile "So Dr. Johnson went to extremes to avoid you, didn't he? Don't take his suicide too hard, it probably had nothing to do with you, Kemosabe," he assured his chief with jovial benevolence.

McCarthy was not in the mood to start any discussion, especially not over a silly remark, so he just picked up some keys and left the office. "I am heading to the Odum-house, if anyone looks for me. I have my phone, call me if you need me."

From his car he yelled back once more to his assistant an order to pick up Doug Bullock and Charlotte Kay Odum for questioning. He was to return in an hour or so, he said.

The Odum house stood silently and imposingly among the huge evergreens. The yellow crime barrier ribbon was intact, the door locked. McCarthy walked around the property, but did not see anything else useful to investigate. He was still waiting for the lab to call him on the shoeprint analysis. On a whim, he walked to the fence where Mr. Wilson stood while talking with him the day before. The mud smeared on the rails unmistakably identified his spot. Behind it were the footprints of his cowboy boots.

McCarthy leaned forward to take a better look at the boot prints. He felt the sudden tension in his neck and shoulders, tighter than a drawn bowstring. Locating the prints of the boots, he almost instantly felt the tension dissipated and he relaxed. The boots definitely were much larger and wider than the print in question near the house. McCarthy was glad and much relieved to find Mr. Wilson's footprints were far from matching the ones he tried to identify. He did not want the murderer to turn out to be the only black man in the Odum's vicinity.

He turned back to the house and entered through the garage. With satisfaction he verified the truck's tires, white lettering proudly advertising 'Bridgestone'. He remembered it well. A few minutes prior he checked out the tractor left by a pile of tree branches, and noted that it also had a similar name on its tires. He was right to think the truck marks came from another vehicle. It must have been a new and expensive one, judging by the perfect imprint.

He opened the door and stepped in the rear hallway leading to the kitchen. The silence following his entry instantly alarmed him: he was absolutely sure he had turned on the home security system before the investigators left. He was the last to leave, he knew he would not have forgotten a basic safety step before the house was sealed. His hand reached for his holster and slowly, silently he pulled his handgun out. He held it in a steady grip ahead of him. He stepped into the empty kitchen and joining family room. A barely audible noise made him turn sharply to face the sofa where Jeb Odum's body was found four days before. He suddenly faced a trembling Vittoria DelRosario holding a few pictures, some clothes, and a make-up bag in her hands.

After the initial shock, Vittoria admitted she crossed the sign "Crime Scene—Keep Away". Though she used her own key to enter the house, in reality she was trespassing. The face of the investigator remained restrained, but his cold stare and stern voice indicated his anger. Fearing the projected consequences, Vittoria decided to come clean. Sitting nervously at the breakfast table, she attempted to justify to McCarthy her illegal break-in.

She told him all she wanted was to remove her personal items. She did not do or touch anything else. She did not want to be questioned any further, neither as Jeb Odum's fiancée, nor as the possible murderer of Jeb Odum. To gain access and to remain unnoticed, she walked up to the house rather than using a car. Yes, investigator Corky's mother loaned her an old Ford, hearing Vittoria wanted to revisit places that had sentimental memories for her. When she was in the main bathroom collecting her make-up, she spotted a man walking outside. She recognized McCarthy and tried to hide first. Then she decided it was safer to get out at the rear door. She was waiting in the back room for the detective to open the front entrance, knowing the loud sound of the creaking front door would camouflage the noise of her exit. She did not expect McCarthy to step in through the garage. By the time she recognized his presence, it was too late to change plans. Her exit route was cut off, she was trapped.

She obeyed his request by putting her bag on the table. One by one she produced a comb, hairbrush, curlers, and laid them next to a jar of Lancôme facial cream, mascara, and a bottle of Bulgari Jasmine de Noire perfume. At McCarthy's questioning she quietly shook her head, indicating there was nothing else left in the bag. Without another word the McCarthy took the rolled-up bag, reached in, and produced a lipstick. It was hot pink. Vittoria was staring at the lipstick, held her breath, and was unable to utter any words for explanation. Her face was pale and panic-stricken.

At the end of a tearful account, McCarthy learned that Vittoria's new landlady was Corky's mother. Whatever Corky said at home of the investigation, he either said it in Vittoria's presence, or his mother told Vittoria during their innocent chatting. Women, especially those with good memory recall, were experts to gather, store, and then recombine tid-bits of information for future use. Men never could understand that innocently dropped words could lead women to major discoveries. Vittoria was intelligent enough to quickly realize how much her lipstick jeopardized her. She knew she had to get it out of Jeb's house before she, the owner of the lipstick, became a major part of the investigation. Little did she know the sheriff already listed every piece of her make-up, clothes, and pictures found in Jeb's house. She never imagined that eventually they would catch her red-handed in Jeb's place, either.

She vehemently denied any part of the murder. Indeed, her alibi cleared her. McCarthy already verified she was at home, in Alabama, when Jeb was attacked. Vittoria defended herself with conviction though McCarthy realized she might have had more than enough motive to harm her fiancée. This was one of his reasons he needed to verify Vittoria played no part in the murder by proxy.

Chapter 36

After Vittoria learned of Jeb's clandestine affair with Lana Hadock, she became suspicious of everything Jeb said or did, and quietly started to investigate Jeb. She admitted, "I had a friend whose neighbor was a private investigator. I approached him, and he called one of his colleagues in Memphis. The Tennessee investigator put a tail on Jeb. Jeb never suspected being followed. He would not in a million years believe I was in the background. Shortly afterward, I got a report I would not have wanted to hear. Apparently, Jeb was pretty carefree in carrying on with another woman. The private investigator did not have a hard time to discover what my fiancée did while I was away. It became clear Lana Hadock was the cancer in our relationship. It devastated me to learn what went on behind my back," then she added, almost as an after-thought, "that was the most painful, but best-spent thousand dollars I have ever paid in my life. Thank goodness, I did. Could you imagine what my life would have become if I blindly kept trusting him? He would never have kept his word and, at the end, I probably would have been hurt much more. To top my emotional devastation, if we had married, I would have lost half of everything I had.

"I was also educated in a hurry on how to mask my emotions but pay close attention to every inconsistent word Jeb uttered or every accordant act he committed. With all respect to you, Mr. McCarthy, in my opinion men are generally simple creatures of habit. By doing or saying something out of character represented just as much of an instant red flag as by doing the opposite. Don't you agree? You must often see it in your line of work, too, don't you?"

McCarthy contemplated an answer, but Vittoria did not wait for him, and continued, "I noted with alarm that, after the fling with Lana Hadock, Jeb suddenly did not mention participating in any church activities. Before this affair was discovered, he was always socializing with the Bible School people or volunteering in the church. Now he failed to bring up even the already scheduled, usual dinners, picnics, or golf practice. He only said the perpetual lawn care tied him down and took all his time. When it was raining or too cold to work outside, he said he kept busy caulking indoors. I bet he could have used up the entire inventory of caulk of a Home Depot; yet, when I visited his house, a lot of cracks in over half of the house showed a desperate need of filling. I did not believe he was not occupying his time elsewhere. On the surface I sympathized with him while inside I noted he kept lying to me." Vittoria smiled sadly.

"Then one day, Jeb gave me his cell phone, to call and locate my own misplaced mobile phone. That's when I discovered Robert Hadock's name on Jeb's frequent-caller list. I knew Lana's husband's name was Robert, who died four years prior. Jeb's conniving craftiness insulted my intelligence: what did he think, I would have not recognized the link between them? In his mind, he was convinced that using a man's name, instead of his wife's, was a brilliant move because it would not have given me any reason to be suspicious or jealous. He only forgot that I have excellent recall, especially when it came to Lana and Jeb. And, by the way, we bought him a new phone together, so he had to enter all his contacts recently. It was not like he kept an old list that he simply overlooked."

"Did you ever confront him? Did you ask him who was this Robert Hadock?" inquired McCarthy.

"No. I did not. I knew already who he was, and did not want to hear another lame excuse, another lie. Instead, I casually remarked to him, it was lucky for him he was not a Democrat, otherwise everyone could have accused him of keeping a list of deceased men as potential voters. He surely got the message, because he just stared at me, without being able to utter a word." Vittoria shook her head.

"Then on one of my visits to Williston I did not see Lana in church. She did not come on the following Sunday, either. When I made a remark noting her absence, Jeb instantly replied, 'Oh, she went to Little Rock for a family visit.' Not a heartbeat of hesitation, he just blurted it out. He knew it, no question in my mind. 'Really? How did you know it?'

"My quick reaction must have been sort of unexpected, because Jeb mumbled something about overhearing it in church. I pressed him further by quietly adding, 'Ahem. Interesting that Lana goes away exactly during the two weeks when I am here, isn't it? Hmm,

I wonder how did she learn precisely which two weeks I was planning to be in Tennessee,' then I dropped the subject. Jeb remained silent. I guess he was caught red-handed, like a child picking his nose in church."

Step-by-step, McCarthy learned about Jeb's unfolding betrayal from Vittoria. He admired her self-control, but also became a bit afraid of her. She was able to cover a lot of her negative emotions too well for his liking. He concluded a simple country boy had no chance to stand against her, especially not when he was macho enough to think he could easily outsmart a mere woman. McCarthy was convinced Jeb had not learned the basic rules of warfare to remain observant and never underestimate an opponent. The man was way too confident of his manipulating skills and the seeming safety given by Vittoria's non-confrontational personality and their physical distance. He never understood that although Vittoria may have talked with an accent, she did not think with one.

The woman sitting across the breakfast table shifted her position, placed her hands softly on top of another, and continued to recall her road leading to lost love. "The following Sunday, Jeb took a new scenic route to church through Somerville. He said he just wanted to show me the country side. Again, to do this was way out of character for a very predictable man. Instantly, I became alert. At first, he drove without particularly looking around but seemed to be quieter than usual. If he wanted to show me the area, it was up to me to see it, because he did not say much. Soon I recognized a distinct change in his behavior. Suddenly, he became tense, real quiet, and failed to point out anything to me. He kept looking to the left as if searching for something. At one point, he even leaned out the window to look back, as if he wanted to see something better, once the car had passed it.

"At the next street sign, I noted the name and number of the street. On a hunch, I found it corresponded with Lana Hadock's address in the church roster. I figured Jeb was evidently checking if Lana's car was on the driveway. Or maybe he was looking for any sign of her being at home. Maybe he just wanted to make sure she was home and not in church. I silently stacked away this discovery also."

"You really had a problem with his church-related contacts and activities, didn't you?" asked McCarthy, although he really did not expect a response.

Vittoria became emotional for the first time, and almost seemed she could lose her composure, as she answered, "You would have had, too, if someone you trusted and loved admitted having an affair with a member of that particular church and then he kept returning there regularly. Just like being compassionate enough to take in a freezing snake, only to be bitten as soon as he warmed up."

A moment later, she continued in her calmer tone, "I knew he never stopped seeing Lana because after I had learned about her, and we made up, Jeb refused to take me to his Church or to Bible class."

"You were not too surprised at that, were you?" interjected McCarthy.

"No, not at that. What bothered me was his lame excuse. 'I cannot take you because I don't know the names of the people there and cannot introduce you.' Puh-lease. Could you believe he attended every Sunday morning service for the last eight-ten years, shared a small class-room with about thirty people, and still did not know any names? I replied that it truly did not matter, we were to go to worship and not to socialize, weren't we? He just stared at me as if he were a mole that suddenly surfaced into a bright sunshine. After a bit of time, he came back with the offer to go to the evening program. I told him, 'Come now, you never go to church in the evening and you are not worried about recalling the names of the evening service attendees? Don't take me for an imbecile.' He ran out of alternatives. I sulked. Regardless, in the end, he won. We stayed home."

"There were lots of Baptist churches in the area; why, practically on every corner there was another one. Couldn't he attend somewhere else, after this embarrassing fiasco with Lana Hadock? He could sing and pray elsewhere as well. Especially when he knew how much it bothered you. That should have been the only resolution," McCarthy remarked.

"Exactly, that was my sentiment, too. He only proved that he did not break up with Lana and was not ready to cut off the ties with her, either, regardless what he said. He just kept her out of sight to placate me. All the little bothersome events cropping up here and there indicated the same. No, the truth was Jeb continued playing a game of betrayal, and he took me for an idiot. Maybe I was a total fool, but he took Lana for one, too. Who knows?" Vittoria wiped her eyes dry then continued.

McCarthy suddenly realized Jeb Odum not only overestimated himself, but he also underestimated everyone around him. As a result, he got trapped in a web of his own lies. He waited patiently for Vittoria's story to end, although he expected more to come, yet. An underestimated, but colorful personality like Jeb probably did a lot more to rap about.

Chapter 37

McCarthy was right, though in reality, he would have preferred the opposite. Oh, yes, quiet and unassuming Jeb Odum had a totally different side which he kept well-hidden from the public. The problem with secrets is that they don't want to remain concealed. Eventually, the true nature surfaces and surprises the witnesses. The degree of their shock depends on the extent of the deceit. Vittoria discovered Jeb's rightful personality and she did not like what she was shown.

"One day we visited Anna, my neighbor. Although Anna heard of Jeb before, she was yet to have met him in person. The visit went on pleasantly enough, until Anna suddenly jumped the question of future plans with Jeb, asking when was the wedding? I expected Jeb to say 'soon' or something to that effect, but he paused for a bit before responding 'not unless I sell my house and need to live somewhere'. Both of us were stunned by this crudely blunt statement. Anna quickly changed the subject, but her attitude distinctly cooled off with Jeb. We left soon afterward, because we all had a gnawing discomfort. Each of us had ill-feelings, though for different reasons. Just the same, the initial pleasant mood of the visit was ruined. Suddenly I saw Jeb losing his mask, and he just stood there, as if naked in a very sharp light. It was not a pretty sight. Naturally, I pouted all the way home. Afterward, Jeb explained I simply misunderstood him."

"I bet that was a shocker to hear," said McCarthy, but he failed to specify whether he referred to Jeb's first remark to Anna or his attempt to divert Vittoria's negative reaction.

"Sure was. Funny, how comments like these bring back memories, and suddenly explain a lot of little, nagging things you stacked away in your mind. You know, the ones that made no significance, or had no particular meaning when first heard, although they might have sounded a bit odd at that time. Yet, you somehow managed to brush them aside or disregarded them.

"His strange statement to Anna made me recall that Jeb once remarked about Lana Hadock also having a house. He said, it was not as big and elegant as mine, but it was a nice little house, especially nice for country folks. Suddenly I realized Jeb might have pursued not a woman, but her house, and his own future and living arrangement. Perhaps the house was the biggest attraction for him in Lana, too. I also had to face the fact that Jeb played both Lana and me simultaneously with the knowledge that either of us would do at the end, as long as he could live somewhere.

"Before this incident we discussed the possibility of moving in together. The problem was we both were homeowners in two different states, far from each other. Jeb could not leave Tennessee though he originally promised to relocate to Alabama. It was a no-brainer: if I wanted to keep this relationship going, I had to eliminate the distance and the temptations he had in my absence."

"Oh, please, after what you have learned about him, you still wanted to keep him? Why not let Lana win him and get the deserved reward of his personality?" wondered McCarthy with both eyebrows raised to the middle of his forehead.

"I guess I thought he would love only me, if I was always present, always with him. I was wrong, I know it now. You see, he was my priority while I was only his option. Anyway, I was offered an excellent package of salary and benefits, if I were to take the job at the Memphis University Hospital. I planned to move in with him. I even considered paying off his ex-wife, getting Jeb's house on our names as soon as we married, and rent my house in Montgomery. I could have done it easily, I had enough cash available. This way he could have saved the house he loved, and we could have been together. Thank goodness, the proverbial something hit the fan before I invested in him more than my emotions and time." Vittoria puckered her mouth into a sad smile.

"In a couple of days, Jeb's ex-wife contacted him and demanded that the house be placed on the market immediately, or she threatened him with legal action for breaking their divorce agreement. Jeb went into overdrive mode of panic and instantly listed the property for sale. Apparently, he resigned himself to the fact that he had no other choice but to get rid of the house. Otherwise, his ex-wife would have predictably returned. He was so shaken up and frightened by Charlotte Kay's unexpected ultimatum that he did not consider or even remember my offer.

"Evidently his ex-wife heard of our plans from their daughter. Which also showed me who Mary Beth sided with, where her loyalty laid. Certainly not by her unobtrusive and, the way I was told, wronged father. Which alone was rather unusual, because children of divorced parents traditionally side with the wronged party, especially adult children, who already had a mature opinion and judgment."

"Look," she turned to McCarthy, "Can you blame the woman for not wanting her successor to move into her old home? I can't. Any woman would have done the same.

"I bet Jeb never dared to offer her to be paid off, either. My plans to move to Tennessee were no longer on the table, but canceled without any further discussion. Instead, I worked as a slave for the entire two weeks of my vacation, and made Jeb's house presentable for potential buyers. While scrubbing, rearranging, organizing the rooms, and making a garden, I had plenty of time to turn things over in my mind.

"I carefully analyzed Jeb's financial status. Although he always talked as if he were a feudal lord or a medieval large land and mansion owner, in reality, he didn't have much. The house was under a forced sale agreement. After all expenses and bank loans were satisfied, the divided proceeds likely would not exceed a hundred or, maximum, a hundred-ten thousand dollars. Jeb had a modest social security, which could have never been accepted as a guarantee to get a loan for purchasing another real estate. If he bought anything, it had to be a cash deal. Out of his sale proceeds, he could not get a one-bedroom condo even in a poor neighborhood. Then he had to add to it the moving expenses and everything else that goes along with getting into a new place. He would have to get some furniture, too, because he did not have two matching chairs left in the house. No, it was not an inexpensive proposition, for sure."

She looked around, sweeping her extended arm in a semi-circle as she indicated the surroundings, then turned to McCarthy, "And you saw this big house. After living in a five-bedroom house on twenty acres land, don't you think this kind of move would have been an unbearably harsh reality for him? To live in a one-bedroom condo? No yard, no lawn, no trees, and no work to kill his time and energy. Just the four walls, an old TV, and a humble social security check. It would have been nearly impossible to get used to something so drastically reduced, so much below the level he was accustomed to, don't you think? Let's face it, his only salvation was finding a woman with a house. He was very realistic to know he had to find this woman while he still had something to impress her with, his home and property. After he sold his house, he had very little to brag with, if anything. In exchange, Jeb was willing to offer this woman the only thing he had: his name in marriage."

McCarthy secretly came to the same conclusion. Now he understood why Jeb constantly kept positioning himself. Of course, he never could make a full commitment to either woman. Whoever seemed more willing to accept his advances, and offered more to him in exchange, was 'in'. The other was placed on the back burner or was 'out'. As long as he was not forced by the sale of his house, he would not have to make a decision and marry either woman. Until he sold his property, he could play a game as long as he managed to keep them apart and on hold. He made them respond to him as a puppet, reacting only when the puppeteer pulled the strings. Simple, honest, sincere, loyal, and God-fearing country boy was only a simple, calculating, country boy, after all.

"A forbidden fruit can get you in an awful jam," remarked McCarthy dryly then questioned Vittoria, "what happened next?"

"What happened? After being his slave for two weeks, I certainly got a payment that was totally unexpected. Jeb snapped at me, 'This is my house, how I deal with it is none of your business'. I swallowed hard and replied, 'You are right. I would never mention again how to list it. I only wanted to help you.' I swore to, and kept my promise I made to myself, to never, ever lifting a finger again in his house. If it was his business, then let him make the work his business, too. Let him buy the rose bushes, plant the flowers, get all the decorations that made his house attractive for the potential buyers. Let him scrub it, stage it, do with it whatever needed to be done. Don't ever expect me to be his maid again. This happened to be a very bitter lesson for me. Yet, interestingly, he only made this remark after I broke my back in his house, and not before he needed me to start the chores. Smart, huh?

"Two weeks ago, he finally sold the house but he did not tell me the good news immediately. I asked him why he did not share his success and joy with me as soon as he got an offer or signed the papers. Can you believe he replied, 'It slipped my mind?' He expected me to believe another one of his lame stories."

"Slipped his mind? Like this happens every day? Nah, I don't think so. He did not want to tell you, or he did not care to tell you. I believe this was more than a red flag for you. It must have been a giant, red, stop sign. Am I right?"

"Yes, you are. Honestly, would he not want to communicate a life-changing event first with the person closest to him? I certainly would have called him immediately. Well, since he died, this really became immaterial.

"In retrospect, there were other red flags in our relationship. I just either found some excuses for Jeb's bad behavior or overlooked them. For instance, when in Italy, I purchased a typical handcrafted item for his sister. I always liked her, though Jeb and his sister were really not that close. Yes, they frequently dined together, but Jeb often made derogatory remarks about their drinking habits which certainly were not too flattering to her or her husband. Regardless, I always considered her my soon-to-be relative. Coming from a close-knit family, I longed for one. She sort of replaced my far-away relatives.

"When we returned from Europe, Jeb told me, instead, we should give my present to his daughter, Mary Beth. He reasoned, his sister never got him anything from her many trips abroad, so he didn't feel obligated to give her anything, either. It did not occur to him it was my present he discussed, and I had nothing to do with his prior experience with his sister and her lack of gifts to Jeb. It turned out, he forgot to get something for his daughter, and it was her birthday. I said I purchased that gift with my own money specifically for another person, his sister. I already had some other present for his daughter. If he pretended my present was his gift to her, I had nothing to give to his sister. Without further comments, he put my present in a gift bag, and gave it to Mary Beth, anyway. I was stunned to silence by his disrespect and outright disregard of my wishes. I had to call my relatives in Rome to buy and ship me a present from Italy so I could replace the one Jeb gave away."

McCarthy casually interjected, "I assume, he did not reimburse you, did he?"

"No, he never offered me any reimbursement. He never thanked me for getting him out of his uncomfortable predicament, either."

McCarthy's remark made Vittoria realize she had been shamelessly used.

"Well, he clearly had no respect for you, your wish, or your property. Yes, you should have paid more attention to his actions. Then you would have seen him in a different light. The problem is, once he got away with being disdainful, it was easy to repeat the same. By tolerating it, you gave him the green light of leeway."

McCarthy listened intently to the factual accounts of betrayal and lies that surely were sufficient for a revenge. Yet, in his guts he felt Vittoria did not kill her fiancée. He just wanted to make sure she did not hire someone to do it for her. If she could hire an investigator, she could have hired an executioner, just as easily, too. But he shrugged off the idea as being outlandish, and his thinking as pure sensationalism. Perhaps all Vittoria wanted was to repay and punish Jeb. Maybe she only waited for her right moment to take that final step. He could see how the stairway of increasing lies lead to the destruction of the relationship. He understood how the need of revenge first formed, then steadily strengthened, and finally materialized in a misled and wronged woman.

Chapter 38

As most detectives learn, McCarthy also knew murder was an ultimate solution to a temporary problem. The crime was committed when emotions overcame logic and thinking. Vittoria DelRosario was very much in control of her emotions, perhaps a bit too much, he concluded. Jeb Odum made the unfortunate mistake to underestimate Vittoria, and allow her controlled facade to mislead him into an imaginary la-la land.

Regardless, Vittoria could not have been the murderer. McCarthy realized, she was far too intelligent to not know the risks of hiring a contract killer. No, she could not have neglected the fact what it would have meant, how it would have jeopardized her integrity and everything she has accumulated. For a transient thrill of revenge, it was not worth taking that gamble.

McCarthy figured Vittoria truly loved Jeb, but her love was slowly chiseled away by an unfaithful man, whose misconduct unfolded gradually. Her love, like most loves, did not die of a natural death. It died many deaths by his repeated betrayal, errors, weariness, and blindness. In return, Jeb's initial infatuation and intimacy died by her cool responses and cold withdrawals. At times, Vittoria secretly hoped to restore the original exhilaration of the relationship, in vain. The recurring evidence of Jeb's dishonesty created an overwhelming mistrust. Doubt and suspicion combined with the discovery of the man's self-serving, alternative motive lead to the ultimate break-down. Once trust was broken, and repeatedly attacked, it simply could not be ignored for long.

Vittoria continued, "Although I got a ring, I only had an empty verbal commitment from Jeb. His words had no reflection on his actions. There was no match between his promises and actions, whatsoever."

"Yep, words simply don't add up if the truth is not included in the equation," McCarthy laconically injected.

Vittoria silently repeated McCarthy's sentence in her mind. She liked McCarthy and his wisdom expressed in succinct statements. She stacked them in her memory bank to be recalled when the future need called for it. After a few minutes sitting by each other without words, each enwrapped in different thoughts but in complete understanding and harmony, McCarthy's voice jolted her back to reality and she started to wrap up her heartbreak.

"The last we talked, he was clearly in a panic and overwhelmed with the sale of his house. He called me the day before he needed to transfer the keys to the new owners and he still had nowhere to go. As long as I live, I would always recall his words. It was as if he had slapped me when he announced, 'Now I am willing to marry you'. I swallowed hard and calmly asked him why he wanted to marry me. He replied, 'Because you make life interesting. Sometimes less so, but always interesting.' This was not what I wanted to hear. Trust me, there is not a single woman on this Earth who would find this either an exciting marriage proposal or a sufficient reason for marriage. He did not say, 'Because I love you and cannot imagine my life without you', or 'Because I want to wake up next to you every day', or 'Because I am happy just to be near you'. I had to face the harsh reality: what he said probably was the truth, and it was all what he felt toward me. I responded, 'No, I do not want to marry you only for this. For me, this is not enough for marriage'. I expected him to correct it, by adding quickly he loved me and all the other reasons, but he angrily retorted my answer with a cold 'good bye' and slammed the phone down. We never talked again.

"Whoa, I did not know that," McCarthy's unexpected shock was obviously genuine.

"Yes, Jeb had changed drastically since Lana entered the picture and periodically returned. She was the worst type of malignancy in our relationship because she was aggressive, tenacious, relentless, and selfish to the core. She succeeded in twisting and bending Jeb as she wished."

"Did you think someone could be stolen if he really loved you? Regardless of how many people or who he met?" McCarthy quietly probed.

"I guess not. Seeing his many recurrent, contradicting acts and attempted cover-ups, finally, I was forced to face the fact that my fiancée had not meant the things he said in the beginning. God, I needed to hear those words so much again, to be reassured of his love, but he didn't repeat them. Furthermore, as his interests changed, then wavered, he easily disregarded his promises. Yet, those very words kept me in an imaginary loving relationship, while the resultant sense of safety allowed Jeb to pursue other women innocuously. He felt secure as long as I was far away. What I did not know, did not hurt me."

"He only miscalculated you, because you did know it. Look, you said that you, yourself discovered it first then confirmed it by your private investigator. Right? And it *did* hurt you. Am I correct?" Vittoria openly dropped a big tear for the first time, hearing the sincere empathy in the investigator's voice.

"You should not be ashamed for what happened because you were provoked and only responded to him. *You were reacting to Jeb, and not pro-acting,* like Lana. Yet, that was you. You probably always dealt with problems in your life like that. You did not do anything wrong, it just was not a particularly effective way to handle a situation. Of course, that does not mean it was not painful and you should not cry," he consoled her, "because you did not deserve it. Nobody deserves to be used. Though, in a way, somehow, we all use others. Just not as crudely as Jeb Odum did, and not without any scruples. Really, this was not the action of a man's man. He had no shame. What you thought you had, was not a reality. His empty promises were used only as vehicles to get him to where he wanted to land. You should always remember that."

"Oh, I do at times," sighed the woman and added, "It's only hard when I do not remember it. You know what bothers me the most? In the beginning I gave him a fair warning when told him how I react to lies and disappointments. Usually I do not like to confront people. I hate fights. I simply withdraw myself and quietly fade away. I told him honestly; yet, he did not pay attention to it."

"Perhaps he never cared enough to recall it. Did it occur to you that your feelings did not matter to him as long as his needs were met?" Vittoria could only stare at McCarthy, his words rendering her totally speechless.

"Tell me, how did Jeb react to your changes? You know, by not moving to Tennessee, not helping in his house, and the rest. Did he change, too?"

"Of course, he did. He noticeably became more aloof and indifferent. He gradually reduced the caring and affectionate expressions. He became distant and alternately outright morose or openly cross. He started to make negative remarks of what I wore. He ignored when I put on a pretty nightgown, and when I pointed it out to him, he simply replied, 'Sorry, I must not have noticed it.' He impatiently shut me up by snapping at me, 'You have already said this before. How many times do you need to repeat yourself?'

"On his last visit he tore into me by saying, 'Do you think I enjoy listening to your cough?' You see, Mr. McCarthy, I work with ill people who carry every bug into the hospital. Unfortunately, in the last five years I had pneumonia three times. Subsequently, I developed a lung condition in the damaged area, resulting in a chronic cough. Periodically, I get a sudden, forceful coughing spell, then once the episode is over, I am fine for another half a day. These spells are embarrassing, painful, and rather uncomfortable to me, but I try to joke by saying, 'Once this hairball is out, I will feel better.'

"Jeb's total lack of empathy and accusatory tone hurt me beyond your imagination. The coldness of his emotions, the total lack of love, and his suppressed anger surfaced for a second. I felt my mere presence irritated him at times to not even tolerate me. This remark really was hurtful to me, because I did not cough on purpose to irritate or disturb him, I just had to cough. In my mind, this remark put the last nail into Jeb's coffin.

"It made me instantly think what if I had cancer or suffered a heart attack? What if I had kidney disease and dialysis or stroke and could not speak or walk? Would he hold it against me? Would he disappear as soon as I had trouble? How much would he be inconvenienced by my illness? After all, cancer could be a real annoyance for a bystander, you know." The last remark was bitterly sneering, it even caught McCarthy off guard. He did not expect that much negative emotion to be allowed to surface from Vittoria's well-controlled personality.

"I cried a lot but forced myself to focus on the sweeter past memories to ease my pain. At the same time, I could not avoid contrasting that nicer past with all of my current wounds, imagined and real alike. Yet, with each of his transgressions I gained more and more ammunition and strength to make a final decision to break up with him."

The time fast approached when Jeb was to learn the consequences of his treachery. During this down-spiraling, he remained oblivious of Vittoria's traumatized emotions and remained confident his fiancée with the big house was a closed deal. He held Vittoria already in his palm, ready to be taken whenever he cashed in his chips. After all, Vittoria pursued him and got him back when Jeb admitted to having an affair. It was safe to conclude that she always would take him back, no matter what Jeb did.

Jeb secretly was satisfied with his quick-witted explanations and shrewd conduct which derailed the predictable end. He was convinced his low-profile and pretentious simplicity hid his faults to perfection. His conviction to be the smartest man in the room was confirmed once more. He could outsmart anyone, and it did not matter what size that room was.

In reality, Vittoria just postponed the inevitable break, while she nervously anticipated Jeb's home to be sold. No question, once without a house, Jeb would have wanted to move in with her. She could not believe Lana Hadock taking Jeb back after he summarily dumped her. She could not be desperate enough after what he put her through. Certainly not soon enough to share her house with him. That left only Vittoria as a potential target. Once Jeb decided to move into her house, she knew her decision had to be revealed, she could not delay it any further.

After learning of Jeb's infidelity, Vittoria could never trust him again. She realized she could not live with him after he broke her trust. This conviction was further cemented by her latest discovery of Jeb's snooping around in her home office.

One day, during his last visit, she found a folder stuck in the top cabinet drawer where she filed all her financial papers. In these drawers were years of various statements arranged in manila folders. Now a strip of the yellow folder was caught in a hastily shut drawer. Knowing she did not open the drawer since she prepared for her tax return in January, she realized the only person who could have done it was Jeb. Jeb was the only other person in her home. He was there alone while she was working. He had plenty of time to search and snoop around.

Vittoria realized she must have returned unexpectedly, and hearing her arrival, Jeb slammed the drawer shut. In his haste, he did not realize what tell-tale sign he left of his search. Vittoria was more hurt than angry by the unexpected discovery. This latest deliberate dishonesty deeply wounded her. The most painful thought was imagining how he had to rush to the other room, only to fake boredom and loneliness as he watched The Big Bang Theory.

While deceiving her, he must have hoped his breathlessness would not give his secret away to Vittoria. He had no inclination that by then she was long beyond the point to even bother confronting him with any questions.

This incident also made Vittoria conclude her fiancée had to be pretty desperate to reduce himself to sneaking, in order to know her complete financial status; yet, not very bright or observant to manage to keep his clandestine review a secret. Apparently, it never had occurred to him Vittoria's home security system was equipped with a video camera.

Once she was forced to disclose his game and his motives, she was sure Jeb could not face her. After all, nobody likes to look into a mirror just to see the wrinkles and liver spots in broad daylight. If they did, dimmers and make-up would not have been invented.

Vittoria logically concluded that if Jeb was confronted with the truth, he would instantly lose his face. Then he had no other choice, but to walk away from her. She was convinced when this happened, he would immediately regroup, turn around, and run back to Lana Hadock. He quickly had to pick up the frayed threads of his busted affair and salvage what was left, even if it took lying, faking, and never recalling his previous nickname of BB ever again. Unless he was willing to get a job, and start building up his finances again, or wanted to live in a small, rented apartment for the rest of his life, he had to get accepted by a woman. Vittoria was confident neither would have been Jeb's choice. Lonely, aging Lana, with a fully paid house, was a more comfortable and safer bet.

In spite of all that happened to Vittoria, McCarthy envisioned her as a survivor. After all, she did not give up or did not give in easily. She kept fighting for what she believed in, as long as she trusted Jeb's love. She did not cave under the increasing emotional pressure. Yet, she remained realistic enough to cash in her chips, without much ado, at the end. When she realized the hopelessness of her relationship, she had the strength to let Jeb go and be alone rather than continue to be used. Against all odds, she remained untouched by bitterness. This type of woman would find a good man eventually. She just had to pick herself up and get going again.

McCarthy eyed her for a while, as if contemplating whether to repeat her the nicest wish he had ever heard. Finally, he decided yes, she should know it, and use it as a guide in her future. He quoted to Vittoria the same words that his late wife said to him when she neared her end, "I would wish you a dance, a dance with your new lover. A dance as intense as your heart." For the first time, Vittoria covered her eyes with both of her hands and let herself go. Only her shaking shoulders indicated her heart-wrenching sobbing.

McCarthy got back to the headquarters later than expected. He sat an awfully long time in his car, thinking about what he learned from Vittoria. If anyone would have watched him, the investigator would have appeared mentally slow, almost as if he lost his marbles. Yet, his jaw muscles rhythmically clenched which were clearly indicating that all wheels and pulleys of his mind were working at maximal intensity.

Once in his office, he added the confiscated house key and lipstick to the already collected items. He quickly glanced at the conclusion of the forensic laboratory report on his desk. He had no time to read the details, because Corky was impatiently waiting for him, with Charlotte Kay Odum in one, and Doug Bullock in the other room.

Before talking with either suspects, McCarthy sternly warned Corky not to talk about the investigation to anyone. "This includes your mother and your house guest, too. Do you understand me? I am not asking you not to, I am ordering you not to. And I expect you to follow it to the last dot. Am I clear?"

Corky stiffly replied, "Yes, sir," and wondered what the hell had happened while McCarthy was away.

Chapter 39

McCarthy observed through the one-way window the nervously pacing Doug Bullock for a while, then decided to talk first to the much calmer Charlotte Kay. After about fifteen minutes, he learned all what he expected could have happened between Charlotte Kay and Doug.

Of course, he knew well that in her presentation the story was likely lop-sided, and that the man's account probably differed in many details. He was not concerned with the particulars though. Instead, he was obsessed with the main events, motivations, and actions. As far as McCarthy could see, the rest was just frills. He knew sometimes it was hard to shoo the unnecessary and not contributing parts aside, but his job was to listen to everything, so he did not complain. When Charlotte Kay started to repeat herself, and placed nothing new onto the table, he left her alone. Once out of her hearing range, he asked Corky to keep an eye on her.

When he entered Doug's room, the wiry young man was sitting in a corner with his legs stretched in front, his arms folded across his chest, and his head dropped forward. He seemed to be bored and resting. McCarthy knew he was playing a role, this was not the same mental condition he observed, the one Doug previously displayed.

After raising his head as if he were awakened by McCarthy's entrance, Doug faked a large yawn before he asked the investigator, "What's up man? You dragged me here after a day of hard work. It better be good, or I am gone."

"Gone? Where, Doug? Back to Jeb Odum's house?" asked McCarthy in an even tone.

"Hey, you cannot accuse me without any proof. You are just fishing. I know my rights and I know what's going on. You make a mistake with me, and man, I'll be worse than a flame-thrower in your most terrorizing nightmare. Just to start with, you know." Doug pulled himself up straight and leaned forward with, what he thought was, a menacing expression, the most threatening he could muster.

McCarthy was amused. "Really? Doug, really? Why?"

"Because you did not do your job to catch the criminal, and now you want to hang me for something I have not done. I have never been to Jeb's house. Have no reason to go there. I don't even know where he lived, except it was somewhere in Williston." Doug was clearly indignant.

"OK, let's pretend it is true, what you said, Doug. Then you must have sent your sneakers alone to Jeb's house, right? Let me see your sole." And he leaned forward to pick up Doug's foot to inspect the bottom of the worn-out sneaker. "Yep, just as I thought and as the lab reported. Nike all the way. I would give a blind dog's eyes to bet the prints fit perfectly, too. Just by glancing at it, I can see the worn-out parts also match perfectly. Do you still deny it, my friend?"

"It means nothing," Doug snapped angrily. "Lots of people wear Nike. Why, the bulls in Pamplona probably run in Nike, too," he snorted.

"Yep, that's possible, but they don't have an ex-girlfriend who testified against them," chuckled McCarthy. The ominous words angered Doug Bullock. He intensely stared into the investigator's face, but was unable to say a word.

"So are you ready now to tell me the truth? Or do you want me first to read you Mrs. Odum's sworn confession? Which one should it be, Doug? You tell me."

"So what if I went to Jeb's house? It does not mean I killed him," Doug clearly changed his tactics, and, instead of being an attacker, he became defensive.

"Hm. Are you admitting now you were at Jeb Odum's house? Apparently, you knew where he lived, didn't you?" asked McCarthy. "Mrs. Odum might have been right, after all, wasn't she?" McCarthy continued to pretend he was told everything by Charlotte Kay, then bluffed even further, "Too bad you had a fall-out with her, didn't you. Otherwise, she would not have sung like a meadow-lark. And sing she did. Oh, boy, did she ever."

"The bitch! What I have to put up with when I have no guns at hand!" blurted out Doug.

"I would appreciate keeping your language civilized," snapped McCarthy at him. "Repeat what you said about a gun."

"Sorry, I was just pi...ticked off." Doug quickly glanced at McCarthy to see whether he noted the new slip. When he did not see any change in the investigator's expression, he was assured and started to relax a bit, thinking he corrected himself just in time. Little did he know that nothing escaped the attention of McCarthy. If he did not seem to notice the slip, it was because he chose temporarily not to acknowledge it. Yet, it was stacked away in some deep nook in his mind, ready to surface at a moment's notice when needed. In the interim, he integrated it into the dynamic make-up of Doug Bullock's personality.

"Mrs. Odum had no right to accuse me. I had no interest in harassing or harming Jeb Odum, but she did. I have all the rights to be offended by her pointing a finger at me when all along it was she who wanted to shake up Jeb." Doug was angry enough to reveal to McCarthy why Charlotte Kay was wrong, and how she got him involved, yet, how he still managed to remain totally innocent.

"Let me tell you how it happened. It was she who first asked me to put God's fear in Jeb Odum if he did not list the house for sale. The whole thing was her idea, not mine. She was so hungry for money, I swear I have never seen anyone as crazy about dough as she was. She wanted to get her money out of the house; any way she could. But there was something more to trigger her anger, to pour oil on the fire. And that something was Jeb's fiancée. She was really upset over Jeb moving her in the house. Charlotte Kay told me Jeb wanted to move a new woman into her half of the house. If Jeb remained there alone and used both halves, that was fine. But the other woman was not to step foot into the house, not as long as Charlotte Kay was breathing. She was determined to block them in this plan, no matter what it took."

"You see, I had nothing to do with it. She planned it all out, then tricked me into doing her dirty work. When it became an open mess, then she pretended to know nothing? It's just not fair. She said it was I who did it all by myself? No way. Better wait. I could tell a lot more about her, too, you know. I just want to remain a gentleman and keep my mouth shut. That's all."

"Yes, Doug, I see what a gentleman you are. I bet you certainly could tell a lot about her, couldn't you? So why don't you? If you want to walk out as a free man, you better start saying what you do know, Doug. Frankly, that free walking away does not look too promising as of now."

Doug sat quietly for a minute and McCarthy let him digest what was said. Finally, he came to the conclusion it was better if McCarthy heard what happened from him then from his angry ex-lover, Charlotte Kay.

Slowly, the whole sordid tale unfolded: how Charlotte Kay convinced him to harass Jeb, urged him to make frequent anonymous night calls, suggested to start stalking and threatening him, and finally demanded him to project bodily harm to her ex unless Jeb sold the house. As he quoted her, "You just have to mess him up a bit. Just enough to get a cast on his leg."

In the interim, Doug, on his own, added to the woman's instructions. He got closer and closer to Jeb's house. Finally, on the last night, he showed up on Jeb's driveway and peeked through the front windows. Jeb woke up, turned on some lights, but never opened his door. That's when Doug got scared, and ran back to his truck, leaving his footprints in the mud. As soon as he jumped behind the wheel, he drove away as fast as he could, never looking back again. He kept calling Jeb on the next couple of nights, but Jeb never picked up the phone. After Doug learned of the murder, the phone calls stopped, and he stayed away from anything that was even remotely connected to Jeb.

"I swear I never, ever, talked to Jeb in person. I swear it on my blessed mother's grave. Believe me, it was not I who harmed him. I don't know who killed him, but it was not me, I swear to you. Maybe it was Charlotte Kay, maybe Jeb's woman friend, I don't know. I only know it was not I. When I left that night, Jeb was very much alive. You yourself said he probably died the following evening. I was not there the following day. I can prove that I had an alibi. You ought to believe me, I swear on anything holy, on any saint, whatever you say." Doug was crying at his last words, obviously desperate to convince the investigator.

McCarthy watched the man's repulsive red face, his tears and nasal discharge merging in the facial crease at the mouth. He knew Doug was telling him the truth. Whatever he heard, correlated with Mr. Wilson's statement, too. Charlotte Kay said the same, except for the motivation. She insinuated that the entire plan to torment Jeb was totally Doug's idea, and she only went along with him because she was deadly afraid of Doug. Of course, she was totally innocent. If Mr. McCarthy would care to recall, it was she who called the police to alert them about Doug.

McCarthy deeply disliked both Charlotte Kay Odum and Doug Bullock. He started to grasp their underlying, basic similarity, which created the original bond between these two characters. That alliance secured them only until each sold out the other, to protect their own hide. Oh, yes, they deserved each other, they were a matching pair. They both played a perfectly complimenting role to each other, according to their low-life.

At the end, McCarthy let both of them go home. The result of his investigation and both passing the lie-detector test made them less likely to be the suspect. Although he still had an uneasy feeling about Doug, he had no hard evidence or reason to keep either him or Charlotte Kay in custody. Watching them close the door, he mumbled half audibly to Corky, "Lord, what a weasel man can be!" He was only happy to not be related to either.

Once behind his desk, he carefully listed and reviewed the events of the day on his yellow pad, then, on a whim, he picked up the phone and called Reverend Babcock for Lana Hadock's phone number.

Chapter 40

Reverend Babcock was surprised to hear the investigator at the other end of his phone. He was more than agreeable to help with the information Mr. McCarthy needed. Afterward he added, "Sir, this might just be your lucky day. Mrs. Hadock happens to have an appointment with me in the church office today at four. If you wish to meet her, come by then. You could talk with her privately in my office if that suits you."

After the initial few casual words, the Reverend turned his room over to McCarthy. Lana Hadock sat in a simple wooden armchair in front of the desk, across the Sheriff. She sat straight, her spine not supported by the cushion in the back. She wore an eggplant-colored, deep purple, winter cowl-neck pullover and a totally inappropriate, flowery, long, cotton summer skirt. The colors in the skirt matched the top, but the materials did not go together. Furthermore, she had on thick, black nylons and a black, open-toe sandal. McCarthy knew very little of female fashion, but even he realized this ensemble was wrong. Oh, for crying out loud, one cannot only complement colors, but clothes have to be appropriate for the season, too. Lana obviously only cared for what people saw and not what they might have thought. McCarthy could not help but pity her, for he only saw an elderly woman desperately trying to turn back the hands of life's clock.

Looking at the aging Lana's hair, he suppressed a smile. He recalled the hairstyle of the seventies, when every woman tried to outdo Priscilla Presley's enormous bee-hive. Lana's was a modernized, toned-down version of the same but in a platinum blond version. From her jet-black, extra-long, false eyelashes to the cherry-red lipstick, everything seemed to be a left-over from that era. The thick makeup aged her, though definitely called for instant attention. McCarthy understood how Jeb Odum could not miss this self-proclaimed, country-Vogue model. He smiled ever so slightly, thinking that hardly any man would miss her, unless he was blind and deaf.

Then he remembered his late wife's beautiful skin which was never covered by layers of heavy make-up, but remained fresh and young, and breathed freely. Almost imperceivably, he shuddered at the mental picture of Lana Hadock without makeup. Instantly he felt sorry for the poor chap who fell into her trap only to discover her true look later.

"You were in the same Bible Class with Mr. Odum, weren't you?" started McCarthy. "As you know, he was found dead. We are investigating the circumstances. What can you tell me about him? Any and all information might be important so, please, tell me everything you remember."

Lana liked the tone, and instantly became satisfied with the respect she detected in the investigator's voice. She thought he must have realized what Lana already knew well: just how important a woman she was. Now she found herself at the center of attention, in the very middle of an investigation, and things depended on her. For the time being, she did not know how much they did, but the sheer knowledge of being in this position made her excited. McCarthy could really recognize a valuable woman, it seemed.

She eagerly started to talk about the Bible Class where her late husband (bless his soul and rest in peace!) was a group leader and where they met Jeb Odum. He was always quiet, but pleasant when someone approached him. After his divorce, and her being single again, it seemed to be God's will for the two of them to get together. She was his soul-mate and completed him perfectly. He was an introvert, but with her chattering, upbeat personality, she could bring him out of his shell. They dated hot and heavy for over two months, frequently met for lunch and dinner, before she agreed with him to let him come to her house. First, she let him beg her for a while, then she graciously granted him the desired favor. All seemed heading in the right direction according to Lana's plans, when Jeb unexpectedly changed.

"Perhaps I was too pious," Lana mused, her long purple nails drumming pensively on the edge of the armrest, "perhaps I should have given in and gone to bed with him. He was a very persuasive, hot-blooded Southern boy, who really went all over me. When he almost forced me to bed, I told him this was my bedroom and only a husband would share it with me, no matter how he tried to coax me to be intimate. He had to realize I was raised properly, and was not the type of woman who would do it before marriage. Yes, sir, that's exactly what I said to him. It was not right to push me like that. The man's priority order was wrong for wanting to hop in bed first and maybe marry later. It should have been in the opposite order, don't you agree? Besides, I was always taught there was never a guarantee of getting married afterward. Am I right? He might have not known, yet, but I had already decided he would marry me. Denying him was the surest way to get him."

McCarthy watched the red lips softly parting, now in clear imitation of Marilyn Monroe's naive sexiness; yet, her steel-hard determination made her a very formidable force behind the girlish charm. It occurred to him that Lana probably was an expert in hooking and landing a fish. He could not resist but ask her, "Have you ever been fishing, Miss Lana?"

Although she was taken aback by the unrelated question, she laughingly replied, "What self-respecting, proper Southern girl would not know how to reel in a fish? You must be a Yankee if you grew up without a fishing pole and a gun. I could teach you how to use either if you ever wanted to try. Was I right to guess you were not born and raised in Tennessee?" McCarthy realized Lana was fishing again, but this time he was the prey.

"Yes, I can see, you are a very accomplished woman," he avoided the direct answer with a compliment. Instead of getting side-tracked, he effortlessly cut her short. He did not want to alienate Lana, he still needed more information. "I bet you held a couple of important jobs in your life, didn't you?" McCarthy himself was good at Lana's game, but he carefully hid his talent.

"Yes, you're correct. I could have been an assistant to any big-wig CEO, even at FedEx or Delta, but I chose to be a housewife to make my executive decisions in my home. The most honorable role for any woman is to be a wife and a mother. Since I was a little girl, this was all I ever wanted to be."

At her next statement, McCarthy had difficulty not to laugh, but eventually managed to listen to her with professional interest. "May he rest in peace until I join him again." What was Lana saying? Probably the truth, he decided. Nothing, but the truth. Well, let the poor man rest, because when Lana arrived, the serene sleep was over, for sure. In the interim, Lana continued, "Although my late husband (bless his soul and may he rest in peace until I join him again!) was the head of the family, as it should be," she quickly interjected, then smoothly continued, "In reality, I made all the decisions, trust me. I still am in charge wherever I go, because people recognize my strikingly outstanding organizational skills. I had been the president of the Ladies Prayer Group, and now I was discussing the roles of a church secretary with the Reverend Babcock. Just to mention a few. How do you like that?"

"Very impressive. I immediately saw that in you. I am most certain Jeb did, too."

"Oh, he needed guidance, no question about it. He was a lost soul before he met me. You know a man needs a good, solid wife with a proper Southern upbringing to get his potential maximized. Maximized," Lana Hadock evidently liked the term enough to repeat it.

"I bet you could maximize it, too," McCarthy looked up from his doodling with an innocent face.

"I tried my best. Just when he was close to make a commitment, his old girlfriend showed up. She stirred up the pot something awful." Her purple nails started the drumbeat again.

"Really? By doing what?" McCarthy played ignorance.

"What? She showed up and, for whatever reason, she lassoed him back. Then tried to keep him on a short chain. Probably cried and begged him, too. It's an old trick to cry. Any woman knows when all else fails, tears always work on a man's sentiment.

"Anyway, he called me late one night and told me he was back with Victoria. He could not hurt her, he said, she suffered enough in life. He discussed with her everything, came clean, and she forgave him. At the end he made the decision to leave me and return to her. He begged me to understand him and, and instead of hating him, feel sorry for him. It hurt him to say these painful words to me. He still wanted us to remain friends and call each other periodically. He still kept calling me 'honey' and he reminded me I was his BB forever. You know, he used to call me BB, for 'beautiful baby'."

"Really?" McCarthy interjected as her words brought back memories of a similar situation with Vittoria and rang with familiarity. "It seems to me, I have heard this before." He kept mum about Jeb calling Lana a 'big butt' or considering it a clever joke by giving 'BB' a totally different meaning to her. Then he was totally shameless to reveal it all to Vittoria… Well, the man was no genius, but no one could accuse him of being honest or inconsistent, either.

"What choice did I have but to accept it? That he also hurt me, did not matter. You have no idea how I felt. The day before, he swore to me he loved only me, wanted to be with me forever, we almost ended in bed, and twenty-four hours later he forgot his declared commitment altogether. I was absolutely devastated. Devastated, I tell you. Especially when I realized that back-biting cat must have laughed at me all the way back to Alabama. Big deal! What was so good in Alabama? That she was a nurse practitioner or something like that? At least I did not wash complete strangers' butts for a living."

"Is that what you think a nurse does?" asked McCarthy.

Lana Hadock just made a self-explanatory, disgusted face, shrugged her shoulder, and dismissed the question altogether. "I saw her, don't you forget. I can read people instantly. I told you, I am somebody who perfectly can assess people at the first glance. Listen to this, Mr. McCarthy. Since we have this discussion, I might as well tell you what people said about Victoria. According to the members of our Bible class, she was classy. Probably, because she claimed to be a debutant in Beverly Hills." Lana leaned forward and with extra significance added, "It's in California, you know. Beverly Hills, that is." Then, leaning back in her chair, she continued, "Big deal. Everyone can see that I am classy, too, after all I get a manicure every other week."

McCarthy had a hard time to decide whether to start laughing or to be stunned by Lana's account, so he did what any wise man would have done in similar situations: he remained silent.

An obviously annoyed Lana almost breathlessly continued, "Victoria was nothing but an old cow. And a skinny cow at that. But I was nice to her, nobody could say otherwise. I even told everyone in church that she looked good for her age, bless her heart. Real good, considering it. I just warned everyone to listen to her speak carefully, because her awful accent was foreign to human ears. "

McCarthy instantly had a flashback of cats fighting in his old Philadelphia alley. Lana had what his wife used to call a 'cattitude'. One accomplished, sophisticated woman and an attractive, steel-butterfly struggling a life-and-death battle. And for what? For winning an aging, bald man with a curved back. For a retired book-keeper, who had one third of a house, and a modest social security. Did being lukewarm, breathing, and having a social security make a man a chick-magnet? He must have had something else to charm these two, something hidden from McCarthy's eyes. Perhaps he was good in bed. Then he brushed the thought away; after all, Jeb was sixty-eight, and there was not enough combined Cialis and Viagra in the pharmacy to keep two women happy for long.

"Maybe Jeb was fascinated by her accent. Or whatever she represented. I don't know. All I see is he returned to Vittoria and left you on a whim. Frankly, he left you high and dry." He deliberately tried to get Lana upset.

The bait worked. Lana winced then shrugged her shoulder. "You're off your ladder, Sheriff. I have other fish to fry, you know." McCarthy was not convinced she meant what she wanted him to believe because Lana angrily responded, "Well, I got even with the sassy, little missy when I ran into them accidentally in the drug store. Jeb did not introduce her to me because he was obviously uncomfortable. So I finally took matters in my hand, and asked her who she was, just standing nearby, and eavesdropping on my conversation with Jeb. Of course, I knew she was Victoria, but I wanted her to see how insignificant she was, by not even making the gossip with her arrival to our church."

"You did? How did she respond?" McCarthy was surprised because he did not know the two women had met.

"Well, she smiled and after telling me her name, she had the gall to say, 'Nice meeting you, Lana. I am sure I will see you in church again.' Ha! The nerve this woman had!" Lana sarcastically imitated Vittoria's accent in an unnatural, sing-song voice.

"In Bible class and church, she greeted me as if we were long-ago separated Siamese twins just being reunited. Jeb assisted her into the chair next to him, and got her coffee. Imagine, into the very chair which I occupied a week before! Into my chair! I declare! I had to sit alone by the wall. That woman really was shameless. Only the gawking eyes could top this insult. Everyone must have laughed at me."

"Hold it for a minute," McCarthy interrupted her, "wasn't Jeb engaged to Vittoria? He acted as he should have, don't you think?"

"No." Lana's word rang with the clarity of a lone rifle shot in the woods. "No. He wanted me, but he had no choice when she lured him away from me. He was nothing but a washrag in her hands."

"A washrag? Is that what you think of Jeb? He was nothing but a washrag?" wondered McCarthy.

"What else? He left me, didn't he? But he did not know who he was dealing with, did he? He sure learned a hard lesson and paid for it dearly. But, then, you pay if you play." Lana's shrugged her shoulder again. Her voice had no warmth, only an empty victory of an imagined gain over her opponent.

"Care to tell me what you really meant by that?" asked the investigator, now fully alert, and expecting the truth to be revealed. But Lana backed up smoothly and, as a slick eel, started to slip from his closing grip.

"He died, didn't he? That's enough of a payment. I have heard he was murdered. Is that correct?" She did not shed a drop of tear though she tried her darnedest to convince McCarthy she was on the brim of tearing up.

"Is that all you meant, Miss Lana? Yes, he was murdered. But that's not all we need to know. You could tell me if something is on your mind or bothers your soul. I understand you, believe me," assured her McCarthy.

"Oh, please! You think I murdered him? For real? You really think that? No. I did not. Sorry to disappoint you, Mr. McCarthy. Jeb was already dead when I saw him last."

"What? What did you say? When was that? Let's start from the beginning. Tell me slowly, and tell me all," he instructed her. The idle chatting suddenly was over, replaced by the cold investigation of a senseless murder. Was the killer sitting in this room? McCarthy was almost sure.

Chapter 41

After a few moments of paralyzing silence, staring into each other's face, expecting the other to talk, McCarthy ended the waiting game. "OK. So you talked with Jeb Odum after he left you, correct?"

"Yes. We decided to remain friends. He told me all about Victoria. I think he felt trapped by his previous obligations and promises. He could not get out of the engagement easily. But he still kept calling me, and we saw each other, too. Don't forget, we attended the same Bible class every Sunday and we saw each other in church. We kept talking each time. First not much, but as time went by, we talked more and more.

"I knew I had to assure him of completely understanding his awful predicament. I also had to point him out that it was she, his fiancée, who made this ungodly mess. He heard me say over and over that I did not blame him, but only pitied him for getting his life ruined by this strange woman. I truly felt obligated to point out to him how Victoria robbed him of his manhood by turning him into a mere puppet and a clown. Everyone could see that. Surely, he had to know everyone ridiculed him behind his back. I had to reveal to him that the general consensus was he was nothing but a cuckold. Yes, he was a disrespected, hen-packed, half-a-man in everyone's eyes. Then I always assured him I was the only one who never laughed at him. Instead, his misfortune with this abusing fiancée brought me to tears."

As she came to this point, Lana seemed evidently proud of herself. She righteously raised her head and with clear self-satisfaction nodded a few times to add extra support to her words.

McCarthy kept watching her without interruptions, though it occurred to him it was most likely Lana herself who needed the assurance and not the investigator. All he could think of was how sheep were herded and led to the slaughterhouse. The sheep did not know what was waiting for them at the end, just like Jeb Odum was blind to see the traps Lana's words meant for him. McCarthy actually started to feel sorry for Jeb for the first time. His eyes got slightly narrowed but his silence prompted Lana into talking again.

"Instead, I promised to support and assist him, if he only made a sincere effort to get out of this toxic engagement. I pledged to wait for his return to me once he was free of her. Each time I declared to him I would never hurt him as much as Victoria did. He was clearly pining after me and responded with renewed interest. In no time, our relationship became more than just a friendship. No fore'ner woman was pulling a fast one over this Southern Belle," she said, grinning with total conviction. McCarthy almost visibly shuddered hearing Lana's substitution for 'foreigner'.

Then, almost as an afterthought, Lana added, "Not even when she was haughty enough to call herself 'Vittoria' instead of saying it decently as it was supposed to be pronounced, 'Victoria'."

For a second, McCarthy found himself speechless, and could only stare at Lana. Then the investigator won over the shock of the private man, and he continued as if he never heard the last remark.

"So you two were getting back again? But Jeb Odum went to see Vittoria regularly. He spent at least two weeks with her each time. And periodically they vacationed together, too, so he had to be away for a good chunk of time. Didn't you know that?"

"Oh, please, that didn't mean a thing. He tried to break up with her but had to do it carefully. And that took time, you know. After each visit, he returned to me, anyway. I told you he was hankering after me. We did a lot of things together, not only the usual church stuff. Interesting things, like when we went to get our gun license or learned shooting. These were the important things for a man to do, not the movies, theaters, museums, cruises, and parties that his fiancée forced him to attend. The fancy little Victoria and all her superficial effects wore off in two or three days after Jeb's return, anyway, and he became lovey-dovey as usual. "

"And you never realized Jeb had the best of both worlds? He played both of you as if you were seasoned violins. Didn't you realize he simply carried on this game until he decided who deserved the only goods he could peddle with, his name and his body? What else could he offer to a woman? Vittoria certainly had everything, and much more than what Jeb had or ever dreamed any woman could have. I understood she had a big house, fantastic looks, and European sophistication, made good money, was a great socialite and cook, and loved Jeb. He could not give her a thing more than what she already had."

"Except a husband. But why would a man buy a cow when he gets the milk free?"

McCarthy almost bit his tongue not to reply with an old joke Corky told him recently, "Or why should a woman buy a whole pig just to get a little sausage?" But he suppressed the urge and remained professionally detached, "Go on, Miss Lana."

"And don't forget, I have a comfortable home, too. Perhaps mine was not right next to that famous Shakespeare Theater and Park like Victoria's in Montgomery, but it was a nice house, just the same. And it was right in Somerville, the county seat of Fayette. It is a big town, you know; and by golly, it's on the brim of becoming a metropolis. The last I heard we had a bit over three-thousand population. Can you imagine? Nobody could say a thing against either Somerville or my house. I decorated it myself in a mixture of country cottage and shabby chic style and, for an additional nice touch, embellished it with Holly Hobby. "

Then she added with confidence, "Also, I was here, and she was far away. A bird in hand is worth more than two in a bush, as the good proverb says. I am sure I read it in the Bible. I would have to look it up where and tell you, in case you were interested."

"Wow. That is not going to be necessary, Miss Lana, I trust your knowledge. After all, you studied and read the good book enough to know it, right?" asked McCarthy in a smooth tone, seemingly devoid of sarcasm.

Then letting some steam off, he continued, "All the same, what you said was very interesting. A unique and an interesting view. It gave me answers to a lot of questions that I would have had to ask otherwise. Anyway, all I tried to say was that Vittoria was accomplished on her own, she did not need a husband to complete her. She had far more education and far more accomplishment than Jeb ever did. Frankly, she was way above Jeb in just about everything."

"Oh, yeah, if you say so. Maybe that's exactly what the man could not take. He might have had the initial challenge to chase something unattainable, but once he got it, it was too much trouble to hold onto, don't you reckon? I made sure Jeb understood that next to her he was a second fiddler only while I made him number one. With me, he saw himself as a real Prince Charming in shining armor.

He said it never dawned on him how she only tagged him along, while I looked up to him. I repeatedly explained this to him until he admitted it, too. What self-respecting, Bible-fearing man would like that arrangement?"

"What self-respecting, Bible-fearing man would cheat on two women?" retorted McCarthy with equal bluntness.

"Well, I also came to that same conclusion lately. I wanted him to level with me, and break up with her once and for all," replied Lana.

"It was time to end that old relationship and finally get going on with my plans. When he did not pick up his phone for two days, and let both his cell and home phone ring day and night without answering, I feared he went to Alabama again. It turned on the crazy in me. I decided to check it out.

"I saw his truck in the garage, I knew he had to be at home. I went to the front entrance, but he did not answer the bell. I looked through the side door, and saw him sitting on the couch, watching TV. I thought he did not hear me in the loud noise and knocked on the glass. When he still did not move, I tried the door. It was unlocked. To my total shock, I found myself with a dead man in the room. I didn't know how he died, but I instantly knew if I were found with him—God forbid!—anyone would have blamed me, thinking I have killed him. God sees my soul, they would have found out I had enough reason to murder the cheating bastard. He was a warped man. A warped, warped man."

Lana was obviously getting angry. Her red lips drew into a thin line, and her facial lines became tight. The soft Southern Belle and the innocent Marilyn Monroe impersonation gone, McCarthy saw only glacial, raw emptiness in her eyes. He watched her with excitement, expecting the thick plaster of make-up to crack and chunks falling off of her face at any moment. Only the heavily sprayed hairdo remained intact, perfectly motionless, just like a yellow football helmet.

She picked up the story again. "What was I to do, but divert all attention? I did not know if anyone saw me coming up to his house or not. I saw his wine glass half filled with red wine. I grabbed another glass and slushed a little wine in it. This way anyone could have presumed he had a visitor. Then I thought better of it. On the bathroom counter I found Victoria's lipstick and dubbed it on the edge of the glass. Let them think it was she who done him in. I declare, she had enough cause to snuff his life out, didn't she? Nobody could doubt it. And she deserved the consequences fully. Just because she did not let a good man go, he had to die. It was she who really murdered Jeb; I don't care who carried out the very act. She cheated me out of my future. She deserved to pay some price. For good measure, I also smeared a bit of the lipstick on the side of his neck. Gosh, it was like marble. Cold and hard. I could not kiss him, I just barely touched his neck with my finger to mark it with the rouge." Lana visibly shivered.

"Then I put his glass in the refrigerator as if he had saved it for later. I left the other glass on the kitchen counter. I wiped clean every place I touched to remove any of my fingerprints. Before I left, I tripped his alarm. I drove away from there as if Lucifer and Satan both were on my heels."

"I would not be surprised if they were," remarked McCarthy dryly. "Look, Miss Lana, you have to come to the station and take a lie-detector test. Are you willing to come on your own, or should I send a legal invitation?"

"I told you the truth. I have nothing to fear. I will go. But I have to tell you, everyone knows me in Somerville as one righteous women, and everyone would come to my defense. Don't forget, I am an active member of the Bible class and an important, elected officer of the church. I am as innocent as an angel, as Gabriel himself, and I will not be kept for long in either your station or in purgatory. I assure you, when I leave, I will not have to shut the door, or turn off the light there, because there will be many more left behind me in that place. So you pick your day and tell me when you want me to show up, and I will be there."

After agreeing on the time, McCarthy let Lana go. She was safe, her house and all her comfort needs securely kept her in the Williston vicinity. After all, Somerville was but a short distance away. People jokingly said a hefty young man could probably throw a stone from Williston and hit the first fence in Somerville. The older men used to say a spit would go that far if the pinch was big enough. The only place Lana Hadock could go was to see her relatives in Little Rock. She could be easily traced there, too.

McCarthy mused, recalling an African proverb: "The cheetah which chases two zebras goes to bed hungry." *Well, Jeb was a 'cheetah', no question about it,* he chuckled quietly. *Yes, it was Jeb Odum, who did not get a chance to chase any zebras now. Both zebras got away from him for good: Vittoria's zebra with a hard-earned heartache, and Lana's with a disappointing victory.*

McCarthy now had learned that Lana was behind the lipstick smears, but she was not the criminal who killed Jeb. He learned early on in his career to follow the road where it led and not to find an easy way which suited his conviction. Now he had to follow the twisting path back to square one. Yet, by eliminating Lana from the list of possible killers, he learned a lot about the murdered man. McCarthy was to set out to discover another fork in the road of investigation, a fork that was not uncovered yet.

It looked like Lana Hadock, Vittoria DelRosario, Charlotte Kay Odum, and Doug Bullock got eliminated one by one. McCarthy decided to visit again the deeply printed cowboy boot marks left in the dried mud at Jeb Odum's house. He hoped once he found the owner, he would also face the murderer. He was the only one left on his list of suspects. By now he was convinced that the cowboy-booted stranger arrived in the fancy truck and it was him who left the new tire prints as a tell-tale of his fatal visit.

Corky and McCarthy spent the next hour reviewing reports from the crime lab. The truck that made the tire marks was still unidentified, but the few sneaker prints matched Doug Bullock's Nikes. No question, the worn-out areas, as well as the manufacturer's design were identical on the print, just as they were observed on Doug's feet. Sometimes even Mother Nature could assist the investigators unexpectedly, like when she provided first a soaking rain, then brilliant sun to quickly bake the gooey clay into a perfect negative. Too bad that the cowboy boots were not yet matched to anyone. McCarthy was sure that secret would be revealed in time, too.

The lab confirmed that the pink rouge marking on the dead man's neck and on the edge of the glass unquestionably came from Vittoria DelRosario's Lancôme lipstick. Unfortunately, the tube was handled by far too many people, so not a single, definite fingerprint could be lifted off of it.

For the time being, McCarthy accepted Lana Hadock's admission on how the lipstick got onto the wine glass and Jeb's neck. He realized, the hurt and revengeful Lana was not an exception of a woman who ever wanted a payback. She might have been taught in her Bible Class that the Lord has claimed, "Revenge is mine" but when it came to her own life, Lana did not want to wait for the Lord.

She realized the good Lord was far away and was slow in payback. On the other hand, Lana was nearby and reciprocated fast. She acted at the first opportunity to score. The demons in her dark soul wanted to see her enemy being punished and suffering, right in front of her eyes. Now, and not later. She certainly was not willing to wait for an eternity or miss her chance to enjoy the retaliation.

Lana's choice might not have been the most expected way to get even; yet, her motivation was age-old: being slighted for another woman always opened the darkest crevices of a heart. McCarthy would have thought, among all the possible types of revenge, this was the least likely to be selected by a faithful Baptist woman. But, then, Lana proved over and over, she was not exactly faithful to her religion, either. Any woman who chases a man until she can manipulate him into cheating, lying and deceit, who shows the least amount of hesitation to break up a formal engagement while faulting the wronged party for her own immoral desires and actions, has only hypocrisy for religion, and herself for God. Too bad, Jeb Odum died, for they deserved each other.

Besides, McCarthy gathered, in Lana's opinion in love and loss there was no rule but one: 'anything goes'; therefore, it was totally justified for her not to take prisoners, but annihilate the opponents. Whether she said the truth, and all the truth or just part of it, McCarthy did not know. He did not worry for it would eventually come out in the lie-detector test, anyway.

If he were a betting man, McCarthy could have put his neck on a chopping block, he was so convinced Lana did not lie. Lana Hadock probably deceived quite a few people under the cloak of pretended righteousness. She also kept committing underhanded betrayals in the shadowy protection of her church and the Baptist community. Yet, McCarthy knew she could not have been Jeb's murderer because she was way too self-conceited not to take credit for her own actions. Her pride was her ultimate pitfall.

There was no need to call for assistance from Sherlock Holmes, yet, in order to untangle this murder. McCarthy felt confident he had other, untraveled roads ahead of him which might just lead him to the killer. He would not let Jeb Odum's murder sink into a dust-covered, cold-case file. He was convinced he could resolve this case, himself.

Chapter 42

When Jake Odum showed up at the Sheriff's Office, everyone expected him to inquire about his younger brother's death. Kevin Cogan was behind the desk; being the youngest recruit, he still had to learn each phase of the work. He immediately updated Jake about the investigation which essentially had not much news.

Jake silently listened and pushed his cap back on his head with his thumb before he said a guttural, "I see," which was as noncommittal as any answer could be. In Kevin Cogan's interpretation, it was but an acknowledgment of his well-presented summary. To his polite inquiry, "Is there anything else, sir, anything I could do for you?" Jake bobbed his head in agreement. "I want to know if you found my son, Billy Bob, yet."

"Let me see," and Kevin picked up a spiral registration book which listed all incoming calls. "Odum, Odum, William," mumbled as he turned the pages and traced each entry with his index finger. "Here it is," he blurted out with the joy of discovery then added in a disappointed voice, "sorry, this was about your brother, not Billy. No, nothing, sir. But don't you fret, Mr. McCarthy is working extra hard on your request."

"What am I working extra hard on?" asked McCarthy in an upbeat voice as he stepped into the reception area. "Hello, Jake. Good to see you. What can I do for you?" he asked the visitor.

"I just dropped by to see whether you heard from Billy Bob."

"No, Jake, nothing. He seems to have vanished since he left Gracie's house in Arizona. She did not know what happened to him, either. When Billy left her, he did not say where he was headed. Gracie thought the skinny young man with him was called Robby or Bobby, but did not know his full name. Anyway, the police artist made a reconstructive portrait from her description and posted it next to Billy Bob's picture. Every police, sheriff, and highway patrol in a thousand-mile radius got a flyer. So far, no response, nothing. But don't give up, Jake, he will turn up one day. People don't vanish without a trace. Only in a television show. We'll find him."

"Good, because the Missus cries her eyes out. Do what you can."

"Sure, Jake. How is the little lady since the cast came off? Is her arm working good?"

"Yep, it's fine. She is doing just fine."

"I talked with her at the funeral last. Gosh, I am sorry for her father. Was it sort of unexpected?"

"Well, sort of, it was. His mind was goin', but at that age everyone's mind would be goin', right? The doctor said his heart gave out at the end. He slept more and more until he did not wake up one morning. Nice death. I don't want nothing worse when my time comes."

"Don't think of that, Jake, you are still a young rooster! You have a lot more years ahead of you."

"Well, one never knows. I am ready, whenever. Not that I am in any hurry, mind you. I have far too many chores, yet, to finish. I have no time for no death, that's all. But the good Lord knows that."

"Good. Keep that attitude. So, when is that big get-together? Christopher came by and told me you planned a giant BBQ or something like that to honor your father-in-law, and I sure don't want to miss it. You make the best ribs in town. Better than in any fancy restaurant, and I mean not only in Memphis, but probably Nashville and Knoxville, as well. Like the best in the entire state of Tennessee!"

"Yep, that's what I heard," agreed Jake. "Come on by Sunday afternoon. But bring some news, so the Missus would lay off of me, would you?" asked Jake and turned to leave.

"I sure will try my best," called McCarthy after him as he slowly walked to disappear in his room.

Later that day, Kevin Cogan rang the phone on McCarthy's desk. "Boss, there is a Sheriff Hands from Texas on the line, calling you. May I transfer his call?"

"Who? What does he want? Did he say?" started McCarthy, then resigned himself to his fate, adding, "Never mind, just transfer the call. I'll take it."

He talked on the phone for a while, then called Corky to tell him the news. Billy Bob Odum was found, but he was found dead. Apparently, this occurred about a month ago. Wade Hands was not sure whether Billy died in Mexico or when he crossed the border. He did not know how he died, either. Most likely it was a drug-related retaliation that led to his end. Or maybe he got involved in the very lucrative gun-smuggling to the drug cartel across the border.

Apparently, the sheriff's informant discovered Billy became part of a drug smuggling ring and was running a smoking hot job when he met his end. He probably was plain cocky and inexperienced enough not to realize the dangers surrounding him. Most likely he also tried to make fast money on the side, by taking on an extra task, without Robby's knowledge and advice. Probably he got involved with an illegal import-export of weapons which destroyed his budding enterprise. For that fatal involvement, Billy paid with his life. Either way, just like hundreds who disappeared before him, his body was never found.

Wade Hands was sure about only one thing that surrounded Billy's death. There was a lot of money that played a role in his demise. It was all about the almighty dollar and the fast track to get the coveted wealth as quickly as one possibly could. Unfortunately, many people were willing to destruct, kill, and to put an end to anyone or anything for money.

Oh, yes, anything for money. For any amount of money, and often for much less than for what Billy hoped to get. What a tragic combination it was that Billy's money-hungry desire linked these heavy-handed investors, unconscious crooks, and antisocial individuals. Running after the mirage of coveted riches only made him run into his end at the hands of some reprehensible criminals.

The Texas Sheriff explained to McCarthy that he accidentally stumbled upon Billy's picture in Robert Falls' home and recalled seeing this man on the posted 'Missing Person' flyer. He recognized Robert Falls as his companion, too. He called to notify the Williston, Tennessee Sheriff Department as this was the apparent contact and the source originating the flyer.

It just took him a while before he could make the call. First, he wanted to verify the facts by his undercover agent. Then he tried to convince the agent to return and discover where Billy's body was disposed. At least get a location, if he could not return with the remains. After all, Billy must have been someone's son, brother, or husband, Sheriff Hands argued. Somewhere there must have been people who loved him and cared for him. His family needed closure.

He also had to finish a job in Arizona before he got back to Texas. At the first moment he got a break, he contacted Chief McCarthy.

In return, McCarthy thanked the Sheriff for his courtesy in his usual steady voice. He only hoped his tight chest did not give away his breathless surprise. He never could get used to hearing news of death, especially not murders of people he knew, no matter how many years he had to confront the tragedies in his job.

After the call, McCarthy sat stunned, staring at the black phone. How on earth could he tell this news to Jake and his wife? How could anyone tell the parents their son was dead for over a month? And they barely knew how he died, and still did not know where he was buried. If he ever was buried. McCarthy was familiar with the crude and cruel ways the drug cartel got rid of their enemy. Surely, he could not reveal all these facts on Sunday, in the midst of the BBQ, when half of Williston was all around the Odums.

Gosh, it was not enough that Billy Bob left them worried to death for months, not knowing about his whereabouts. It was not enough that Mrs. Odum broke her arm and lost her father, that her brother-in-law was just murdered by an unknown assailant, and now add this to it? How much was too much for a woman's heart to take? She seemed to be a fragile, aging woman who relied on the strength of her husband. McCarthy felt the time might just have arrived when she needed all the support Jake could provide. Kasia Odum suffered so much misfortune recently that her life resembled an ancient Greek tragedy. Now McCarthy had to add the further shocking news of her child being killed. McCarthy surely did not look forward to facing the Odums. But who said life in a uniform was easy?

Eventually Corky came up with the good solution of notifying Monsignor Stanley Wolan, from the Polish Catholic Saint Stanislaus Church, and have him be present when McCarthy told the Odums about Billy Bob. The old couple knew and trusted the priest, and in return, he certainly would be able to give spiritual guidance and support to them in their gravest need.

McCarthy stayed for the entire evening at the Odum's. They sat and talked, cried, and hugged each other. It was heart-breaking to see a strong man age in front of one's eyes, and suddenly be reduced to a broken-spirited and pale shell of himself. It was almost unbearable to watch the silent flow of tears of an aging mother, and the incredulous expression on the wrinkled, ashen face of an old grandmother.

Jake Odum's obvious suffering was fully clear to everyone. His grief was almost unendurable as it was magnified by his own guilt of wishing never to see his son again. He blamed himself for Billy's death by saying things in anger that he did not truly mean. He suddenly recalled what he heard from his parents long ago, "Be careful what you wish for because you may just get it."

Suddenly Jake realized there was not much else left for his remaining years, but toiling the cotton growing, eternal land, with the help of his remaining two sons. He sure as hell got his unintentional wish fulfilled now.

Hearing this tragedy, for the first time Kasia seemed stronger than her husband. Although she was devastated by the loss, she had a child-like trust in God's will. She also had the mother's forgiving soul, especially towards her youngest child. Knowing her husband was a good man, she was able to find kindness and mercy in her heart to overlook his unfortunate angry burst. Yet, deep down in the hidden corners of her soul, she did not exonerate him totally. For the rest of her years, each time Jake touched her, she felt an ice-grip squeezing her heart in a relentless clutch.

Children never could understand the pain they cause to their parents unless they became parents themselves, and their children hurt them. Then they had to reach into the depth of their soul to bring out forgiveness the same way their own parents pardoned them before. They had to rely on the existing bond of deep love connecting them, in the hope it was strong enough to forgive and forget. Ah, love could do everything, even if it seemed impossible.

Afterward both Ron McCarthy and Monsignor Wolan felt emotionally spent, but thankful, for this was not their own family tragedy. Just the same, they still had heavy hearts for sharing the tragic news with Jake and Kasia.

Chapter 43

The morning following McCarthy's visit with the Odums, even before the sheriff headquarters opened their door, Mr. Wilson was already waiting on the steps. He seemed his casual self, slowly chewing on the young shoot of a long piece of grass, making it travel from one corner of his mouth to the other. This time, the old straw hat was pulled down on his head to shelter his eyes from the rising sun. Only city folks would wear sunglasses for protection; a decent man used his hat instead to fend off rain and the sun alike.

"Well, I am glad you woke up, it's almost seven o'clock. Half a day is gone, and you're just coming in? You sure should be thankful not to be a farmer," he started with a big smile spreading on his shiny black face, but abruptly stopped chastising the two approaching men when he recognized one of them was McCarthy. "Good morning, Mr. McCarthy. I came to see you, and I sure am glad you came in early." He turned to greet the other approaching officer "Good morning, Captain Corky, to you, too. T'is a nice morning, ain't it?"

McCarthy invited the early visitor into his office. He called Captain Corky to join them. Then he changed his mind and escorted Mr. Wilson into the conference room, where he could record every word. Before he sat down, Earl Ray Wilson produced a long object in a rolled up, stained newspaper. The two men curiously watched him as he carefully opened up the slender package. It contained a blackened, triangular, metal file. Mr. Wilson never touched the file, only the edge of the wrapping. He placed the file on the desk, partially still wrapped in the paper. The newspaper was rusty brown where it touched the file. Both McCarthy and Corky seemed to be captivated by Mr. Wilson's every movement. They intently listened as he accounted of his discovery of the file. This was the type used to smooth off rough patches on hard to reach, metal surfaces. The file that could have caused the unique type of wound, and ultimately the death, of Jeb Odum.

"D'you reckon' Mr. McCarthy at the last time we talked I tole' you there was a young man workin' on Jeb Odum's house? The one who repaired and hung them big shutters on his upper story plate glass winders? I even wondered whether he got paid or not," started Mr. Wilson.

"Yes, sir, I sure reckon I do." McCarthy always found the language most appropriate to his company and situation.

"Well, it seemed like he ain't got paid, after all. He came to git his money the other day but found the house cordoned off, and wanted to know what happened. So he came to the fence and hollered over to me to git the load down. I was out, in the back, helping my son to tune up old John Deere because it just did not want to start. So I gone back to the fence 'coz he axed me. I figgered I learns somethin'.

"By the way, his name was Derek Bagwell, and he came from Memphis, near the airport. I myself thinks he stayed with some relatives, maybe an uncle. Yeah, I is sure that's what he tole' me. He did not know Jeb Odum was killed dead. He was mighty surprised hearin' what happen' if I may say so. Mighty surprised, indeed."

"Well, he could have pretended to be shocked, you know. Are you sure he was not faking it? Was it for real?" asked Corky.

"Nope, he was not putting on no show. Or if he was, then he was a darn good actor, for sure. Darn good, I tells you. I tole' him to go to Jake, he probably would give him his due money. Jake was a good man; he was not fixin' to cheat a poor guy out of a few bucks. Derek did not even know Jeb got himself a brother, or where Jake lived. No sir, I can sincerely says that's the truth. I was the one who tole' him 'bout Jake's farm. I explains him it was just yonder, and if he squinted his eyes, he probably could read his big sign of "Land of Cotton" from where we stood. We talked a little more, mainly about Jeb and the work Derek did done on his house. Then he axed me if I knows some of his tools were missing, and how he could git' them back? Now I knew nothin' about no tools, nohow, but pretended I did, just so I gathers some information. You know, it would be like assistin' you in the investigation."

"Well, thank you, Mr. Wilson. That was smart thinking," complimented McCarthy and secretly sweated the projected, possible, butchered-up outcome. But Mr. Wilson was shrewd enough not to compromise any new discovery. Corky was not as convinced as the other two seemed to be.

Ray Earl Wilson calmly continued, "Derek says he was missing a long metal file, triangular at one end, but pointed in a sharp tip at the other. I knowed what he meant."

"Like this?" asked McCarthy with renewed interest, bobbing his head toward the newspaper wrapped blackened tool.

"Yep, just like that. Or, shall we say, this exact one. 'Coz this sure was the very same file Derek was missing." He thoughtfully dragged his words out even more than it was his habit while keeping his unwavering eyes on McCarthy's face.

Mr. Wilson nodded his head as he continued. "Derek said he never went much into Jeb's house, he did not need to, 'coz his work was all on the outside of the building. He usually started early. Well, he was a decent feller, he didn't wanted to disturb Jeb. Derek kept his toolbox and ladder in the old gazebo overnight. On the last day before he left, on Wednesday that is, he tole' Jeb he was not coming back until Monday to finish the job, 'coz he had to go to court. I think he owed for some tickets or maybe for child support. Somethin' like that. He say he had all them money he needed for the case to settle, but after he finish all the work for Jeb, he wanted to be paid. Right after, 'coz he was poor-short on money. He expected his pockets to be flat empty after the hearin'."

Mr. Wilson half-way turned his head, chatted with his tongue before he continued. "Yep, you goes to Court with a pocket full of money and comes out flat as the Mississippi flood zone after the water receded. The thieves, and here I was referrin' to them lawyers, made sure you paid your last red cent, even if they had to cut it out of your livin' flesh. Nothin', but thieves, who are lazy even to get off their butts. They just sits in them fancy offices and empty them pockets which is brought to them. I tells you, they are nothing but hyenas, every one of them. Well, we all knows how they operate, ain't we?" he grinned. "Of course, Jeb agreed to pay the kid on next Monday, but he got himself killed on Wednesday night, so Derek got no money. That's all. That's why I ain't been wondering' no more."

"Wait a minute, Mr. Wilson that could not be all. You sent Derek Bagwell to Jake, didn't you?" asked Corky.

"Yes, and I am plenty sure Jake was fixin' to pay him all right. Derek got happy as a puppy with two peckers as soon as he heard he might get his money. Anyway, since he did not comes back, I figgered he must been satisfied just fine at the end."

"Did you get Derek's home address? Or any of his personal information?" Corky was getting anxious, and his voice began raising to a higher pitch. Only McCarthy remained remotely unemotional like a solitary iceberg which was accidentally swept into open waters. All along the muscles on his jaw were clenching and releasing rhythmically.

"Nope, I 'fess I don't, but I gots his name. He lived with his relatives in Memphis, but said he originally comes from some place in Arizona. He was easy goin', when he finds hisself low on cash, he stops to do odd jobs to support hisself. He comes in an old, beat-up Chevy, more in rust and dent than red paint and shine on its body. Let me tell you, that little car had seen much fewer good days than you and I put together. That's for sure.

"Listen, Mr. McCarthy, it gits interestin', real interestin' here. Derek also tole' me Jeb had a visitor late afternoon. It was another man straight from his home of Arizona, so they strickes up a good conversation while awaitin'. This man comes to look for Mr. Odum, too, but Jeb was not home, so they just sits in the gazebo and chews some fat. Then Derek had to leave but the other man says he was continued waitin' for Mr. Odum, he don't care how long it took. He had some business with him, somethin' important to talk over, he says. Whatever that business was, Derek don't know, but the man seemed pretty sore 'bout it. He never tole' Derek nothin' what it was 'bout. Well, Derek was Derek and he did not git' it, but I figgered it all out."

"You did, huh? Good for you. Want to share it with us?" started Corky, but McCarthy interrupted him by saying, "So Derek Bagwell left, but the man from Arizona stayed. Do you recall his name?" asked McCarthy and hoped Mr. Wilson did not forget to ask this important question. After all, he became an assistant investigator, whether McCarthy wanted him to be one or not.

"Now, what kind of help was I if I don't ax for his name?" Mr. Wilson clearly was incensed. "Of course, I knows it. He was Robert. At least that's all what I reckon Derek call him."

"Robert. Robert what?" Corky barely could control his voice and facial expressions to cover his annoyance mixed with curiosity.

"That he didn't say," Mr. Wilson flatly replied.

"Geez," started Corky, "if he were the murderer, we just let him slip by," but McCarthy's raised hand stopped his indignant tirade.

"Derek? He ain't no killer, is you lost your mind? Is you a few crayons shy in the box? When I says more, you sees I is right," Mr. Wilson was rightfully indignant. After all, he did not reveal all he knew and wanted to say.

"OK, Robert No Name, that's it," came McCarthy's obviously disappointed response. "At least, did he say anything else about what they talked about? How he got there? Could you describe him; how did he look? Like was he tall, short, skinny, fat, young, or old? You know, something to go by when we look for him. At least did Derek see his car?" McCarthy's questions came as rapid firings.

"Whoa, slow down, Chief. Derek said very little. Accordin' to him, this Robert was about forty, skinny, and too well-dressed, even for Arizona. He was a skinny man, not too tall, but with unusually narrow and small hands and feet. Not the kind that works in the fields, for sure. Com' to think of it, even Derek repeated this a few times, so he must have founded this odd.

"Now I 'fess, I don't know nothin' what men wears in Arizona nowadays, but a shiny gray suit and alligator cowboy boots aren't exactly blendin' into the attire of the country folks in Tennessee, I reckon. D'you agree?" he turned to McCarthy.

Seeing a hint of smile and plain agreement on the face of the chief investigator and his assistant, Mr. Wilson eagerly continued, "In addition, he further calls for a lot of attention to hisself by drivin' a fancy, big truck with brand-new, over-sized tires. And the rear tires was doubled. You know the kind of truck that's custom-built to git its carriage raised high above them wheels. Like the owner is announcin' to the whole world he sittin' on a throne while ridin'."

"Aha, so Derek left in a rickety, old, small car, but this Robert arrived in a big, fancy truck." The mention of new tires definitely raised the possibility of leaving the special tire tracks in the mud. And it must have been this man whose small alligator cowboy boots left their prints in the dried-up mud, too.

"Oh, yes. One more thing. This Robert pumped Derek 'bout Mr. Odum's son, though Derek kept repeatin' he never knew nothin' 'bout the Odums had a son. Derek also tole' Robert he was sure Jeb had a grown-up daughter, but never heard him mentionin' a son. Regardless, it seemed Robert was fixated on the son and returned to this subject all the time. Finally, Derek gave up sayin' anythin' to him, and just sits there and listen with one ear. You know, just enough to appear that he pay attention.

"Evidently, somethin' made this Robert plenty sore about Mr. Odum and how he treated his son. He was much convinced it was the father with his straight-laced, church-going, pious behavior that made his son runs away and finally to meets his end. I figgered that must have been the business this Robert had with Mr. Odum. The only strange thing was that he kept referrin' to Jeb as Jake Odum.

"So Derek and the guy from Arizona just sat a spell in the gazebo, waiting, Derek did not care much because he got confused in the very beginning of the rantin' about Jake and Jeb, then some ramblin' about an unknown son, and so on. I can attest to that 'coz, until after his return on Monday, he never even knew Jeb Odum had no brother. You recall, I tole' him first about Jeb havin' a brother when I sent him over to git his money from Jake," Mr. Wilson ended the account.

"Well, Derek Bagwell might not have understood what was going on, but I think I do. You see, Jeb never had a son, but Jake did. And Jake's son disappeared, indeed, a few months ago. Nobody knew where he went, what he was doing, or where he could be found. Jake and his Missus were plumb worried but could not do much else. We sent out a missing person's flyer and finally we had to end the search when all leads went cold. Two days ago, we got the sad news from Arizona of his tragic death," McCarthy concluded. "I think I know what happened. Before I tell anything more, Mr. Wilson, where did you get this file?"

"Well, I ain't git it; it was actually my son who did. We has no choice, but before we could git the good old John Deere started, we has to hoist him up to see what ailed him. It never had no problem like this before, and whatever we did from the top, it made no difference. So we has to look from below to see what happen'. We works quite a bit already when one of the tires slippes off of the support, and the whole hefty tractor felled to the ground. Fortunately, neither of us were layin' underneath at that time, or we sure would not be talking here now, Mr. McCarthy. No, sir, we sure would not."

Mr. Wilson raised an index finger as if emphasizing the incredible escape before he continued, "I bet it even shooked the ground a bit. It most certainly rattled my ears with the clinkin' of metal. And d'you know what the whole trouble was? You would never figger' it out, I bet. This piece of metal file. The tractor picked it up, and this darn thing stopped the whole production. The tractor works fine ever since we git it out, not even half a sputter out of it. Yes, sir, just as if it was cured all of a sudden."

Earl Ray Wilson was obviously proud of his fine equipment and the job he and his son did to restart the engine. "Shucks, junior rans over this darn file and picks it up; but, really, it's not the boy's fault. Not at all. You could not see a blessed thing in the big grass, no way. Whoever threwed it, threwed it far enough, aimin' it right into the tall weeds. He sure knowed what he was doin'."

"Where did your tractor break down, Mr. Wilson?" asked McCarthy curiously.

"Why, it did just about where we spoke the other day. Right by the fence, near the side entrance to Jeb's house. Why you ax me that? Don't it make no difference?" wondered Mr. Wilson and started to think the chief had not much common sense or practical ways to solve problems if the tractor's break-down was more interesting to him than the file found in the weeds.

"A lot, indeed, it made a lot of difference," replied McCarthy. "You see, if I wanted to get rid of something in a hurry like this metal tool, I would toss it over the fence into another man's yard. Right into the thicket, so it was well hidden. At least for a while, or at least until I was safely gone. Now if you came by to mow the weeds, the tractor would sure pick up the discarded metal piece and clog the rotating mower. The place where your tractor stopped working was the place where the file landed. It was by the gazebo, across from the side entrance of Jeb's house, you said. Correct?"

"Yes, sir, it sure was," replied Mr. Wilson in awe.

McCarthy's logical string of events started to shed light on the obscure events. Mr. Wilson watched McCarthy in awe as his interest increased. Now he saw clearly the path that lead all the way to Jeb's murder. "Go on, Mr. McCarthy, let's hear the rest. I follow you, for I knowed what you means," Mr. Wilson encouraged him.

"Yes," McCarthy was also certain, "now it all makes sense to me. It was this Robert who stole the file from Derek's tool box after he was left alone in the gazebo, and then he attacked Jeb with it. Who else could it have been? He was there alone, he was angry, and was waiting for Jeb's return. Once he mortally injured the older man, he tossed the weapon across the fence as far as he could, and took off in his fancy truck in a hurry. I bet he is gone by now, if not back to Arizona or even to Mexico, but getting close to it."

This seemed reasonable and rational to both Mr. Wilson and Captain Corky.

It was Robert's misfortune that no rain fell since he attacked Jeb, and the Wilson's decided to clean up the yard. After all, the commotion next door brought a lot of visitors to the Odum-house. These people could quickly form a not too flattering opinion about the neighbor if he did not take care of his land. Mr. Wilson and his sons were proud people who did not want to lose their hard-earned reputation. John Deere served the Wilson's well for years, but the biggest favor it did to McCarthy and Jeb Odum was when it broke down.

Earl Ray Wilson's grandparents were sharecroppers, but his parents already owned and worked their own land. Way back, in his family tree, Mr. Wilson claimed to have ancestors who worked as slaves on the cotton fields. Mr. Wilson was the first of his clan to enter middle school, and although he only finished fifth grade, he set an example and a goal for his children. His achievement dwarfed by the fact that his oldest son attended college on a full scholarship. No wonder, Earl Ray Wilson, and his entire family were proud and respected people not only in the black community but in all Williston.

"I reckon I might of guessed it, all right, but I still fail to see what did poor Jeb do to deserve to be kilt?" lamented Mr. Wilson. Corky just sat there, unable to utter a word, staring from Mr. Wilson to McCarthy and back.

"Nothing more but looking like his brother."

"I'll be a monkey's uncle!" Mr. Wilson's surprise was hard to miss.

"A mistaken identity!" blurted out Corky. "Yes, everyone knew these two looked more like twins than brothers. They were alike like two eggs, similar in appearance and even in their habits."

"They also lived close to one another, don't you forget that," interjected Mr. McCarthy, "So if not specified by a full name, any direction to the Odums could have been given to Jeb's house. What a tragedy!"

"I bet Jeb Odum was surprised by a stranger waiting for him when he got out of his truck. Not knowing who he was, why he came to Jeb's property or what the man wanted from him, Jeb probably made the first inquiry. Before he got any answer, the man confronted him, 'Are you Mr. Odum?' and Jeb replied, 'Yes, I am. What do you want?' He likely was still wondering why the man approached him."

"I'm positive he instantly attacked Jeb verbally, like 'What did you do to your son, Jake Odum? Did you know how you ruined Billy's life? Did it ever occur to you that it was you who made him lose his family and to become homeless? You pushed him into a world he was not prepared for; he did not know. Ultimately, he paid with his life for your heartless ways. It was your sin that killed him. I loved him. I would have stayed with him forever, done anything for him, but you robbed him of his life. You also robbed me of my love.' Something of that nature.

"Jeb probably turned his back on this rabid, frothing mouth and quickly opened his side door to escape the madman. That's when the enraged Robert must have lunged forward, 'Oh, no, you don't get away that easy. Don't you ever turn your back on me. Listen to me, you scumbag, you miserable praying hypocrite; you don't deserve to live, you don't deserve to breathe, you deserve to die just like Billy did.' Robert yelled at the older man with hatred.

"He grabbed Jeb on the right shoulder with his left hand to spin him around. Simultaneously, he plunged the file held in his right fist into Jeb's middle, a bit below his ribs but aimed up toward his heart. Jeb fell to the wall from the blow but was able to open his side door to get into the house. The crazy lunatic who attacked him was gone in a flash."

"You don't say! This man was crazy!" shouted Corky.

"We all go a little mad sometimes," Mr. Wilson slowly added.

McCarthy cautiously picked up the long file by holding it from its middle. "Do you see this dark color covering it from the sharp tip for almost its entire length? The lab would tell you it was Jeb Odum's blood. On the handle, the microscopic shredded skin particles would implicate Robert Falls. Robert Falls, who was spooked by Sheriff Hands when he delivered the news of Billy's and Miguel's tragedy. Robert Falls, who, in his anger, took off in a hurry to find Billy's father and take revenge for his lover's death. Robert Falls, who did not know there were two Odums living nearby each other and that it was not Jeb Odum who was Billy's father. At the end, it was Robert Falls who killed an innocent man."

Corky was crushed by the developments. He already heard of Lana Hadock's sneaky interference but was still willing to bet at the final show-down that it was she who turned out to be the true murderer. The more he listened to McCarthy, the further his secret dream of becoming the new Chief Investigator of Homicide seemed to slip. He missed the clues, no question, he missed them big time. He tried so hard and, in spite of all his valiant efforts, it was McCarthy who solved the crime and not Corky. At the end, McCarthy won.

McCarthy continued in an even tone, "I don't think I am far off by saying, once he stumbled in, Jeb Odum checked his left side where he suffered the blow. He had only a drop of blood but seeing only a tiny bleeding, he was not alarmed. He put on a band aid and considered it done. He must have thought the man punched him with his fist, maybe scratched him with his ring a bit; that was all. On the other hand, he was shook up from the sudden assault, hurt deep inside from the blow, shocked by the unknown attacker, and the confusing accusations the man kept hurling at him. Why did he keep calling him Jake? And what did he have to do with Billy Bob's disappearance and death? Why did he have to pay for a father's sin when he was not even Billy's dad? His head was getting more and more filled with cobwebs, making it hard to concentrate and focus.

"Jeb poured a little wine for himself, tasted it, but suddenly he did not feel like drinking any. He left it on the kitchen counter. He dragged himself to the sofa and fell on it. Unexpectedly, he felt awfully tired. He must have been getting short of breath. It occurred to him if he could calm down and just rest a bit, maybe fall asleep, he would bounce back again. The last thing he remembered was to turn on the TV. Remote control in one hand, the other pressed tightly on the wound, Jeb closed his eyes to take a little nap. By the time Lana Hadock came by, Jeb Odum was not in this world."

The three men sat speechless, looking at each other, and then staring at the file: a decent, working man's tool which turned into a fatal weapon in a murderous hand.

"That was great work, Chief," said Mr. Wilson, extending a well-worn, large hand to shake McCarthy's right. "That was as good as high cotton gets. No wonder, you is the head of the investigating team in Fayette County. Well, just one more thing, you is one of us, so let's not forget that! You is the best, you belongs to Williston."

"Not for long, Mr. Wilson. But thank you, just the same. I love Williston, and I love this area. I would like to remain here longer, but they are moving me to Memphis in May. Memphis is crime-ridden, and parts of the city reached critical breach in safety. In a way, it is understandable. With the economy remaining so poor, the jobless, loitering youth have no hope to make a positive change. They are not able to improve their deplorable living and lives. Instead, they are getting angrier and angrier, and more and more frustrated. Furthermore, the lawlessness, resentment, and smoldering unrest are whipped into a frenzy by the reckless politicians and the even more irresponsible media. You know what happens if you mix recurrent, inflammatory remarks and mob mentality. Nothing good can be expected.

"True enough, people are less tolerant and more volatile when threatened and insecure. Just like a cornered, wild animal would be: one could be sure it turned on anyone if there was no route left to escape. As a direct consequence of the deplorable situation, the number of assaults are increasing. Some are nothing else but clear imitation of other crimes, while others are original, vicious, and unique. Either way, they are getting more frequent. Yet, this is not an exception, you are right, it is all over. It's not an unparalleled phenomenon, it happens in every large city which has this kind of population, not only in Memphis."

"So you are being moved to Memphis now?" Mr. Wilson did not believe his own ears. "Just when did you prove to them big-wigs you could solve a murder in two weeks? Since I was knee-high to a grasshopper, I reckon, no one had done it like you did, Mr. McCarthy." His worked-out, large, black hands reached out to grab McCarthy's hand as if in support or as in an attempt to keep him in Williston. For a fleeting moment, it occurred to Corky that Mr. Wilson was expressing his condolences.

"Exactly for the same reason," agreed McCarthy, "they needed me there and offered me a job I could not refuse. Though I still would have to come back once or twice a month to supervise the local department. But don't you worry, my friend, you got the best man to be the chief who surely would deserve your trust. I have recommended Captain Corky to fill my post. I am certain he would excel in doing a terrific job."